FIFTY-ONE

Chris Barnham

For Laura
—travelling with me into the future,
one day at a time.

PROLOGUE

Koblenz, Germany 1952

The sun moved out from behind a cloud and the river flooded with light. A white-painted steamer wheeled around in the middle of the Rhine, easing toward shore. White birds swooped over its stern like scraps of wind-blown paper.

Lewis Brockley was glad to feel the sun; it was, in truth, a little too cool to sit at the low wooden table outside the Rheinanlagen café. The waiter was unable to suppress a quizzical eyebrow as he put Brockley's coffee in front of him, obviously considering it eccentric—antisocial, even—for a British tourist to sit alone outside. Brockley muttered something about the view, nodding at the far bank where gray cliffs rose steeply from the water, topped by the ancient fortress of Ehrenbreitstein.

The waiter glanced at the matchstick pile of scaffolding clinging to one corner of the fortress. Repairs were still being made after the damage inflicted by the Americans' bomb eight years before. He made a clucking noise and shrugged his shoulders as if to say— *View? I'm sick of it.* Then he went back inside.

Brockley sipped his coffee and for perhaps the tenth time since he sat down, surveyed his surroundings the way he was trained to do. He looked back along Rheinuferstrasse, the broad avenue beside the river, automatically registering everyone in sight; a middle-aged couple about to turn right into Rheinstrasse, a woman in a headscarf pushing a pram near the clock tower, and beyond her a tall man in a gray overcoat leaning on the embankment wall.

Closer to where Brockley sat there was another man in a dark coat and hat, a scarf covering his lower face. Brockley wondered if he'd seen him before. Surely it wasn't the airman arriving early? The man stepped into the church entrance and out of sight before Brockley could get a good look at him.

In any case, his attention was snagged by the sight of Nancy Ahmed settling into a seat outside the Augusta restaurant, further up the river bank. Nancy wore the knee-length wool coat they had 'borrowed' from the OffTime wardrobe warehouse before they'd Jumped back to 1952. She was precisely on time and betrayed no sign of recognizing him. *Perfect, Nancy.* Everything—so far—was going to plan.

On the table in front of him was a German-English dictionary, and beneath that a ring-bound notebook. Brockley picked up the notebook, and after glancing around to check he wasn't observed, leafed through the key information for this afternoon. His research said he had perhaps fifteen minutes from the arrival of Heidi Kastelein until the American airman turned up.

He needed to spot Heidi as soon as she appeared. After that, everything depended on what he liked to think of as the high-octane, tried-and-tested Lew Brockley charm. Fortunately, it looked like Heidi had a thing for older men, if the American was any measure. If Lew failed with Heidi, Plan B was for Nancy to distract Frank Darnell—the American—when he turned up.

Lew was confident Nancy wouldn't need to come to the rescue. He could distract women well enough; after half an hour in a bar, he usually got a girl's number, if not a firm date. The early stages of a relationship were never a problem. It was the later stages, sustaining her interest and his, where he ran out of gas. That's where experience had shown Brockley that he fell short.

There were other areas of life where he'd fallen short, such as knowing who to trust in the Office, and being in the right place at the right time to save his partner's life—that kind of thing was where he should've raised his game. But it was too late to worry about that. He was in the right place at the right time now, no doubt about that. Pull this off, and everything would be different.

A movement caught his attention where Rheinstrasse opened onto the avenue alongside the river. A young woman walked into view and stood for a moment at the metal railings overlooking the water.

That must be her.

Seagulls fluttered behind her like spring blossoms blown from a tree. She wore a knee-length gray skirt and a thin cream jacket, with a purple headscarf. She carried some books under her arm. The woman glanced up at the church clock and then along the avenue to the café where Lew sat. She walked toward him. Right on cue.

She was the one he'd been waiting for: Heidi Kastelein, a young German woman whose English lesson today had been cancelled. If events were left undisturbed, in the next fifteen minutes, she'd meet the American, Frank Darnell, who had yet to appear. They'd leave the café together, and she'd become his German tutor. Romance would blossom, and they'd get married. In seven years' time, if events were left to run their course, they'd have a son who'd grow up to achieve very great things.

Lew didn't intend to leave events to run their course.

He left his table and strolled toward the café entrance. Reaching the door a few paces ahead of the woman, he pulled it open and stepped aside, holding it for her and giving her a wide smile.

"Vielen dank," she said.

"No problem."

The woman hesitated for a beat at his English, looking at him closely for the first time. She had pale green eyes, like seawater in a sunny lagoon. Not bad...maybe pleasure could mix with business. She smiled, nodded, and walked inside.

Lew shivered. It must've been his imagination, but it was as if everything around him moved. The sky, the river, and the pavement beneath him swung heavily about as if he was suspended on the end of a rope while the rest of the universe turned on an invisible axis. He felt a spasm of dizziness and leaned on the door jamb. A dust cloud of memories filled his head. He pictured Jacob Wesson running down a London street toward a burning building, the sky boiling with searchlight beams and tracer bullets; a blizzard of confetti around a young bride outside a church...the same woman running away, as the flying bomb screamed its dying wail across the same sky.

Lew could again taste the whisky he drank with Jake that last evening. *Take care.* That was the last thing he'd said to his partner. *You both take care.*

He didn't take care; that was the problem. He didn't take enough care of the people he should've protected. There was nothing he could do about that now. Some things couldn't change. Other things, however, could. That's the thought he clung to; the thought that brought him and Nancy to this café by the Rhine at this precise moment, when the future hung above them, unseen and untouchable, but more massive than the castle across the river.

The young woman walked into the café and Lew was about to follow her inside when there was movement behind him; a scrape of shoe on pavement, a brisk intake of someone else's breath. A hand gripped his left arm, and something was pressed hard into his lower back.

"Surprise." A familiar voice whispered in his left ear. "Keep calm, Agent Brockley, and we'll all be fine. Let the door close; we need to take a little walk."

"Jesus, Kavanagh! You're like shit on my shoe. You get everywhere." Lew resisted turning his head, but he hardly needed to. The man he had glimpsed ducking into the church, covered up with a coat, hat, and scarf. Of course he looked familiar.

"I'll take it as a compliment," Kavanagh said. He tugged on Lew's arm, and they both turned away from the café. The gun moved from Lew's back, but Kavanagh had one hand inside his coat, pointing at Lew. "Let's walk nice and easy away from the café, and let the lovebirds meet like they're supposed to. You can signal Agent Ahmed to join us. I spotted her too, of course."

The horror on Nancy's face was clear even at a distance. Lew beckoned her. She stood up and dropped a coin on her table, then came to join them. Kavanagh made her walk alongside Lew, with him on their right covering them both.

"If you like," he said, "we can watch history unfold before our eyes. We'll stand at a safe distance and watch them meet."

"You're such a charmer, Kavanagh," Lew said. "Not happy just to win, you want to rub our noses in it."

"You deserve the full service, Brockley."

The three of them stood at the river wall, some forty yards from the café. The misery on Nancy's face reflected what was in Lew's head. None of them spoke as they waited to watch the event Lew and Nancy had come to prevent— the first meeting of the parents of Axel Darnell. Axel Darnell who would grow up to become the world's best-known physicist. The man who in eighty years' time, now that Lew and Nancy were unable to stop the meeting, would invent the first time travel device.

Facing this final failure, Lew's misery swept over him like a damp fog. He leaned on the river wall and couldn't help his mind slipping back over the events that led them here. So much had gone wrong it was hard to keep track. He now knew how much of what went wrong was a deliberate part of someone else's plan. But he couldn't have known that when it started—all those months ago in his time, and nearly a century in the future—when he and Jake were called to see Ed Robinson and given the Churchill mission.

PART I

THIS PLAQUE COMMEMORATES

THE FIFTY-ONE PEOPLE

KILLED BY A VI FLYING BOMB

WHICH LANDED ON THE

MARKET PLACE IN

LEWISHAM HIGH STREET

ON THE 28TH JULY 1944

-Brass Memorial plate in the pavement of

Lewisham High Street, South London

I

London, 2040

Jacob Wesson met Ed Robinson in one of the Office meeting pods. The external glass wall looked out onto St. James' Park. The sky was lead gray, and patches of muddy snow clung to the grass. The interior wall of the pod was also glass, and on the other side the OffTime offices were emptying; people were shutting down computers, grabbing coats, and disappearing into the early evening. Jake knew this meeting with his boss would make him late home. He realized with a guilty surprise that he didn't mind. Lately, there didn't seem much reason to rush home.

Ed poured coffee into three cups. Before Jake could ask who was joining them, there was a confident rap on the door, and Lewis Brockley strode in. He nodded to Jake and Ed and sat down. Jake wasn't surprised to see him, and he took Lew's appearance as a good sign. They'd worked together several times, and Robinson meeting with them together suggested a new mission was on offer.

"Jake, Lew. How are you both? Been a while."

Robinson was solidly built with a completely bald head, like a bowling ball perched on a wardrobe. He chewed, as always, on an unlit cigar and held a thin file he was obviously itching to hand over. There was a lot of gossip about Robinson's service history; people said he was with the Office from the time it was set up and involved in the swashbuckling Ops of the early days. Office rumor said he led the famous 1929 mission to stop Israeli agents assassinating Hitler.

"Fine, Ed," Jake said, filling the silence left by Lew. "I could survive a bit more excitement. I don't like it too long at the desk." Some people thought Jake had a glamorous job, but he couldn't remember the last time he was involved in an actual operation.

"You and Hannah all right?"

"We're fine. Why wouldn't we be?" Jake couldn't avoid a sideways glance at Lew. He wasn't sure he wanted to discuss his marriage with his boss, and he certainly didn't want to do it in front of Lew Brockley.

"Will we get around to my love life too?" Lew asked.

"I don't suppose Ed's got the time," Jake said.

Robinson's face betrayed nothing. He had this way of keeping quiet, this mastery of the provocative silence, which usually made Jake say more than intended. At least with Lew present that wouldn't happen.

"It's nothing to do with Hannah," Jake went on at last. "I could just do with a change."

"Change?"

"Don't get me wrong, Ed. You know I love the work."

"We all do, of course," Lew chipped in.

Robinson sucked a little harder on his cigar, a slurping sound the only sign he was still part of the conversation. Honestly, Jake didn't know how he got away with having that thing in the office. He never lit it, but couldn't you get cancer just from having it nearby? Ed seemed to operate to his own rules. Maybe saving Hitler's life cut you some serious slack.

"It's important, obviously. The work…" Jake trailed off as his shoulders drooped. "It's just that sometimes you can't see how it all fits together. Does what we're doing make much difference?"

"It makes a difference, all right." Robinson's fingers drummed lightly on the file, which he'd placed on the glass tabletop.

"We know the official line," Lew said.

"What's wrong with the official line?"

"Nothing wrong with it," Lew said. "We have to stop people messing with the past."

"But?"

"I didn't say there was a 'but.' I just wonder sometimes whether the threat is quite that bad."

"What, you think it's a bogeyman story we spread to scare the public?"

"No. It's just I find it depressing, what we have to do." Lew, normally so laid-back, waved his arms as he warmed to a subject close to his heart. "When you think what we could be doing with time travel. The whole of history is there to be studied, and we end up playing cops and robbers; some people spend their time dreaming up ideas for interfering with the past, while we do what we can to stop them."

"Lew's a big history guy," Jake said, trying to lighten the mood as Robinson stared at Lew. "He'd rather be exploring the ancient library at Alexandria than chasing after terrorists."

Jake was unsure whether Lew knew as much of Robinson's history as he did, and the motivation it gave their boss. Early in Ed's career, before anyone dreamed of the need for a branch of the police to fight Time Crime, Robinson was a young copper in London. He was on the streets in July 2021 when eight young guys carrying bombs in rucksacks traveled into the city. Four hit the Tube, while two blew themselves up in Whitehall, in the entrances of the Cabinet Office and the Treasury. The last two placed the cherry on the fanatics' cake by forcing their way into a nursery and a primary school in Westminster.

Robinson was near King's Cross station when the bombs went off, and he'd ended up on the front pages of the newspapers next day, photographed helping an injured woman across the road to an ambulance, his jacket wrapped around her shoulders, her face painted red with blood and charred clothes hanging in rags. The experience marked Robinson. You could tell it was always with him, the memory of what it was like when criminals cut loose and the determination never to let such a thing happen again. Robinson had, in many ways, been a kind of friendly uncle to Jake, but there were times he glimpsed the cold steeliness below the surface, the hard core built inside Ed Robinson by fear and pain encountered at a young age.

"I'm interested in history too, Agent Brockley," Robinson said. He spoke softly, but his face tightened with a hint of anger. "It teaches me there are too many people who want to destroy things. Once, these guys only had explosives and Tube trains. We could stop that kind of attack because all you needed back then was more security: scanners in the stations, sniffer dogs, and cameras. Not so simple now."

Jake understood. The world had been made a lot more complicated by Axel Darnell and his team at CERN. When they started throwing particles around in their lab under the Swiss mountains they hadn't known where it would lead. First, there was the proof that particles traveled back in time, then the early experiments sending objects back and forth. After that, the big step forward with the first pioneering trips into the past and the famous photo of Julius Caesar's assassination—before trips that far back were banned.

It didn't take long for governments to panic about what might happen if time travel was not tightly controlled; if nutjobs like the July 2021 bombers could go anywhere, anytime, the possibility was high of someone assassinating George Washington, or rescuing Jesus from the cross. The 2029 Time Act outlawed time travel except for government-approved research, security, and law and order purposes. OffTime was set up to stop illicit use of the Darnell System, guarding against Time Crime. Everyone could sleep soundly knowing the Time Cops were stopping anyone from interfering with their great-grand-mothers.

It worked, so far as Jake could tell. The world hadn't yet awakened to find the history books all changed, with Hitler now just a murdered minor politician—a footnote in the history of communist Germany. On the other hand, if history changed, how would anyone know?

"Anyway, I won't keep you gentlemen too long from your work," Robinson shifted gear, his tone suddenly brisk. "I've got a mission for you."

"Yay," said Lew. "We're not worthy."

"What is it?" asked Jake.

"There's more detail in here." Robinson tapped the file on the table. "Read this in a minute, but it can't leave the room. I've downloaded the orders on your palmers so you can brief yourselves later. But here are the basics." Robinson opened the folder and glanced at the first page. "The backroom boys picked up unauthorized temporal Jumps into late April and early May 1941."

"London?" Lew leaned forward.

"Yes. A history scholar like yourself, Agent Brockley, won't need me to tell you how crucial a time this was in the war with Nazi Germany, with Britain fighting alone and in danger of invasion."

"So what're they trying to do?"

"They've already done it, of course," Robinson said. "We've checked it out, and the system says it's at least 90 percent likely they're behind the assassination of a politician, a guy called Winston Churchill."

"Should I know him?" Jake didn't share Lew's interest in obscure periods of the past, but the thoughtful expression on Brockley's face said he'd heard of Churchill.

"Well, he was prime minister for a year, as I'm sure Agent Brockley could've told you," Robinson said. "I've had it checked out: if Churchill isn't shot after a year in the job, he turns out to be an inspirational war leader."

"How can anyone know that?"

"You know I can't talk about that, Jake. But you can trust me on it. Churchill shouldn't die, and your job is to save him."

"Hold on." Lew frowned. "What're these guys trying to achieve by killing Churchill?"

"I assume they want Britain to lose the war."

"But the Allies won without Churchill," Lew said. "So they failed."

"Maybe their computers aren't as good as ours. But we still need to undo the damage," Robinson said. "Look, the details are on file but a couple of things I need to say now. First, it's very important you follow the schedule in your orders. I mean precisely—time, place, everything. You need to be where the orders tell you when they tell you. At all times."

Jake nodded. Lew remained still. Neither spoke, and Robinson peered once more at the cigar in his fingers before putting it away in a desk drawer.

"I'm sending four of you," Robinson went on. "There's you two, with Jake as mission leader. You'll be joined by Hannah Benedict and Nancy Ahmed."

"Hannah?" Jake asked. "Is that really necessary?"

"Nancy's a good pick," Lew said. Jake found that predictable; Lew had a reputation with the female OffTime agents, and he wasn't the only one in the Office who thought Nancy was a striking recent recruit.

"But Hannah," Jake said again. "She's got the experience, but shouldn't I get a say, as mission leader? And she's my partner."

"You are having a say," Robinson said. "And I've listened. But it's my call, and I've made it. We wouldn't be much of an organization if the boys on a mission got to choose the girls, would we? Now," he stood up to leave, "get yourselves briefed. I want you ready to go uptime by this time tomorrow."

II

London, 2040

After Robinson had left, Jake and Lew spent a few minutes leafing through the file, passing papers back and forth without comment.

Paper files were rarely used; when they were, the admin team seemed to take pleasure in organizing them badly. Jake needed to flick through most of the papers to get the sense of it. There were some grainy black-and-white photos. One showed two men walking along a crowded street talking, oblivious to the surveillance. By the look of it, they'd been snapped from some distance away. One of the men had a thick beard and a bald head. The other guy, visible only in profile, was smooth-faced with blond hair.

In another photo, the same men were beside a road, and the side of a vehicle was visible—a flat wagon with crates of bottles on it. The words 'Royal Arsenal Cooperative Society' were printed on the side. The driver sat on a raised seat at the front, holding two lengths of rope in his hands. Jake recognized it at once: a horse-drawn milk cart.

In addition to the photos were several printed email messages. They were mostly surveillance reports on the men in the pictures. There'd obviously already been some OffTime activity to trace the unauthorized Jumpers. Several names were mentioned, but without any certainty who they belonged to; references to a Gerrold and someone called Byers.

Then there was a three-page summary report, which gave times and places where they ought to be able to intercept these guys. The basic plan was to scare them off, so they never got near Churchill. That was to be done in Blackheath, in south-east London, about six miles out from the center where the illegal Jumpers seemed to have based themselves. If that didn't work, the backup was to get close to Churchill in the days leading up to May 10th, when he was shot outside 10 Downing Street.

"What do you think, Lew?" Jake said, at last, pushing the papers aside and leaning back in his chair. Outside, the sky over the park was darkening fast, color draining from the trees as the daylight died.

"Well, it was a critical time in the war. According to the file, if Churchill's prime minister instead of Halifax he's able to draw in American support sooner."

"Yeah, yeah," Jake said. "But Hitler still invaded Russia in June, taking the heat off Britain after six months of the Blitz. Who needs Churchill?"

"Search me," Lew said. "Maybe Mrs. Churchill and the children he might've had? Though he was nearly seventy, so maybe more children were unlikely. But if Robinson's had it checked out, I believe it. This is one bit of history that'd be on that database no one talks about."

The government never confirmed it, and most staff in OffTime weren't cleared to know about it, but persistent rumors said in the early years of time travel the Office had set up a huge database to record the authorized version of the past, based on analysis of the key events that shaped the modern world. People said this historical truth facility, assuming it existed, was housed in a secure building deep in the past, in a location that at some time in history was destroyed, leaving no archeological evidence. It made sense. So, when in doubt, people like Ed Robinson could check the 'authentic' version of the past.

"I guess," Jake said. "Anyway, I wasn't asking what you thought about the history, more about the mission."

"Seems simple enough," Lew said. "I'm not sure why Robinson's set it up the way he has."

"Me neither."

"And if you don't mind me saying Jake, I don't know why you let him do that to you."

"Do what?"

"Tell you your civvie's on the team and then shut you down when you object."

"I don't object."

"I would," Lew said. "Nothing against Hannah, but if you're in charge of the mission, he should ask you before deciding. Why let him get away with that?"

"It's complicated," Jake said.

But it wasn't complicated, really. Both he and Lew knew how much he owed Ed Robinson. Jake's parents were both killed in the July 2021 attacks, and Ed had known them. When they were gone, orphaned Jake began a slide that could easily have taken him to prison or worse. Jake remembered those days like a film he'd once seen—the fights at school, the way he'd mouthed off to his teachers, bunking school and walking the streets all day, pockets stuffed with stolen cigarettes.

One day, Ed turned up at his foster parents' house in Brighton. "I knew your mother," he said. "It would break her heart to see the way you're going."

Within weeks, Jake was in a new school, a boarding place in the Sussex Downs, away from the kids in his usual neighborhood. A charity scholarship paid his fees. Ed Robinson made the calls.

Ed remained his mentor through school, and later, as Jake earned history and criminology degrees at Reading University. True, things had been cooler and more formal between them in the last couple of years, since Ed got his latest promotion and started hanging out more with the Brass on the eleventh floor. But whatever the ups and down between them, Jake owed Robinson big-time.

It was well after seven when Jake left Lew to make the arrangements for tomorrow's Jump, and headed home.

Delays on the Tube made him even later. There'd been a shooting on Whitehall—the Met boys stopped someone with the wrong ID, probably an illegal from one of the outer zones. He was probably just a petty thief, but the poor sap made the mistake of running. The cops took no chances so close to Parliament, cleaning him out in front of several of London's dwindling band of tourists. Officially, the plods only used stun guns, but five stun guns at once tend to leave a guy terminally stunned.

Even when the chaos at street level cleared, there was the normal snarl-up on the Tube, made worse by the wait to walk through the scanners. These always seemed pointless to Jake; it had been years since anyone had blown themselves up on the Tube. There were more imaginative ways to cause mayhem these days.

"You're late," Hannah called from the kitchen as he entered their apartment and hung up his coat. He gave her a brief peck on her cheek.

"Robinson wanted to talk. By the time I left, the Tube was mobbed."

"Ah, the 1941 job," she said. "I'm already half packed." Hannah gestured with her chin, and now Jake noticed the canvas carryall on the floor of the living room, a small pile of clothes next to it.

"You know about it already?" Jake said. "I was hoping I could surprise you."

"Ed told me this afternoon."

So, Robinson briefed Hannah before talking to him and Lew. No wonder he was so keen to override any arguments. Maybe Lew had a point about the way Ed was treating him.

"Let's talk about it over dinner," Hannah said.

"What is it? Smells OK."

"Chicken. And I've poured some wine."

"Is it real?"

"The chicken or the wine?"

"Both."

"Who can tell these days? Best not worry about it."

The dining table was beside their fifth-floor window. In the summer, they'd slide back the doors and move the table out onto the balcony. Tonight it was too cold, but they had the curtains pulled back, with a view across the river. The skyscrapers of the Canary Wharf financial district were a mosaic of colored lights; they interlaced with the flashing lights of skimmers taxiing the high earners to and from work, keeping them from having to mix with the ordinary people who earned a fraction of their wage and probably paid more tax.

The only thing that marred the view was the dark, skeletal shadow of the Shanghai Bank building, a jagged semi-circle still visible in the side from the bomb damage of 2035. Jake heard the Bank and the Mayor's office were arguing over who was responsible for the Christian bomber getting in, and the building wouldn't be restored without a court case.

Their conversation about the next day's mission didn't take long. What was there to say? They'd both read the same briefing. Jake could hardly tell Hannah he tried to get her taken off the team, but Ed overruled him. His attention drifted to the night view outside.

"After this Jump, how long do you think you'll stay active, Jake?"

"I've never really thought about it," he said.

But he *had* thought about it. What if he hadn't joined the Office, where would he be? He sometimes imagined a parallel career, maybe in academic research, or in old-fashioned police work solving the present-day murders that were so often neglected in favor of the glamour of fighting Time Crime.

Most days at OffTime were a bore, just an office job like any other. The thing that kept him there was the occasional buzz from the Jump; the shiver down his back and the hairs standing up on his arms when he stepped into the Darnell Suite. That brief flash of terror at the momentary lurch of the Jump, when you couldn't help blinking, however hard you tried, and you didn't know what you might see when your eyes opened again.

His answer didn't seem to satisfy Hannah. She put her wine glass to her lips and looked out the window. There was something pained and reproachful in her glance like he'd hurt her once and she was remembering it.

"Why do you ask?" Jake said.

"I just wondered if you ever thought about us," she said. "Our future."

"I'm not sure what you mean."

That wasn't true either. Jake wondered when he'd stopped being honest when he spoke to Hannah. It had crept up on him without his noticing. Because he knew exactly what she meant. As an OffTime agent, contraceptive shots were compulsory. Everyone on service uptime had to be certified infertile to a date at least a month beyond the expected end of their mission. There were all kinds of mistakes agents could make in the past: letting slip the knowledge of future election results, talking about Shakespeare before anyone heard of him, making critical remarks about Hitler in the days when he was still popular. Most of these mistakes could be put right. But getting your great grandmother pregnant, or if you were female, coming downtime with Casanova's bun in your oven, these things were very definitely frowned upon.

Younger agents had a regular three-month injection, older ones who already had families usually had their tubes snipped or tied. It was one of the reasons there weren't many couples of Jake and Hannah's age still on missions to the past. Most were younger, or older. It was one of the sacrifices when you signed up to work for OffTime; not a big deal for a young man dreaming of seeing the Colosseum in Rome when it was newly built, or standing close enough to smell Cleopatra's perfume as her bearers carried her gold-trimmed chair through the crowd. It was just part of the price of admission, along with the tiny chip they implanted between your shoulder blades, to help the tech guys track those who Jumped back in time.

He'd been Hannah's civvie for nine years, and he knew when their latest five-year contract expired next year, Hannah expected them to make their partnership permanent. Just like old-time marriage. Romantic.

Jake didn't know if it was what he wanted, but he guessed it would just happen. It was strange how life went—when you're young, you spend all your time thinking about what you're going to do, where you're going, the things you'll see when you're older and out on your own. Later, without noticing it, you realize you slipped into the world of work and responsibility, and things just seemed to happen to you.

Somewhere along the line, there must've been choices to make, other paths Jake could've chosen, but he couldn't remember them. So, yes, he knew very well what Hannah wanted to say. And why her face clouded over and stayed clouded when he didn't answer as she wanted.

When are you going to give up time travel? Stop the contraceptive shots?
When are we going to have children?

"Let's see how this 1941 job goes." He put his hand on Hannah's arm. "Maybe talk about it after that."

"Sure, let's wait until we're back from 1941," Hannah said. She withdrew her arm, her face tight. "That way you'll have had a hundred years to think about it and I might get an answer."

She picked up the wine bottle to refill their glasses, but the bottle was empty.

III

London, 1941

Amy Jenkins had her coat on before the minute hand on the clock above the door clicked onto twelve. A loud bell in the corridor signaled the end of the working day at the Liverpool Victoria Insurance Headquarters. Amy slipped out from behind her desk and was first out the door, running down the back stairs while other girls headed for the lift.

By the fifth chime of the bells of Southwark Cathedral, on the far side of the river, she was running across London Bridge, skipping between crowds already streaming away from the financial district. Her shoes were in the pockets of her coat so she could run quicker. Some of the girls laughed at her for this, but Amy didn't care. She loved this moment of liberation at the end of the working day, and she wanted to run as fast as she could, her hair streaming back from her face, coat flapping in the wind. Once that bell went, it was her time, not her employer's, and she wasn't wasting a second.

Mum and Dad teased her about her impatience. Dad said it must be the Irish bit of her ancestry, the part that gave her the red hair and green eyes. All her life Amy felt she wanted something important to happen, but nothing ever did. She would never admit it to anyone, but she was excited when the War broke out eighteen months ago. She giggled as she tried on her gas mask and gladly shared duty with a spade when Dad dug the trench in the garden for the Anderson shelter. It was such a change from endless, unchanging days typing dull insurance documents, and evenings helping Mum with the cleaning and the cooking and listening to the wireless. For the first time in her life, no one knew what was going to happen next. Anything was possible.

When the skies filled with bombers and the Luftwaffe began night after night of bombing, Amy quickly decided what she wanted to do. One morning, she was on the way to the station and passed a row of ruined shops that looked like they had been squashed from above by a giant fist. The back wall of the terrace still stood, but everything else was a heap of smoking bricks and wooden planks. Here and there, bits of furniture stuck out of the rubble: four chair legs pointing at the sky, the corner of a mattress. Wardens and firefighters swarmed over the wreckage, pulling away chunks of masonry. There were shouts from further down the road, where a group of wardens tore at the heaped rubble. Amy thought she saw an arm sticking out.

"Here, darling, help out." A warden near Amy helped a man along the street. "Help this gent to the ambulance, on Albyn Road."

The ARP warden looked impossibly glamorous, unshaven and with a half-smoked roll-up in the corner of his mouth. The injured man said nothing, simply leaned on her shoulder and shuffled along beside her. They were almost at the ambulance when he asked to stop. He said his arm was hurting. For the first time, Amy looked properly at him—the right sleeve of his jacket was flapping and torn. He had lost the arm in the blast.

"Dad, Mum," Amy said that evening. "I'm going to join the ARP."

The three of them were in the kitchen, listening to the news on the wireless. Neither of her parents spoke for a beat. Her mother looked up from her sewing, her father turned the volume down.

"Are you asking us or telling us?" Mum said.

"I just think I can do a bit more...for the war effort, I mean."

"You can help me a bit more if you've got spare time," Mum said.

"What does Alfie think?" Dad asked.

Alfie was Amy's fiancé. In a few weeks, he would be her husband. Everything was fixed for the wedding in May at St Mary's church on Blackheath.

"I haven't told him yet. Anyway, it's up to me, isn't it?"

"Do you want to be digging dead people out of bomb sites?" Mum said. "And two wardens were killed last week in Catford. They were checking the cinema for damage after a raid, and it got bombed again while they were there."

"You can get bombed sitting at home," Amy said. "Anyway, Dad, there's a war on. You always say we've all got to do our bit, don't you?"

"You're not wrong." Her father gave her mother a long look. She dropped her gaze to her lap and resumed her sewing. "Good for you, Amy," Dad said and turned the news back up.

Amy's first night with the ARP was a week later. The Air Raid Protection station was upstairs in the library building, near the hospital. She jumped off the bus a few minutes before seven, walked briskly up to the doors and pushed inside. A gray-haired man in a shabby tweed jacket sat at a desk inside the door. She handed him her identity papers.

"Miss Jenkins. Glad to have you on board." He shook her hand. His skin was soft and lined like old parchment. "I'm Captain Rogers. I run the station. I'll show you round and get you kitted out. I'm afraid we won't be able to chat long, I've got a feeling Mister Goering's going to keep us busy tonight."

Rogers was right about that. At eight-thirty Amy was in the small canteen at the back of the building. She was drinking tea, chatting to two of the older women in the station, Mrs. Morgan and Mrs. Buckingham. Neither offered a first name, and Amy didn't ask. The women were in their fifties, both already widowed by the war. Neither looked like they did much in the way of air raid work, but they made tea and sandwiches, and they knew the name of every warden who came in. There were four other people in the room. The atmosphere was friendly, with a buzz of conversation; for a few minutes, the reason they were there and what the night ahead might hold was forgotten.

There was no siren, but all at once everyone stopped talking. Mrs. Morgan put down her teacup and half-stood. "Oh dear," she said. Amy was about to ask what was wrong when a low drone reached her ears, like a grumbling deep in the throat of the city. It got louder, and when Amy looked down at her tea, a pattern of tiny circles quivered on the surface of the liquid. Too late, the nervous whine of the sirens started up. No one moved in the ARP station, they simply sat and looked at the ceiling as the roaring noise came nearer. Amy thought nothing could be louder or more frightening.

Actually that wasn't right, because she soon heard something worse. The aircraft noise moved down a notch, and it sounded like it had passed overhead.

Amy was conscious of a movement at the corner of her vision; perhaps one of the men at a neighboring table relaxing slightly.

"Get down!"

They all heard the whistle of falling bombs—dead souls screaming to be let out of Hell—before a giant hand reached out of the earth and thumped the side of the building. They were all on the floor, and there was a series of loud crashes. Powdered plaster and brick rained over them, stinging the backs of Amy's legs.

The explosions stopped, then started up again farther away. No one moved for a few minutes until there were sounds of banging and shouting from outside the building. Amy jumped to her feet and ran to the front door. A man stood there with a child in his arms. It looked like a little girl, but the small form was so covered in blood it was hard to tell.

"For God's sake." The man cast his eyes about without focusing on anyone in particular. "Help us. A bomb."

Behind him and across the street, smoke rose from a block of flats. Two of the men from the canteen now joined her. She didn't know their names. Captain Rogers also emerged from somewhere within the building, setting his helmet on his head.

Amy turned to the men behind her. "Come on. Let's go."

"Wait a minute," Rogers said. "We need the all-clear."

"You're joking."

"Look here young lady, I run this station, and I think I know the regulations by now. I need to know from Central that the raid has passed."

The man who had banged on the door still stood in the threshold. The child in his arms shifted, raising a hand to her bloodied face before giving a weak sigh and letting her arm drop.

"There are people over there who need our help." Amy looked fiercely at Rogers and then at the two men standing uncertainly between them. "We can go help them, or we can stay here and wait for a phone call. Which do you think Hitler would prefer?" Amy turned and ran into the street. The two young men followed.

The block of flats was silhouetted against a sky paled orange with firelight. Amy expected to see heaps of rubble, but there were only a few bricks scattered on the ground. The three of them went into the dark building. At once, Amy spotted the metallic gleam of the bomb. It had come straight through the roof and crashed down several floors without exploding, ending up in the ground floor room where people had been sheltering. Women and children had been sitting on the floor, while some men played cards at a table. The bomb had fallen right into the middle of them. Everyone was sobbing and groaning, covered in bricks, rubble, and dust.

Amy ran forward and started digging people out, quickly followed by the two men. They uncovered the head and shoulders of a young man. His eyes were open, but he didn't move. They pulled him out of the rubble with their hands under his armpits. He came out too easily, and Amy realized the lower part of his body was missing. He was dead, of course. He couldn't have been more than seventeen or eighteen years old. Amy dragged him outside and put him against a tree in front of the building. He stared upwards at the inky sky. Amy wanted to close his eyes like in the movies, but she couldn't bring herself to touch them.

"You leave him to me, love." A hand touched Amy's shoulders, and she turned to face Captain Rogers. "Go on. You're right. They need our help."

They worked in the ruined building until nearly dawn, joined eventually by half a dozen more ARP, and ambulances from Lewisham Hospital. Everyone was covered with brick dust and powdered plaster, making them look ghostly until sweat scoured thick lines down their faces. There were seven dead in the ground-floor flat, and they pulled a young girl from the wreckage. As they carried her outside, she kept screaming her legs hurt...but her legs were gone. Amy wouldn't shake that memory off for days.

When they finished, Amy was so tired she sat on the grass in front of the flats for a long time, not noticing how cold the night had become. There were ice crystals on her skirt. Captain Rogers approached her and held out a bottle of whisky.

"There you go, dear. This'll warm you."

Amy took a small sip and coughed it out. Then she gulped a larger mouthful and swallowed, her throat and chest burning as the liquid ran down inside her.

"I'm getting married next month."

Amy didn't know why she said it. During the night, she had thought of Alfie several times, wondering what he would think of her shifting rubble and pulling bodies from the wreckage. Alfie was also doing a night shift, at the rifle factory where he worked. It was his last. He had received his call-up papers. After the wedding, he was going to work a couple of weeks in her office in the City before he joined his unit in Bromley.

"Good," Captain Rogers said. "Lucky man, whoever he is."

"Is it always like this?" Amy's voice was tight and squeaky from the alcohol.

"Not always, no." Rogers gave her a lopsided smile. "Sometimes it's worse."

IV

The 1941 Op was due to Jump at nine, and the mission team was in the Office's Darnell Suite by eight. It took half an hour to sort the paperwork and get their time-sickness shots before the four of them passed one at a time through the airlock and into the Jump Room.

Jake had never Jumped with Hannah before, but he and Lew had worked together many times. A little taller than Jake, maybe six-foot-three, Lew was wiry and muscular with receding dark hair. He was a few years older, and Jake liked to remind him of it. Lew pretended he didn't care, but Jake had noticed his partner occasionally resorted to a pair of reading glasses; sneaking them out of his jacket pocket when he needed to read small print before hiding them again.

Nancy Ahmed was barely more than a trainee, young and keen. An Oxford Criminology graduate born in Edinburgh, she still spoke with the soft musicality of the eastern lowlands of Scotland. Jake didn't know Nancy very well, but he hadn't missed the way Lew approved of her inclusion when Robinson told them. He suspected Lew might've had more in mind than her Oxford degree. Nancy had dark brown eyes and hair the color of raven's wings, with the faintest tint of olive in her skin the only clue—apart from her surname—to her family's Indian origins.

"Are you sure I can't get closer to the action?" Nancy asked as they stripped off their clothes in the locker room. The Darnell Suite had seen better days, and the flaking paint on the walls and the chipped tiles in the showers dragged down Jake's mood. Surely it hadn't been this shabby when he started working with the Office.

Showers were necessary, as anyone knew if they'd ever done a Darnell Jump. Jake had never quite grasped why when it was explained in training, but living things had to go separate from inanimate objects. If you carried anything of a significant mass when you tried to Jump, it didn't work. Jake had learned the hard way that a Jump was possible if you wore normal clothing, but it made him Time Sick. He'd spent several hours puking up his guts, despite the vaccinations. Once they became veterans of Jumping, old pros like Wesson and Brockley offered junior agents the same advice: go naked, preferably after scrubbing every gram of dust from your body. The hardcore pros shaved their heads and cut their nails to the quick, but Jake never felt the need to go that far.

Some people got away with a very light covering, something natural, like thin cotton. But Jake never risked the cotton cloaks. He long ago decided to Jump buffo and knew Lew did too. He didn't know about Nancy, but he guessed Lew was hopeful she'd follow suit. She was, after all, something of a looker. Jake glanced guiltily at Hannah, a few feet to his left in front of her own locker. She was half-undressed, sitting on the bare wooden bench with her head bowed over a page from the mission briefing.

"You've read the file, Nancy," Jake said, closing his locker door. "None of us gets close to the targets unless we have to. And if that happens, leave it to Lew and me. Usually, if they know someone's on to them, they clear out. Job done."

"If they're even there."

"They're there."

"But soon they won't be," Lew said. "OffTime to the rescue."

Jake went in the booth first, giving the others a mock salute as he closed the door. Disappointingly, Nancy had opted for the calico cloak option and looked like a Halloween ghost. Inside the metal booth, Jake stood in silence for a few seconds. He got the nervous flutter in his chest, like he always did. There was a brief flash of violet light and a puff of air in his face, like a balloon popped silently nearby. He lurched sideways as if the ground shifted a few inches.

As always, Jake found that however hard he tried, he couldn't shower enough for a Jump. Arriving in 1941, his stomach clenched like a fist, and he bent down and vomited into the shadows at his feet. He wiped his mouth with the back of his hand and stood up. It looked like he'd arrived just as planned, in a small alley just north of the river in the eastern part of London's banking district. It was early in the morning, and the strip of sky above the alley was as clear as black velvet, with a hint of gray-blue creeping in from the east. The OffTime researchers had done their job and found the right time and place for Jake and the team to arrive undisturbed. The last thing they wanted was for some night duty copper to find them struggling into their clothes in the dark. It might be hard to talk their way out of that.

With a soft popping noise, Lew Brockley was on his knees beside Jake, like he'd been pushed up through an invisible trapdoor.

"All right?" Lew asked. He glanced at the smudge of Jake's vomit on the dark pavement.

"Fine." With another couple of pops, their bags came through, and they pulled out their clothes and dressed. A minute later Nancy joined them, her cotton robe swirling as she appeared, like washing on a line. She remained on her hands and knees for a few minutes, coughing up her breakfast.

"You gotta Jump naked, kiddo," Lew said gently. "Listen to the pros."

Nancy looked up at him fiercely but said nothing. Jake wondered whether he should find a moment to have a quiet word with Nancy about Lew. He was divorced, and it sometimes seemed he was on a mission to work his way through the younger women of the Office. Lew always seemed to be out with someone new, if he wasn't working up to asking someone out or recovering from the latest girl to dump him after a handful of dates. Lew had a jokey, easy charm that meant women took to him quickly. The problem seemed to be when they got to know him a bit better, and things got more serious.

Hannah appeared last, unclothed like the men, but with something sternly unerotic about her nakedness. She appeared out of a bubble of purple light a few feet in front of them, standing upright with her hands on her hips. She didn't move until her bag flopped into existence at her feet when she bent down and pulled out her clothes.

"You OK?" Jake said. He wondered whether he should step forward and offer to help her. He didn't move, unsure how Hannah would respond in front of the others to a show of manly solicitousness.

"Fine." Hannah was pulling on a pair of convincingly 1940s-looking nylons. She didn't look up.

The smell got Jake like it always did. The air before 1950 smelled sweet—hardly any car exhaust and no odor of too many millions of people. Even here in one of the biggest cities in the world, which had been bombed repeatedly in recent months, the air was clean. Admittedly, there was a hint of powdered masonry along with the metallic tang of burnt coal, but the absence of the century yet to come was obvious.

Jake finished dressing last and checked the coast was clear before they left the alley. Their instructions, which Ed Robinson had been so insistent they stick to precisely, were to split up and travel to Blackheath in pairs. Although they had good-quality forged papers, the thinking was that traveling all together at this time of day might draw suspicion in a way that two couples walking separately would not. Lew and Nancy set off first with Jake and Hannah giving them a ten-minute head start. Hannah fiddled with something in her bag. A fragile silence edged into the alley.

"You okay?" Jake said. "Not nervous?"

"I'm fine. Why shouldn't I be?" There were several answers to that, but Jake didn't think this was the time for any of them.

Lew and Nancy were out of sight when Jake and Hannah left the alley. They walked east toward Tower Bridge. It was six miles to Blackheath, and they planned to walk it rather than risk public transport this early in their stay. The more you mixed with the locals, talked to them and used local currencies, the greater the risk of a mistake—especially when you'd just arrived. Briefing before the mission, no matter how detailed, could only take you so far. Better to take some time to ease gently into 1941.

They walked in silence, passing some early risers—office workers walking toward the City behind them. No one took any notice of them; most people walked with their heads down, collars up against the chilly east wind coming off the river. The wind pushed at the two sausage-shaped barrage balloons attached to the south end of the bridge, leaning them over to the right-hand side, making the thick cables creak noisily where they were fixed to the chains that connected the roadway to the towers.

On the south bank of the Thames, they walked away from the river and onto Old Kent Road. Here the street scene livened up, with dozens of people on bicycles and more walking on the broad pavement. A double-decker tram rattled loudly up the middle of the road, iron wheels screeching on the tracks, sparks raining from overhead power cables. They passed horse-drawn carts delivering supplies to the shops. Jake studied the shop fronts as they passed, trying not to appear too curious. There was little resemblance to the London he knew; virtually no familiar names and hardly any products he recognized.

Outside a fruit and vegetable shop, a man in a grubby apron arranged a jumble of ugly-looking objects on a broad table. They looked like small rocks, covered in dry dirt. A sign read: 'New Pot's.' Another shop was something called an 'ironmonger,' while another was clearly meant to be some kind of meat-seller, although there was nothing visible in the window except loose straw and egg-boxes. This shop was not yet open, but there was already a short line of women outside, most with straw baskets over their arms. The women were all thin, with pinched, tired faces.

As they walked, Hannah's silence prompted Jake to wonder about their relationship. It was obvious what she and everyone else thought. They were an item—Jake and Hannah, together now and always. Looking back, the years they'd been together didn't seem to have any coherence—no sense of driving forward, more a feeling of drifting from one thing to another. At no point did they make plans for the future; every step was always just the next thing, the obvious thing to do. They met at university, fell in love, made a home, and started jobs together at the Office...every inch the golden couple of OffTime. They had good friends, enjoyed holidays together, ate out sometimes but other times enjoyed cozy meals at home. There was every reason to expect life would carry on like that. Why shouldn't it?

Jake couldn't say there was ever a dramatic turning point, a moment when their love began to fade. It was more, on his part, that there was always something missing. That wasn't to say he felt discontented; mostly he didn't. He cherished Hannah and enjoyed the times they spent together. She was pretty, intelligent, and kind. She loved him and wanted to make him happy. He supposed they'd always be together.

It took Jake and Hannah over an hour to walk to Blackheath. The journey took them through New Cross—by this time of the morning, a confusing bustle of trams, buses, and crowds of people shoving into the railway station—and on through Deptford Broadway. They passed the end of the High Street, and Jake glanced down it.

"We could walk home from here." He hadn't spoken for some time, and Hannah looked surprised to hear his voice. She showed no comprehension as she followed his gaze up the High Street.

"Our apartment," Jake said. "It's at the far end of that road. We could walk there in ten minutes."

"And then wait ninety years for it to be built."

"True." They walked on.

"It all looks so different," Hannah said. "No traffic except trams and bikes. And those factories." She gestured at the high brick walls on their right. "In our time, there are apartment blocks there."

"No advertising," Jake said. In 2040, you could barely move without screens or holograms pestering you to upgrade your computing power, improve your teeth or skin tone, or book your next skiing holiday in Antarctica.

"Well, there's some." Hannah pointed across the road. On the side of a tall red-brick house was a painting of a chubby-looking girl holding a cup in front of her. Large block letters above her head read, "Ovaltine. Prevents Night Starvation."

"Cute," Jake said.

"How are we doing on time?" Hannah said.

Jake glanced at his watch. "Looks like we're maybe a minute ahead of ourselves."

"Slow down a little," Hannah said. "Ed was very insistent about exact timing, though only God knows why."

They reached the edge of Blackheath, passing through a small triangle of houses bounded by the main road on one side with a smaller street and the open expanse of the heath on the others. The houses here were small and pressed tightly together, each with a single window and door on the ground floor and two windows above. One or two houses had small front gardens, with long mounds of bare earth where the occupants had dug their air-raid shelters.

"Oh, watch out!"

There was the crash of a door slamming, and something struck Jake in the back. He stumbled into Hannah, who was walking in front of him, but he managed to stay on his feet.

"Sod it!"

Jake turned to find a young redheaded woman on her knees behind him, picking up coins that had spilled from her purse.

"Sorry, Mister." She looked up at him. "Excuse my French. I didn't see you. In too much of a hurry, as usual." She laughed.

Jake glanced beyond her to the blue door of the house she must've emerged from. It had a number 10 on the door in crudely painted black letters. The window immediately beside the door had no glass in it, only a large sheet of wood with strips of black tape across it.

"Let me help you." Jake bent down and picked up a bronze coin and handed it to the girl.

"Thanks. Sorry again." She stood up. Jake glanced down to notice that her skirt had ridden up onto her thigh. There was a smudge of red on her knee. The girl followed his gaze onto her bare leg and hastily brushed the hem of her skirt downwards.

"Are you okay?" Jake said. "You've got a cut there."

"I'm fine." Her cheeks were pink. "Got to go. Late for work." With that, she spun on her heel and ran up the street. She had long hair, tied back in a ponytail. It swung from side-to-side as she receded into the distance as if waving him goodbye. Jake turned to find Hannah looking at him intently.

"Another woman you've swept off her feet." She turned away and continued walking. Jake watched her for a few moments, his brief collision with the world of 1941 leaving him breathless and excited, as if the young woman from number 10 had jolted him with several hundred volts of electricity. Almost immediately, Hannah had reintroduced him to the dull gloom that hung around them in 2040.

V

London, 1941

As dictated by Ed Robinson's fussy orders, Jake's team made their base in Blackheath, a few miles down the Kent railway from the center of London. The suburb sat south of the wide expanse of open grassland from which it took its name. The heath stretched north, bisected by the A2 trunk road toward Dover until it reached the walled park at Greenwich. Blackheath itself had a church, some shops and pubs, and still looked very much the village it had been until London's expansion swallowed it at the end of the previous century.

The team took rooms in a boarding house with peeling flock wallpaper and spots of rust on the metal radiators. There was no shower, and the only bath was on the floor below. No en suite, even in the best room any of them had, the one Lew jokingly referred to as the 'honeymoon suite,' shared by Jake and Hannah. It wasn't much of a joke; Jake was well aware he and Hannah were acting nothing like newlyweds. Nancy and Lew made do with tiny single rooms on the upper floor.

The first two days were uneventful, to the special frustration of Lew, who had not jumped back to the 1940s before and resented wasting what was probably his one shot at the wartime years by spending boring days in a shabby house in a dull suburb. They had not yet managed to get a handle on the people they had been sent to intercept. That was not in itself a surprise. There was only so much detail available to the guys in 2040—you might know the person you wanted to find was in the area, but you couldn't always pinpoint an exact time and place. Their orders had sent them to a pub down the hill in Greenwich, and to two different addresses in Blackheath, where OffTime's so-called intelligence suggested their quarry could be staying. Maybe they were, but the team had seen no sign of them.

Their orders were to stick to the Blackheath area for four days. If, and only if, they failed to locate their targets before the 10ᵗʰ of May, they had to relocate to Westminster. They would need to be nearer to Churchill for the actual assassination date. But the government district would have tighter security, with greater risk to their cover, so it was best not to move there too soon.

It was around ten thirty on their third morning. Jake was alone in his room when Lew returned from the first outing of the day.

"Usual story," Lew said, dumping his rucksack on the bed. "Whole lot of nothing. This is a pretty small place. Hard to believe they're here if we can't see them."

"They'll be here," Jake said. While the other three were out, he had been reading over his coded notes for the afternoon's movements, which mainly involved more walking around and searching.

"Hard to believe, in fact, that anything in history ever happened here."

"Nancy and Hannah?" Jake asked.

"Left them at the railway station, watching who comes and goes."

"And they let you come back to the hotel for a well-earned break?"

"Like that's a reward." Lew gestured at the room around them and rolled his eyes. It couldn't be described as the pinnacle of luxury, even for the spartan 1940s.

There was a clatter of footsteps on the stairs, and someone banged rapidly five times on the door to the room—shave and a haircut, the signal they had agreed. Very 1940s. Lew jumped up and opened the door, and Nancy pushed past him into the room, out of breath and a little pink in the face.

"One of them, maybe two," she said. "Definitely the bearded, bald one and the one with him is maybe Byers."

"Where?" Jake was on his feet. "Where's Hannah?"

"She's sticking to them. Staying out of sight. They were heading up the hill to the church. Suited and booted, looking dressed for a wedding or maybe a job interview."

"Well, they're not getting this job," Lew said. Jake saw him slip something dark and metallic in his jacket pocket; his Glock stun pistol. Jake's was already in his pocket. He rarely took it out.

"Lew and I will go find Hannah and check things out," Jake said. "Nancy, you stay here."

"You're kidding me." Nancy had her hands on her hips. Her face was, if anything, redder than when she burst into the room. "Two days of boredom and when I spot them you tell me to mind the shop?"

"Nancy, we don't have time to argue about it," Jake said. He pulled on his stiff 1940s jacket, wondering as always how people wore these thick, heavy clothes. "At this point in the mission, I need the most experienced people on point."

"And how would you and Lew have ever become so experienced if no one let you do anything?"

"We can have that debate back at the Office," Jake said. "For now, you need to do what I say."

"Hate to admit it, Jake, but she's got a point," Lew said. Nancy looked at him, eyebrows raised. "We might need the extra eyes out there more than we need someone back here. Just in the next hour, while we work out the situation."

Jake wanted to shut down the debate and tell them just to do as he said, but Lew rarely spoke against his judgment. When he did, it made sense to listen.

"All right, Nancy comes," he said. "But you do exactly what I say, and no more argument."

Nancy nodded in agreement. As Jake turned to the door, he saw her mouth a thank you to Lew. Outside, they walked briskly through the center of Blackheath village, up toward the heath and St. Mary's church. Jake let Nancy pull a few yards ahead, then spoke softly to Lew. "You're not letting your personal feelings affect your judgment, I hope?"

"The very thought is unworthy of you, boss."

They caught up with Nancy, and she told them a little more about the sighting. "We were across the road from the station. Hannah spotted the first guy as he came out. Before we could move, Byers popped up out of nowhere. They didn't speak, just turned and walked toward the village. We followed them about fifty yards, then I peeled off, and Hannah said she'd stick with them."

"You're certain it was them?"

"Definitely. One of them you can't miss: beard, bald, and taller than you."

"And you're sure there wasn't anyone else? Someone who might've seen you follow them?"

"Pretty sure." She didn't sound too certain.

"What if they're not going to the church?"

"Hannah said she'd stick with them if they went anywhere else, find out where they went then double back and meet us at the church."

They reached the top of the road called Tranquil Vale, and the heath lay before them, flat and empty. To their right, the spire of St. Mary's pierced a dull gray sky. A cold breeze rustled the leaves of some small trees across the road on the edge of the heath, making Jake wish he'd worn something warmer than the jacket. He wondered how people in the 1940s put up with the weather—which was noticeably colder than 2040—with clothes made from such useless fabrics.

"Shame about the weather," Lew said. "For the bride, I mean."

Jake said nothing. He was already scanning the ground ahead, eyes flicking from side-to-side, completely focused on their next steps. A small crowd clustered at the front of the church. The men wore dark suits, and some women held hats in place against the wind.

"We're not exactly dressed for a wedding," Nancy said.

"Maybe we could be the caterers," Lew said.

Jake ignored them both, his eyes on the people in front of the church. As they moved closer, Lew nudged Jake with his elbow, nodding to where he'd spotted Hannah. She was standing close to the side wall of the church, out of the line of sight of the people at the entrance, in front of a stained-glass window. At least, Jake assumed there was stained glass under the sheets of cardboard and strips of tape.

"Where are they?" Jake said when they reached Hannah.

"Nice to see you too, darling."

"Come on, Hannah, we haven't got time to muck about."

"He's inside." Hannah's face was tight and pale. "The tall slap-head with the beard. Byers left and walked east. I lost sight of him behind the church. I decided it was best to stick here."

"Good. Lew, you remember what Byers looked like?"

"Sure."

"And the third guy, Gerrold?"

"Short hair, blond. About your height."

"Blond in the photos." Jake cursed the lack of updated surveillance. "We haven't seen him yet, and he may have changed his appearance."

"I'll know him."

"Right, you and Hannah go after Byers," Jake said. "If you find him, stick on him. Find out where he goes, then loop back here. Don't engage until I say so."

Lew turned to go, but Hannah didn't move. She looked at Jake with a sullen expression, her lower lip jutting out. "What about you and Nancy?"

"What do you mean?" Jake frowned. He glanced quickly again at the front of the church, where more people were getting out of a black taxi. The taxi engine sounded like farm machinery. Maybe it had to run on cooking oil, what with it being wartime.

"What are you doing while Lew and I chase after Byers?"

"Didn't you say one of them was inside?"

"Yes."

"Do you know who else is inside?"

"Of course not."

"So, we don't know what he's doing in there or who he's talking to."

"No, but..."

"That's what I'm going to find out," Jake spoke very deliberately, as if to a child. "Nancy's going to back off from the church a bit so she can keep an eye on whoever comes and goes," Jake said. "As for me..."

"I can do more than that," Nancy said.

"What?" Jake stared at her.

"I can do more than hang around out here. You might need backup."

Jake turned from her to Lew, who had taken a few paces away but turned back when the instant action he expected had failed to materialize. Hannah was standing with her hands on her hips, watching Jake deal with Nancy.

"Lew," Jake said, "will you explain things or do I have to?"

"Explain what?" Nancy said.

"He means we're on a field mission, Nancy," Lew said. "He's the team leader, and he doesn't appreciate having to debate his decisions."

"I'm only trying to help."

"It's not that I don't appreciate it," Jake said. "It's dangerous. When you get to run a mission, Nancy, assuming we make it through this one, you can decide how things get done. And if you're lucky, people will do it and not argue. But for now, it's my call, and I'm making it. If that doesn't suit you, you can go back downtime, and we'll manage without you. Clear?"

"Yes," Nancy said to her shoes, head bowed. Jake threw a fierce look at Hannah. He didn't need to say aloud the words it conveyed: *and you should know better.*

"Right," he said. "As I was saying, Lew and Hannah, go for Byers, Nancy waits here. And as for me…" He looked toward the corner of the church furthest from the main entrance. There was a small, plain window set in the wall, about four feet from the ground. The window was partly open.

"As for me," Jake said, looking at that window. "I'm going inside."

VI

London, 1941

Unseen by Jake Wesson, three people were at that moment in the room beyond the church window. One of them was Amy Jenkins, preparing for her wedding.

"Look, I'll never be ready at this rate!" Amy threw her bag onto the chair behind her.

"Amy! The posy." Her mother snatched up the bag and picked up the flowers that had been on the chair. "You bent one of the lilies."

"Mum, I'm going to bend more than that in a minute."

They were in the room behind the choir's pews, where the choir boys got changed. The St. Mary's volunteers used it as an all-purpose junk room. There were spare chairs and tables stacked high along one wall, and a long rail hung with robes. The remaining space was filled by Amy and her parents, their bags of clothing, and the wedding gifts that guests had pressed on them as they entered the church.

"We're only trying to help, dear."

"Just give me a few minutes to myself."

"I knew we should have got you ready before we left home," her mother said. "It's all very well the vicar saying you can change here, but it's so cramped."

What made it worse was the faulty heating in the room, with an oil heater pumping out heat so strongly that Amy instantly broke into a sweat. Cursing, she had pushed open the window. She ignored the disapproving tightening of Dad's mouth as she did so. She knew very well that there was a war on, but she wasn't the one wasting fuel by putting the wretched heater on in an empty room.

Amy managed to persuade her parents to leave her alone for a few minutes so she could sort out her hair and makeup. They agreed to go out the front and see how things were going with the arrivals.

"Don't come out until we're back," Mum said. "It's bad luck if you're there before Alfie."

"I won't, Mum. Just go."

Left to herself, Amy took off her dress and went into the side bathroom to finish her makeup. She struck a pose in front of the mirror, holding her hair up behind her head with one hand, the other provocatively on her hip. She didn't look too bad. Indeed, at a guess, she thought Alfie would probably prefer her like this—in her nylons, long knickers, and lace-up Basque—than in her mother's patched-up wedding dress. There was always tonight. Amy hadn't quite made Alfie wait for everything until they were married. He had seen her in her underwear, and without it. But they hadn't yet gone 'all the way,' as she thought of it.

There was a noise from the room behind her. A small thump as something was knocked to the floor and a muffled exclamation. Amy assumed it was her mother or father returning too soon. She marched back into the main room.

"Look, how can I ever get ready if you..."

A man stood in front of the window. He looked like he had been replacing some clothing on the rail when her voice surprised him. The window Amy had opened was now pushed shut—he must have come in that way.

"Who the hell are you?"

"It's okay." He held his hands in front of him like a peace offering. He was tall, over six feet, with dark hair. There was something familiar about him, but Amy couldn't place it. "I thought the room was empty."

"Well it isn't, is it?" She stood defiantly with her hands on her hips and then remembered how little she was wearing. She snatched up her dress and held it in front of her. "What are you doing here?"

"I'm, ah, checking the plumbing." He looked around the room and nodded at the radiator beneath the window. "Have you noticed any problems with the heating?"

"Leave it out, mate. Why would you come in the window to check the radiator?"

"Ah. Well, it's quite simple." He took a step toward her, slipping his hands casually into the pockets of his gray trousers.

"Stay where you are!" Amy held her dress in front of her like a shield. "Come near me, and I'll scream."

"Okay, okay." He held his hands up as if warding off an attack. "Look, I don't want to spoil your big day, Miss. I'll just go out that door, and we'll say no more about it."

The man edged sideways and walked slowly toward the door, giving Amy a wide berth. He kept a stupid smile pinned to his face and didn't take his eyes off her. It was the smile that jogged her memory.

"Hold on," Amy stepped in front of the door. "I've seen you before."

"I don't think so."

"Yes, I have. A few days ago. Dartmouth Row, outside my house."

"You've got the wrong guy."

"No, it was you. I bumped into you when I came out. You were with a woman."

There was something odd about this man. What was he doing outside her house so early that morning? She remembered him staring at her bare leg after she picked herself up off the pavement, making her blush. And now he had climbed in her window while she was in her underwear. He spoke funny too; he said 'okay' a lot, and 'guy,' like a character in one of the American detective films Alfie took her to at the Lewisham Odeon so he could put his hand on her knee in the dark. This man wasn't American, as far as she could tell, although there was something American-sounding about the way he spoke.

The woman he was with outside her house was strange too. She was blonde, but with hair cut short, like the girls who worked in the munitions factories. Except she looked like she'd never been near a factory, with her perfect white skin and her lips in a tight curl, as if everything she saw was too shabby or dirty for her to risk opening her mouth.

"Who are you really?" Amy planted her feet firmly in front of the door. "You don't work here, and you're not checking the plumbing."

He took a step back and sighed, spreading his arms again. "Look, I'm in a bit of a hurry, and it's important that I get going. Can't I just leave you in peace?"

"Not until you tell me what's going on."

They were interrupted by footsteps approaching the door. There was a rattle as someone turned the handle and attempted to push the door inwards. Amy stepped to the door and pressed her back against it to keep it closed.

"Who is it? Bride getting ready in here."

"The bride's going to miss her bloody wedding if she doesn't get a move on." It was Dad.

"Nearly done," Amy said. The man in the room with her was staring at her, his face pale. She didn't know what he was looking so scared about. She was the one at risk of being caught half-undressed with a stranger five minutes before her wedding.

"Go away and do something useful, Dad," she yelled over her shoulder. "Come back and tell me when Alfie's here."

"He is here."

"Well, come and tell me if he looks like he's leaving."

Amy and the man opposite her listened as the sound of footsteps died away. She said, "Are you going to tell me the truth or am I going to miss my wedding?"

"Is Alfie the groom?"

"Yes."

"Lucky man." The stranger looked at Amy oddly, making her more conscious of her half-dressed state. "He'll wait. If not, he hasn't got the sense to be married to you."

"Well, what do you know?" Amy felt a heat in her cheeks. "Anyway, I'm asking about you."

"Okay. My name's Wesson, Jacob Wesson. But you can't tell anyone that."

"I can keep a secret, Mister. If you convince me it's worth keeping."

"Seriously," he said. "It's war work. I work for the police, but undercover."

"What does that mean?"

"Plainclothes. Secret stuff. I can't say much about it, but we had a tip-off that someone we're looking for was here."

"At my wedding? Who?"

"I can't tell you. Otherwise, I'd have to kill you."

Amy stared at him, eyes wide. She wondered how quickly she could pull open the door behind her and scream for help.

"I'm joking," he said. "But there really are things I can't tell you. I'm sure you understand."

"'Course I do. There's a war on."

"That's right," Jacob Wesson said. "There's a war on." The way he said it sounded like he'd never heard the phrase before.

"I'm Amy Jenkins." She held out her right hand for him to shake but quickly drew it back when her wedding dress slipped down, exposing the top of her Basque.

"Pleased to meet you, Amy," Wesson said, pretending he hadn't noticed the glimpse of her cleavage. "I just need to check if our suspect is here and report back. Don't worry; nothing will interfere with your service. A quick look round the church and I'll be gone."

"Well, all right." Amy stepped away from the door, still clutching her dress in front of her.

"Thanks for your cooperation, Miss Jenkins."

"Maybe that's the last time anyone will call me that," Amy said. It was an odd thought, getting used to a different name.

Wesson stepped forward and reached for the door.

"Wait!" Amy said. "I don't want anyone to see you leave. I'll check outside." But she couldn't peer out of the door in her underwear; she might give the vicar a heart attack. She turned her back on Wesson and in one quick movement lifted her wedding dress and slipped it over her head, pulling it down and straightening it into place as she turned back to face Wesson again. He looked her up and down and smiled.

"Does Alfie know how lucky he is?"

"You can stop that kind of talk, Mister Wesson, if that's really your name." Amy wagged a finger at him. In her dress, she felt much more in control. "Trying to turn a young girl's head."

Wesson held up his hands in mock-surrender. Amy walked to the door and paused as she reached for the handle.

"Are you married, Mister Wesson?"

"No." He had a distant look in his eyes. "Not exactly."

"You don't sound too sure." Amy wondered how old he was. He looked older than her, maybe thirty or so, but his face was pale and unlined as if he spent a lot of time indoors.

Amy leaned out into the corridor. There was no one in sight, and she heard nothing except the sound of the church organ. Any minute now, she knew, it would strike up 'Here Comes the Bride,' and nothing would ever be the same again.

"Siren's sounded," she said back over her shoulder.

"I'm sorry?"

"All clear," she explained. "What've you been doing during all the air raids, Jacob Wesson?"

"Keeping busy." He moved past her as she stepped away from the door. "Thanks. And good luck, Miss Jenkins." With that, Jacob Wesson slipped out of the room and walked quickly but quietly down the corridor, not looking back as he moved out of sight around the corner and into the church.

VII

Jake was in a corner of the nave of the church, shielded from the view of most of the pews by a thick pillar. He stood for a few moments in the shadows and looked around. There was a gentle murmur of voices inside the church, where maybe sixty people sat in the pews. The church was dark, with many of the stained-glass windows covered in protective boards and wire mesh. There were some candles on metal stands at intervals around the place, which created a nice atmosphere for a wedding, but didn't do much for the light.

Jake saw no sign of the man he was searching for. His gaze lingered for a while on the two young men in the front pew. They both wore dark suits that looked as if they'd been rented in the past hour. One of them, a dark-haired young man with a freckled face, looked nervous and his companion clapped him on the shoulder and whispered something that made them both laugh. The nervous one must be the groom. He looked about nineteen.

She can do better than that.

Jake shook his head to clear the thought away. Amy Jenkins and her wedding were nothing to do with him. He needed to do his job. He walked down the side of the church, shielded from the view of most of the congregation by a row of pillars. The church organ burst into loud life, with the unmistakable opening chords of the Wedding March. There was a rustling sound as the congregation got to their feet.

That was when he saw him; a glimpse of a bald head and dark bush of beard, just for a moment visible on the far side of the room between two people who were standing and craning forward to look for the bride. Jake mentally noted the spot and moved further down the side of the church. He reached the back of the congregation, close to the main doors of the church. He had another glimpse of his target, about twenty yards in, on the far side. He was bending forward, his mouth close to the ear of a man in the row in front of him. Jake stepped forward, aiming to sneak around and take a pew a few rows behind them.

Unfortunately, just at that moment, the doors opened, and the bride walked in with her father. The organ music moved up a notch in volume, and everyone twisted round to look. Jake stepped back behind the pillars, out of the way of the bride, who gave him a brief hostile glance before continuing forward. As Jake moved back out of sight, he caught a clear flash of Baldy's face turned toward him.

He saw me.

Amy and her father were almost at the front now, and most people were settling back down into their seats. There was now a gap in the pew where his bald target had been, and another in the row in front. Jake stepped further into the open and looked round. They couldn't have passed him to the main exit, but he couldn't see them anywhere in the crowd. There was, however, a bit of disturbance in the corner at the front of the hall, to the right of the altar, near the mouth of the corridor that led back to the choir changing room. The people there were slower resuming their seats. Jake saw a man's back retreating into the shadows of the corridor.

Taking advantage of the still-high noise level in the church, he sprinted back up the side of the church and past the door of the room where Amy had dressed. He came to another heavy wooden door. He grabbed the handle and wrenched it round, pulling the door toward him and throwing it open.

"Off Time! Hands up!" He ducked forward into the room, holding his stun pistol in front of him.

It was another storeroom, at the very back of the church. There were stacks of chairs and tables against a wall, and some buckets and brooms leaning in a corner. A door in the opposite wall was open, showing a patch of grass outside the church. Jake ran through the room and outside. There was no sign of his quarry. It was possible that merely being seen by them would achieve the mission's objective. Once the time criminals knew they were rumbled, they often scarpered. But he needed to make sure.

Nancy sat on the grass with her back against a tree. There was something wrong; her head hung forward, her chin almost on her chest, and there was a smudge of red on her cheek.

"Nance," he said. "Are you all right?"

"I'll be okay." She sketched a thin smile. "I don't suppose you know first aid? Mouth to mouth?"

"What happened?"

"The bald one and another guy." Nancy's voice creaked a bit, but she didn't seem seriously hurt. "Just barged me aside. Sorry."

"Which way did they go?"

Nancy gestured with her head, wincing as she did so. Jake straightened up and saw two men running away from them across the heath, toward Greenwich Park. They were already some way off.

"Will you be okay?"

"I'll survive. I'll get my breath back and come after you."

"No, stay here. If Lew comes back, tell him where I've gone. Send him after me."

He ran after them. By now they had about a quarter of a mile on him. Jake was younger than they were, and at least as fit. If he could keep them in view, he'd reel them in. That was how it went for a few minutes. They were heading directly away from him so he couldn't judge progress easily, but their backs looked as if they were growing as he ran. His problems began when they reached the Park and disappeared through the gates. Jake ran faster, breath now burning in his throat.

He stopped a few yards inside the gates and looked round. He was surprised how big the park was, and how busy. There were women pushing prams, couples strolling arm-in-arm, children kicking a ball around on the grass, a full-scale game of cricket in progress on a pale green square. But no sign of Baldy and his sidekick. Unfortunately, bushes obscured the view to his immediate right, and a low hut surrounded by trees and shrubs blocked the view to the left. The two men could've run in either direction and been out of sight in seconds.

Jake had to guess, choosing to go right. He sprinted away from the main gate and round the first clump of bushes. There was a low metal fence around a garden. Jake easily jumped it and continued along a path that curved around a pond. He passed a couple with a small child but saw no sign of the men he was after. Within two minutes he was through the ornamental garden and at the far gate. From here, there was a choice of another exit or a long stretch of the path down the side of the Park. Jake turned a complete circle, looking in every direction. He was stuck. Maybe there was nothing for it but to go back to Nancy and see if maybe they could pick up the trail again. Jake moved back toward the gate, and Lew Brockley ran through it. Lew lurched to a halt a few yards in front of him.

"I saw Nancy. Where are they?"

"Any sign of them out there?" Jake gestured at the gate.

"No, and I had a clear view down the street."

"We need to double back. You go that way." Jake pointed back the way he'd come, through the fenced garden. "I'll go around the outside. Meet at the next gate. About two hundred yards. Keep your stunner handy but out of sight."

Jake looked from side-to-side as he ran. His eyes scoured the park around him. There were too many places to hide: thick trees, the raised platform of a bandstand, clumped bushes. He was angry with himself for losing track of them, but even more for the clumsy way he'd given himself away back in the church. Stumbling in and revealing himself might have the welcome effect of frightening off the enemy, but it also gave them time to change tack, moving onto whatever Plan B they had in their back pockets.

An angry cry, followed by another voice shouting…and then silence. It came from the far side of the ornamental garden, where Lew had gone.

Jake vaulted the low fence. He sprinted between a crop of tall rhododendrons to emerge into a wide grassed area. In front of him were two flower beds, newly planted with blue and orange blossoms. He ran through them, heading toward a thick copse of trees. His Glock was in his hand. He didn't remember taking it out, but he wasn't putting it away, despite the chance of being seen by civilians. He should slow down and check what he was running into. Acting on impulse and making so much noise risked alerting whoever had shouted. But that thought was outweighed by another: his partner was in trouble.

Into the woods, and he saw them straight away. Lew was on his knees, leaning forward against a tree. He had one arm across his stomach, and his face was down. One of the men from the church stood behind him. He looked as if he'd just hit him and was about to do so again. The bald one stood a couple of yards away.

Jake came upon them fast, giving him an edge of surprise. He couldn't remember what setting his Glock was on, but he squeezed the trigger. He jerked the gun up and away as he did so, trying to give Lew's attacker a good blast without catching Lew. There was a blue flash, and a pale glowing ray swiped across the guy's chest and up into the leaves above. He gave a strangled squawk, like a chicken struck by a falling fence post, and fell backward.

Jake wasn't so lucky with the other one. He caught a glimpse of movement as he turned toward him. Before he could raise the Glock, he was struck in the chest by the other man's bald head. Jake's opponent wasn't the lightest of men, and his weight, combined with the impact of Jake's back hitting the ground, punched the air from Jake's lungs. His hand was empty, the Glock lost somewhere in the bushes. He got his hands in front of him and was able to push the clutching hands away from his throat, but he felt weak, and his attacker bore down hard with all his weight.

Jake relaxed his arms for an instant, causing Baldy to lurch closer to him. At the same time, Jake twisted hard to the left and thrust his head up. His forehead hit the other man in the nose, not as hard as Jake would've liked, but with enough force to make his attacker grunt and flinch backward. Jake pushed, and the man went over sideways, with a dig in his crotch from Jake's knee as a bonus. This might not have been enough to break his grip, but Lew chose that moment to make his re-entry. There was a muffled thump and a large shoe with a black-trousered leg attached thrust past Jake's face and struck his opponent on the shoulder.

He was quick for a big bearded baldy, Jake had to give him that. Instead of resisting the twin blows from Jake and Lew, he rolled with them. Jake leaped up to go after him but stumbled slightly and for a moment took his eye off him. When he stood up, his enemy was fifteen yards away, facing them warily. The other guy, the one Jake had Glocked, was on his knees, shaking his head in a dazed fashion, but recovering.

"Stay right there," Baldy said. He had a hand in the pocket of his jacket.

It was impossible to know whether he had a weapon or was bluffing. Jake held his hand out at his side, keeping Lew back. For a moment, there was quiet in the small clearing among the trees, except for the faint groans made by Baldy's mate as he pulled himself upright.

"OffTime agents," Jake said at last. "I can show you ID if you like, but I'm sure you don't need it."

"Off-what, mate?" the man said. "Off your head, coming after us like that. You've got the wrong guys."

"Next you'll be telling me you know nothing about Winston Churchill, Axel Darnell, and the Office for Time Crime Prevention."

"Everyone's heard of Churchill."

"And the rest."

"You're making a mistake, pal."

"Why did you run?"

"What?"

"Back at the church. Why run, if you're so innocent?"

"I thought you were someone else." Baldy glanced sideways, to his mate who was now on his feet watching the exchange. There was something in their faces Jake didn't like, a smirking hint of confidence they didn't deserve as if this was going to their script rather than his.

"Take your hand out of your pocket," Jake said.

The other man didn't move, except for a swift glance at his comrade. Jake risked a quick glance aside himself, wondering where his Glock went. And why Lew didn't have his gun out. Surely, they couldn't both have lost them.

"We better go, Kav," the second man spoke for the first time but fell silent at a sharp glance from the bald one.

"I said your pocket, Kav." Baldy reacted to Jake picking up on his name, but not as Jake expected. He smiled. "What's in your pocket?"

"Confetti. I was going to a wedding."

"You expect us to believe—" Lew spoke for the first time, but he didn't have time to complete a sentence. Baldy pulled his hand out of his pocket and thrust it toward them. Jake flinched and threw up his hands, as the other man turned to run.

On one thing at least, the one called Kav was telling the truth; instead of a rock or other hard object hitting him, Jake lunged forward through a cloud of tiny pieces of colored paper. Baldy had indeed had confetti in his pocket.

Jake and Lew ran after the two men, who crashed away through the bushes. Kav had a hand to his mouth, and his mate was tearing off his jacket as he ran.

"Jake, they're Jumping."

The second man went behind a tree. There was a low popping sound, and a brief flash of purple light threw a faint shadow into the bushes nearby. The man reappeared briefly on the other side of the tree, and Jake saw him fade away into a Jump. He looked for a moment like a silent wind was blowing up from the ground, rippling his trousers and shirt. One moment he was there, grinning his relief at getting away, and then he dimmed like a light bulb about to blow. Jake saw leaves and branches behind him before, with a puff of wind in Jake's face, he was gone.

"Get Baldy!" Jake shouted, but they were too late. There was a violet tinge to the air across the small clearing. The man called Kav mouthed something inaudible, his face twisted in triumph, and then he flowed swiftly upwards and popped out of sight.

Jake and Lew converged on empty space, with a few scraps of confetti still drifting sadly down through the air.

VIII

London, 1941

After the brief and abortive excitement of Greenwich Park, Jake's mission quickly returned to the boredom of its initial days. There was no further sign of their quarry in Blackheath, and the team spent increasing amounts of time in central London, eliminating the possibility of Kav, Byers, or anyone else getting close to Churchill. They worked through the list of times and locations in their brief, but there was no trace of the enemy at any of them. It looked like the encounter in the Park had already changed events and pushed the prime minister's assassins off track.

They checked out of their lodgings on the 10th of May, after nearly two weeks of mostly bored discomfort. They traveled separately by train to London Bridge and stashed their bags in Left Luggage. Their orders were to do a day's worth of sweeping the government district in Westminster, just in case the plotters improvised a backup plan. Jake doubted they would. He was sure that once they pressed the panic button in Greenwich Park, the danger was gone. But orders were orders.

They saw nothing unexpected, and the footsore team regrouped at the north end of London Bridge as a nearby church bell began tolling five. The Office had scheduled their return Jump for five-thirty. For some reason, known only to the geniuses who planned these missions, the Jump point was not the alley they arrived in, but a space between office buildings about half a mile west of there. Everyone was tired, and no one had much to say. Except for Nancy, who was keen to show her can-do nature, as always.

"Is it always like this? I get two weeks in cold and dirty 1941, and all I see of the action is a fist, and then they're gone."

"The main thing is we stopped them doing what they planned," Jake said. He and Lew were leaning on the embankment wall, gazing down at the oily

Thames beneath the bridge. Hannah sat on a stone step a few yards away. She and Jake had exchanged barely a word all day. He wasn't looking forward to the inevitable conversation when they got home.

"I feel like we should've gone after them or something," Nancy said.

"If there was any way of going after them, we might have. But there isn't."

"Can't you Jump with someone if you grab hold of them? That's what I heard."

"I think so," Jake said. "The Darnell Jump will take two people together if they're touching. But it's risky; you've got no idea when you're going or what you'll find when you get there."

"You ever tried it?"

"No, and I don't want to."

"Never mind chasing after them." Lew straightened up and leaned back with his elbows on the wall. "What frustrates me is going back without really seeing anything."

"What else do you want to see?" Nancy said. "One powdered egg is enough for me."

"Lew's been like this all day," Hannah said. "When we were in Westminster earlier, all he could say was, did I know George Orwell lived in a house near here? Or, oh look, there's the House of Commons before the Germans burned it down."

"Lew's our history guy," Jake said. "Most agents don't care what year they get sent to, as long as they can get back in good time to spend their bonus. But Lew wants to have tea with Isaac Newton."

"Yeah, and I sometimes wonder what they taught you at that expensive school, Wesson," Lew said. "No curiosity."

"Can you teach curiosity?" Nancy said.

"Ask me when we get home," Lew said. "My point is, we should do something better with what Darnell gave us. There's so much to learn, and we have to chase round after idiots who just want to destroy."

"Why, Agent Brockley, who would've dreamed you were such a visionary?" Nancy said. "Underneath that hard-boiled act."

"Speaking of going home," Jake said. "Are we clear on the Jump site?" He gestured at the office buildings across the street, some of which were now pouring out streams of home-going workers, pulling on coats and hats as they made for their buses and trains.

"The Liverpool Victoria office is the tall building with the steps up to the doors." Lew pointed across the wide road junction. "That path to the left of it, that's where we need to go."

There was a loud wailing noise from above them, like the ghost of an animal in pain. Within seconds the sound was echoed from across the river and all directions.

"Shit!" Lew pushed away from the bridge wall to stand upright. "Air-raid siren."

"Bit early," Hannah said. "It's not dark for hours yet."

"Maybe Hitler's watch is fast," Jake said. He looked a question at Lew.

"They didn't always bomb at night," Lew said.

"Christ, what about defenses?" Nancy said. "They just let the Germans fly over and bomb the shit out of them?"

"And is today one of those times?" Hannah said, ignoring Nancy and Jake and staring hard at Lew. "For a daylight raid? You're the history guy."

"I don't know. I didn't check."

"Don't you think it would've been worthwhile?" Hannah said. "I mean, you being so interested in the 1940s and all."

"Maybe you had two weeks to get ready for this, Hannah," Lew said. "I got less than twenty-four hours."

"Surely the planning team checks all this out?" Nancy said. "Our orders were pretty damn precise."

There was now a low rumble beneath the continued shrieking of the sirens. Airplane engines. Most of the departing office workers were still heading for their transport, many breaking into a jog. A few had turned to go back inside, presumably taking shelter.

"What do you think, Lew?" Jake said.

Lew looked at his watch. He knew what Jake was asking: what was the risk of the raid pinning them down here and preventing the pick-up?

"Pick-up in twenty minutes," Lew said. "Keep out of sight and be ready to get in position right on the dot?"

There was a flight of stone steps at the side of the bridge, leading down to the river embankment, where a wide footpath ran beside the Thames. They ran down and took shelter. Small pieces of grit scraped under Jake's shoes, echoing under the low ceiling of the bridge above. The noise of the sirens was slightly reduced down here, where the damp air smelled of the river.

All at once the sirens fell silent, and Jake could hear the team's breathing, fast and loud before it was drowned by the rising growl of the bombers. He imagined he could hear the heaviness of the planes with the ugly grinding of the engines, almost see the swollen metal bellies of the Heinkel bombers, stuffed with high explosives eager to spill onto the city below. The roar grew louder, until the sound was all around, coming up through the stone slabs of the pavement and seeping out of the thick granite pillars of the bridge. Another sound joined in: the chaotic crash of anti-aircraft guns, some booming sharply from nearby, others muffled and further away.

The noise eased slightly, and Jake felt a brief surge of relief at the thought that the attacking planes, or at least the leading group, had passed over. Maybe today's bombs had some other city's name on them. Then he heard something else.

"Down!" Lew shouted. He grabbed Nancy's shoulder, pulling her downwards. She resisted, pulling away.

"Get down! Cover your head."

Jake and Hannah dropped face down and put their arms over their heads. Peering upwards, Jake saw that Nancy was slow to follow.

"Listen!" she said, and then she heard it: as the roar of the bombers ebbed, another sound crept into hearing, a faraway whistling, growing fast in pitch and volume. Realization hit her face like a slap with a wet cloth. "Shit," she said and dropped to the floor. Lew threw himself beside her, his upper body curved around her head, elbows clamped at the sides of his head.

The sound of bombs landing nearby was like having your head inside a bass drum. The ground shook and the air filled with brick dust. Fragments of masonry stung Jake's cheek. He clamped his eyes shut and kept his face down as explosions went off among the buildings north of the bridge, and marched along both banks of the river like the footfall of giants.

After the initial cluster of explosions, there was a pause. The first wave of German planes must've passed over, and for a few moments the crash of guns eased off, leaving a fragile quiet.

"Everyone all right?" Jake said.

Nancy lifted her head from the floor and mouthed another silent 'thank you' to Lew. He patted her shoulder and struggled to his feet with Jake and Hannah, brushing dust and grit from his clothes. He looked again at his watch. "Ten minutes to pick-up."

Nancy stood up and slapped brick-dust from her hair. "You know what I said about getting close to the action? If I say it again, just shoot me."

"Lew, what do you think?" Jake said. "Stay here longer or get in position now?"

"Stay here. Listen." Lew pointed upwards.

The growl of another wave of planes was rising. They all moved further under the shelter of the bridge and sat with their backs against the wall. This time was different. The engine noise rose up the scale, accompanied by the clatter of gunfire. As the planes passed overhead and began to move away to the west, Jake braced himself for the thunder of more bombs. But no explosions came, instead, an irregular pounding, like someone had tipped a box of heavy books off the top of one of the nearby buildings, letting them fall to the street.

An object bounced in under the bridge, skidding to a stop about six feet away. A stubby cylinder about fifteen inches long. As it came to a halt, it gave off a fizzing sound and spewed a shower of sparks from one end, which rapidly strengthened into a fierce white tail of flame. A wedge of white smoke poured upwards, mushrooming under the bridge above.

Lew lunged forward. He tore off his coat and wrapped it round his hand to pick up the flaming cylinder. Holding it far from his body, he ran to the embankment wall and threw it into the river. There was a brief flash of fire and steam.

"Incendiary bombs." Lew leaned back against the river wall to recover his breath. "They drop explosives first to smash up the buildings and create kindling. Now they set it on fire. Look."

Outside, beyond the shelter of the bridge, all along the river bank and up on the road above there were columns of white smoke, and in a few places, the flicker of flames as buildings began to catch fire.

"Gonna be a long night," Lew said.

"Lucky we're going home, then." Nancy looked from Lew to Jake and back again. "We are going to be able to Jump, aren't we?"

"Course we are," Jake said. He touched a hand to his cheek. It came away with a smudge of blood from a small cut. It must've happened when the pieces of masonry showered them.

They crept out from under the bridge and climbed the steps to street level. The difference of a few minutes was startling. Fires were everywhere; in some places, incendiary bombs still fizzed, in others, there were larger sheets of yellow and red flame as buildings caught fire. The bank building on the far side of London Bridge had fallen in on itself, with chunks of brick and glass strewn on the ground. A few people stood in the road, taking no notice of the confusion around them, and it looked like there were bodies among the shattered masonry and timber. Dense smoke hung over everything, and pieces of charred paper and cloth drifted down like burned feathers, brushing their cheeks and sticking to their clothes.

"Fuck. Look." Lew pointed ahead. The insurance office building that marked the pick-up site was pouring black smoke from its upper windows.

"We can still get to the alley at the side," Jake said.

"Wait." Lew pointed up and to the east, where there was a line of planes high up, moving fast toward them. Dark shadows spread behind and beneath the aircraft as hundreds more incendiaries tumbled toward the ground.

They sprinted back to the bridge and took shelter again as another hail of firebombs pelted the city streets with that curious plop-plop sound, quickly stirring up new thickets of fire all around. This time no incendiaries came near the team, and they ran back up the stairs as soon as the worst of the wave passed.

The insurance office building was now burning strongly, and a smaller building next to it was also on fire. A fire engine was angled across the road junction, and firefighters were hurriedly unrolling hoses. The second burning building looked like several incendiaries hit it, and flames were already gushing from it. As they crossed the road, Jake felt the heat of the flames, even at this distance, like a huge beast breathing on his face. The team walked rapidly toward the insurance building. Hannah was leading, followed closely by Nancy and Lew, with Jake bringing up the rear. He had his head down to avoid falling cinders, focused only on the back of Lew's legs.

Someone was shouting, repeating the same phrase. At first, Jake couldn't make out the words but was distracted enough to stop and look around for the source of the shouting.

"Agent Wesson!" He looked down a side street, past the second burning building. Another office block across from it was also burning hard, making the street boil with smoke and heat haze. There was someone down there, but he couldn't see clearly through the smoke and rippling heat haze.

"Agent Wesson! Code One!"

Jake glanced ahead. Lew and the others were now thirty yards ahead of him. None of them had heard the distress call, and Jake could hardly credit it himself, it was so unexpected. Code One was the OffTime call when an agent was down and needed help. If you heard it, you had to help.

"Code One." The smoke cleared briefly, and Jake saw a man down the street past the burning building. He was too far away to see clearly, but Jake knew he had seen the man before somewhere. He was waving urgently. Jake held a hand up to shield his eyes and looked again beyond the firemen and the blazing building. Between him and the waving figure, in an otherwise empty junction, there was what looked like a small heap of clothing in the road. There was something familiar about it.

Jake glanced again at his receding team. Lew had turned back and seen Jake far behind. He shouted something, inaudible over the roar of fire and planes overhead, and a chain of explosions behind them as bombs walked along the far bank of the river. Beyond Lew, Nancy and Hannah scuttled toward their destination, bent almost double. Through the curtains of smoke, Jake could see the narrow passage where within minutes OffTime's Darnell machinery would pull the four them out of 1941 and back to 2040. He wondered if he could already see a violet tinge to the air.

"Go!" Jake shouted, gesturing Lew to keep going. He had a margin of error for the Jump, possibly up to twenty minutes. He could go to the aid of the mystery OffTime agent and still get out. "I'll follow!"

Jake ran down the side street, waving at the firemen as he approached. One of them saw him coming and held out his arms. He was shouting something, but Jake couldn't hear over the noise of the fire. Beyond the fireman, the man who called him was now nowhere in sight, but the bundle in the road was struggling to stand up.

Jake dodged round the firefighter and kept running. The burning office building flicked a petulant tongue of flame at him. Smoke gushed from windows above his head with a roar like an oncoming train. There was a loud bang, and a high window exploded outwards in a shower of sparks, pelting the road behind him with broken glass in a musical cascade.

IX

London, 1941

Amy was halfway across London Bridge when the sirens screamed into life. Good sense said she shouldn't go back because the financial district was a much juicier target for the bombers than further out into south London, where she was heading.

Alfie. He's still in the office.

He worked a later shift than Amy. As she stood on the bridge, undecided, the first bombs began to fall, with loud explosions behind her and in front of her, and a tall plume of water shooting up from the river to the right.

A man ran past her, almost knocking her over. "Get off the bridge!" he shouted. "Are you mad?"

Amy ran back toward the office, ignoring the scattered popping sound of incendiaries on all sides. She reached the building too late; it had taken a direct hit, and the upper floor was a roofless brick façade. Incendiaries had already burrowed in deep, and flames spewed from several windows and the main door.

"Alfie!" She meant it as a call to bring him to her, but she could hear the despair in her voice. Amy knew, even as she did it, that trying to get back inside the burning building was the worst thing she could do in the middle of an air raid. The heat and fury of the fires felt like the Germans had tired of simply bombing London and found a way of opening a trap-door beneath the city, allowing flames directly up from Hell.

There was no way in. The wide double door of oak panels, through which she walked each working day, was gone. In its place, an ugly bouquet of black smoke and livid yellow flames churned horizontally out into the road. Amy ran at it, trying to beat her way inside, but the Devil breathed on her, and she was thrown back onto the road. The asphalt was cool against her back and arms, and she felt if she just lay there for a few seconds, maybe she'd find the strength to try again. That was the easiest thing to do, just rest until things calmed down.

She closed her eyes and didn't open them again until she felt someone grab her shoulder and pull her upwards. A man was bending over her, his mouth moving soundlessly as the fire roared behind him. She'd seen this man before, although sadly it wasn't Alfie.

"Oh, it's you. Still working undercover?"

Afterward, Amy knew she should be grateful to the stranger, Jacob Wesson, for pulling her away. If she'd been left alone and had found the strength to get up from the road, she might've tried again to go inside the burning ruin. She'd never have come out. At the time, all she felt was anger when Wesson helped her to her feet, standing so his body shielded her from some of the heat from the fire behind him.

"Come on." His words were barely audible over the roar of flames eating up the interior of the offices she worked in. Wesson gestured with his head up the street. "It's clearer up that way, where the fire truck is. Let me help you."

"My husband's in there."

"You can't go in." Wesson stood in her way. As if to back him up, there was a loud crash behind him. The building shuddered, and a second-floor window vomited a violet sheet of flame over their heads. Wesson clutched her shoulders and pulled her head down against his chest.

For a moment, all Amy wanted was to keep her head down, shut out the firelight and the noise. Something about the way Wesson held her felt safe and right. She was amazed to find that amid the danger and chaos she had a strong memory of being back again on her wedding day, nearly two weeks earlier. She was surprised to find her strongest image of the day was not of Alfie or the service in the church, but of this stranger who appeared from nowhere in her changing room before disappearing again.

Amy felt a sudden spasm of anger with herself, indulging in these frivolous memories at a time like this. The street was on fire, and her husband was in danger. "Let me go!" She pushed herself away from Wesson. "I've got to find him."

"He's not in there," Wesson hung on to her and yelled in her ear. "There's no one there."

"There are lots of people still there."

"No, they got out. Some of them went under the bridge back there. Others went to a shelter."

"What shelter?" Amy studied Wesson's face. Hitler's fire behind his head gave him a flickering halo of flames. He had a smudge of blood on the side of his face from a scratch on his neck. Deep down, she knew he was lying to save her. But maybe the part of her that still wanted to live persuaded her to listen. "Where did they go?"

"Isn't there a shelter near here?"

"Well, yeah." As they spoke, Wesson edged Amy back along the street, and she let him. His hand on her shoulder was reassuring. "Near Cannon Street station," Amy said.

"That's the place," Wesson said. He looked anxious about something other than the continuing air raid, looking all around them as they hurried along the street as if searching for someone. He looked at his watch and seemed to make a mental calculation, his lips moving soundlessly before he nodded and said, "Come on, I can take you there."

They moved past the fire engine and continued along the embankment. There were no more planes overhead, so no new bombs fell, but the city around them was a scene from a fevered nightmare. Along the far bank of the Thames, warehouses were ablaze. It was still daylight this early, but that was hard to believe under a sky seething with thick smoke.

"How far do you think?" Jake shouted close to Amy's ear, as they ran at a crouch along the embankment.

"Couple of hundred yards." They were keeping close to the river and as far as possible from the burning buildings.

"When we get there, you go inside the shelter. I need to go back for someone."

"You can't do that," Amy said. She studied his face in disbelief.

"It'll only take me a moment."

"So, you stop me trying to help, but it's all right for you to go back?"

"I can't explain," he said. He looked again at his watch. "You go in the shelter, I'll join you as soon as I can. And your husband. Trust me."

They reached a junction with a side street, Allhallows Lane, according to the sign. In front of them, the railway tracks from Cannon Street station passed over the road on a tall viaduct, continuing over the river. One of the pillars of the viaduct held a sign with a large blue arrow, and the words 'Air Raid Shelter.'

"Here it is!" Amy said. Wesson had his arm on her elbow. She reached a set of steps, leading down to a metal door. "Down here."

Wesson let go of her arm, and she moved a few paces ahead of him, preparing to bang on the shelter door. Amid the still-chaotic noise of the burning city all around, she caught a new sound: a high-pitched hum, which came from everywhere rather than any one direction. There was a sudden flash of purple light, bright enough to cast her shadow down the steps in front of her.

"Go ahead," Wesson said behind her. "I'll just…"

His voice cut out as if a silent door closed between them. Amy felt a lurch as if the world jerked sideways a fraction of an inch. She turned back, and for an instant thought she could see him still there, but a gust of air hit her in the face, and she blinked.

Behind her, the shelter door scraped open. But when she opened her eyes, Jacob Wesson was gone.

X

London, 2040

Nancy and Hannah Jumped a few seconds before Lew, rippling up into London's noisy Blitz sky. He was about to run after Jake when the Jump seized him too, and he was back in the Darnell Suite in a shower of violet light. His stomach tried to leap out of his throat, and he fell to his knees, splashing the tiles with his lunch. He was vaguely aware of Hannah and Nancy groaning down there with him.

Too angry to be nauseous, he jumped to his feet and hammered on the door. "Where is he? Where's the fuck-up who thought it was fine to bring us back in the middle of an air raid?"

He stood back from the door, glancing round to see if Jake had appeared yet. Maybe the tech guys needed extra time to grab him, with Jake running away from the pick-up point. Why did he do that? What did he see?

It was easier to pick someone up when they were exactly where you expected them to be. But Lew heard the techies could still grab someone even fifty yards from the pick-up point, so long as the time was right. Even if they missed him the first time, they should've been able to track him and get a new fix.

"Come on!" He kicked the door, bouncing in place on the balls of his feet. "Get in here. You could've got us killed."

"Lew, where's Jake?" Hannah was on her feet, wiping her mouth with the back of her hand.

"He'll be here in a second."

"He ran off, where did he go?"

"Open the fucking door!" Lew gave it another kick, and this time there was a metallic rattle from the other side, and a hiss of air from the seals as it slid open. Nancy was now on her feet, and the three of them faced the opening door like the front row of a ragged jury.

Ed Robinson stepped through the door. He stood with his feet planted like Napoleon ready to face down the mob. His face was grim. A white-coated technician hovered nervously behind him.

"Agent Brockley, Agents Benedict, and Ahmed." Robinson nodded at them in turn. "I'm pleased to see you back safe, but I'm afraid we have a problem. We've lost Agent Wesson."

Hannah drew a sharp gasp of breath. Nancy put a hand on her arm.

"Lost him? How?"

"Get yourselves cleaned up," Robinson said. A small muscle in the side of his face twitched. "We'll meet in the control room in ten minutes."

They filed into the control room a few minutes later. Hannah and Nancy were arm-in-arm, and Lew couldn't tell who was comforting whom more. The tech crew arranged plastic chairs in a semicircle facing the control desk and its bank of displays and touchscreens. Robinson gestured them into the seats with his cigar while he stood before them with his back to the screens.

"I don't need to tell you something has gone wrong. But I want to tell you what we know about the problem."

"We just want to know where Jake is," Lew said.

"Naturally." Robinson glanced at Hannah, who sat with her head down, hand over her mouth. "You'll have questions, and I'll try to answer them. But I suggest you hear what I can tell you first."

"Now," Robinson went on. "We got the first information that something was wrong about an hour ago." He nodded at a white-coated man to his left. "Doctor Jarvis called me, and I came to the Darnell Suite at once."

Jarvis, a fiftyish man whose thin comb-over failed to disguise a balding head, remained bent over his desk, his fingers moving rapidly over the touchscreens.

"It seems there was a problem with the tracking signal," Robinson said. "Doctor Jarvis and his team had difficulty keeping a trace on all four of you before your return Jump. A couple of times they lost one or other of you completely. It seems something may have disrupted the trace, but we don't yet know what."

"Maybe it wasn't such a great idea picking us up in the middle of an air raid," Lew said. "Just a thought."

Robinson gave him a look like he'd farted in church, and said, "I agree, conditions on the ground don't seem to have been ideal." He put his unlit cigar in his mouth and immediately took it out again. "I've got someone looking into that."

"Not ideal?" Nancy muttered quietly. "You try a firebomb raid sometime."

"Nevertheless," Robinson went on. "We got you back despite the, ah, conditions. There is no obvious reason why we couldn't have got Agent Wesson too."

"He didn't come to the pick-up point with us." It was the first time Hannah had spoken. She looked like she couldn't decide whether to be angry or upset. "He ran the other way."

"Yes, we picked that up on the tracker; three of you close to the Jump point, one further off and moving away as we activated the Jump."

"Is that it?" Lew said. "Jake was too far away? Just get him with a second sweep."

"Unfortunately, it isn't that simple. I want to show you something. Jarvis." Robinson nodded at Comb-over Guy next to him, who did something to the screen in front of him. "Here's what the main panel showed at the time of the pick-up." Robinson gestured at the screen on the wall behind him. There was a series of five concentric red circles, the small one in the middle dark in color, the others becoming progressively paler as they radiated out. A digital time display at the bottom of the screen read 17:27:30.

"The view is centered on the alley where we picked you up. At first, all four of you are well in the target zone and moving toward the middle." Robinson's cigar pointed to a cluster of four dark blue spots, just inside the outer circle at the bottom of the screen. "Run it, Jarvis."

There were no surprises for Lew in the replay. The four spots remained bunched together, moving up the screen, and then stretched out, before one of them moved away from the others, sliding rapidly across the screen to the right. Lew remembered the heat of the flames, the noise of the bombers overhead and Jake shouting something before he ran away.

"One of you moved away from the others," Robinson said. "That was Jacob Wesson. What was he doing, do you know?"

"It was very confusing. There was an air raid going on, maybe you heard."

"Agent Brockley, we're all as keen as you to ensure that Jake returns safely. One thing that might help is for you to give us all the information you have."

"There was a fire truck in front of the building," Nancy said. "Jake ran toward it. Some firefighters tried to stop him, but then he was out of sight. I didn't see him again."

"Thank you," Robinson said. "You will each have a full debrief after we've finished here. Anything you can remember could be crucial. But first, let's finish this."

Robinson gestured again at Jarvis, turning to the screen behind him. The three blue dots still sat in the middle circle, but Lew was watching only the fourth one, which moved across to the far right of the screen.

"Now, here's where we activate your Jump." As Robinson spoke, a small cross appeared on one of the blue spots. The spot flared purple, before disappearing from the screen. The same thing happened to each of the spots nearby, leaving the small red circle empty. They all now watched the last blue spot, on the edge of the screen.

"This may surprise you," Robinson said. "Jake was further away from the center of the target zone. So, it took longer for the signal to lock on him. But he was inside the outer limits of the target zone."

As he spoke, the final spot moved again, tracking back toward the center of the circle. The timer counted past 17:30 and kept going. The blue spot passed near the center of the circle and carried on, down into the bottom left corner of the screen. Lew couldn't estimate how far that meant Jake moved. At 17:36 a cross appeared on Jake's blue dot, but there wasn't the immediate purple glow the other three had shown. Instead, the cross faded for a couple of seconds, before reappearing. Then, just for an instant, the blue spot disappeared completely before coming back, with the cross on it, and flaring purple. It stayed like that for longer than the others, and then it was gone.

"He Jumped," Lew said. "Jake Jumped?"

"That's why we couldn't get him with a second sweep," Robinson said. "He Jumped already, a few minutes after you."

"But..." Hannah spoke, turning a baffled look to Lew rather than Robinson. "If he Jumped, why isn't he here?"

"We've double-checked with a sweep of the hour after you Jumped," Robinson said. "Jake isn't in 1941 London anymore."

"So where is he?"

"That's just it." Robinson chewed on the end of his cigar, his forehead creased. Hannah stifled a moan, but Lew was briefly distracted by the expression on the face of the technician, Jarvis, who avoided his gaze. He looked like a man who'd just been told his growth was malignant.

"Jacob Wesson Jumped out of 1941," Robinson said. "But we don't know where he Jumped to. We don't know where—or when—he is."

PART II

XI

Time and Again: Scientific Progress and Moral Dilemmas
Extract from a lecture by Sir Sanjeev Kumar, Branson Professor of Science
Ethics at Cambridge University, 17 February 2039.

…with any new technological development debates rage about its impact. Progress is not always linear, and the balance sheet of positive and negative effects of change can take decades to compile. Most observers would now agree that the Industrial Revolution of the eighteenth century had a beneficial impact. Cheap and efficient energy, mass production and distribution of manufactured goods, advances in science and medicine; these changes meant that in the twentieth century most people were richer, better educated and healthier. But things looked different to artisans thrown out of work and home by the first mechanical textile production, to factory workers crammed into the slums of nineteenth-century Manchester, and children forced into mines, mills, and chimneys.

The verdict of history cannot be rushed. Hence the confused debate about the Darnell Process. Some argue that the capability to place modern human beings in actual historical settings is a blessing. The advantages for research and advancement of knowledge are obvious. On the other hand, many would, if it were possible, destroy every existing piece of Darnell equipment, and every scrap of supporting technical information, to ensure the machines could not be rebuilt.

To what extent will Darnell's discovery be seen as blessing or curse, or messy in-between? Perhaps this observer might be permitted a personal observation.

Any tool is potentially harmful in proportion to the kind of damage that people are prepared to contemplate doing with it. In the years following World War Two, many commentators feared that humankind now had in nuclear weapons a tool that could destroy much of life on earth. Atomic bombs have not, so far, done the damage that we feared, because most people can see no justification for risking their use.

One might argue that the ability to visit past centuries, possibly to have a physical impact on history, is a development more threatening even than nuclear weapons. The attempts of governments to control access to the process suggest they agree.

It is easy to see the blessing that time travel could be in a settled and calm society, one at ease with itself and its history. I do not think I risk controversy in observing that this is a society we no longer enjoy, if ever we did. A visitor from 1945 (if time travel were possible into the future instead of just the past) might recognize the decline of science and reason, and the rise of intolerant faith and impatience with deviation. Our visitor might also find familiar the abiding fear of crime and terrorism that places western societies on an almost permanent war footing. But they would struggle to work out who we were at war with, shocked to find the extent to which the threat comes from among us, from dissident elements of our own population, rather than an external enemy.

What our friends from 1945 would not have anticipated is the extent to which social solidarity has broken down in our times. This is fast becoming a world in which a sense of entitlement and lack of personal responsibility go hand in hand with an unquenchable thirst for novelty and impatience with difficulty and complication.

The way we manage our relationships is emblematic of the muddled world we have made. Commentators in the second half of the last century agonized over the decline of marriage and traditional families. In the twenty-first century, civil partnerships have made relationships provisional and time-limited. Hardly anyone gets divorced because they don't have to. It's like solving a crime wave by making robbery legal.

What has this got to do with my theme, the mixed blessing of Axel Darnell's wondrous device? My point is this: we now have the power to change not only the physical fabric of our world but also the roots of our very consciousness, the past events that have made us and our world. That power is controlled by governments that cannot prevent their citizens killing themselves and blowing up parts of London.

And this almost unimaginable power to reshape the past, present, and future—to make decisions that could influence all of us forever—is in the hands of people who are increasingly unable to make decisions in their personal lives that last more than a few years.

XII

London, 1943

Jacob Wesson didn't have time to speak when the Jump took him. Amy Jenkins was a few paces ahead of him. Jake saw the back of her head light up purple. The street and burning buildings rippled around him with the customary puff of air against his face.

Then he was on his hands and knees in darkness. His stomach clenched and his throat burned with acid, but he managed to avoid throwing up. He looked left and right to make sure he was safe, but saw nothing. It didn't feel like the Darnell Suite. His hands rested on a hard surface that was cold and gritty. The air wasn't like 2040 either; it smelled simultaneously too fresh and yet polluted with the ancient carbon smell of coal and burnt oil.

Jake pulled himself to his feet, groping around him in the dark with outstretched arms. His left hand encountered the smoothness of what felt like painted wood; he patted his way along it until he touched the colder roughness of a brick wall, and then a flat plate of metal and a light switch. Jake pushed it downwards, and a bare bulb six inches above his head flared into life with a suddenness that made the door in front of him leap into being. Jake winced with the brightness, then forced his eyes open and studied his surroundings.

He was in a storeroom, with a low ceiling and a solid wooden door. There were some metal buckets and what looked like brooms and other cleaning equipment in one corner. Grubby overalls hung from hooks on the wall beside the door. Jake stepped closer to the door and put his ear to it, hearing a distant rumbling sound which quickly faded away.

The door didn't fit very closely into its frame, so Jake switched out the light to return the room to darkness and put his eye to the gap. He could see a few yards of a corridor, with a low curved ceiling and a picture on the wall opposite. It showed a man and woman side-by-side in uniform beneath the words "Serve in the WAAF with the Men Who Fly." The man and woman didn't look like they were going off to war; with their flushed faces and idiot smiles, they looked as if they were about to slip into the bushes to have sex. No doubt that was the subliminal message intended.

The door handle turned easily and Jake stepped into the empty corridor, checking in both directions to make sure he wasn't observed. He was in a London tube station. Beyond that, where—and when—remained a mystery. He seemed to have Jumped away from the street he'd been on with Amy Jenkins. How far, he didn't know. As to whether he had moved in time...he didn't know that either, but he obviously hadn't gone far. The poster on the wall told him he was still in wartime London—at least ninety years earlier than where he ought to be.

He gently touched his thumb between his shoulder blades, feeling as he so often had the hard lump of his tracker chip under the skin. His best bet was that someone at OffTime would quickly get a trace on him and he'd be picked up and swept back to 2040.

The corridor took him to a steep flight of spiral stairs and up into the ticket hall of London Bridge underground station. He was on the other side of the Thames, no more than half a mile from the place he'd Jumped. At the exit to the street, there was a man in a flat cap selling copies of the London Evening News. The main headline read "Allies Pound Hamburg and Berlin—Heavy Damage to Hitler's War Factories, Naval Base." Jake walked past and doubled back into the station, walking close to the newspaper seller. The date above the headline was Monday, November 22nd 1943.

Jake had Jumped half a mile across London and two-and-a-half years into the future. He had no idea why. Every return Jump he'd taken had sent him downtime to the exact location he started from. He'd never experienced a Jump that shifted him in space as well as time, nor had he heard of anyone else doing it. Nor had he ever heard of anyone falling short in their return Jump after a mission. He had no idea how it could've happened.

That wasn't all he didn't know. He couldn't be sure that OffTime knew he was here, or how long it would take them to pull him out. He was confident they'd track him and rescue him. Indeed, it was most likely he'd be picked up within minutes. However long it took them to locate him, they could then target a pick-up at the earliest point of his time here. This gave rise to a worrying thought: did the fact he hadn't already been pulled out mean he hadn't been found? Ever?

It wasn't a pleasant thought, but it was one that bore down heavily on him during the hour he hung around the station, gaining nothing except suspicious looks from the railway staff. He was reluctant to move too far from his arrival location, but there was a limit to how long he could sit around waiting for the boys in 2040 to bring him in.

He walked into the London Bridge mainline station and bought a ticket to Deptford. On the short train ride, he went over in his mind what he needed to do. Jake's team for the 1941 mission, as with every OffTime Jump, had hypno-conditioning on what to do if something went wrong. It told him where to go, what kind of place to stay in, and where to find work until rescued. It also included the coded messages he should put in newspapers so his colleagues in 2040 could trace him. Until now, Jake had always assumed this was like the demonstrations on airliners of where to find the life jackets. It might comfort passengers to know they were there, but he'd never heard of a plane crash where anyone's life was saved by pulling a life jacket from under the seat.

Jake wasn't aware of any agent being marooned in the past, let alone saving himself with an entry in the personal ads. But what choice did he have? He'd follow his briefing, and at least his rescuers would be able to predict where he was and what he was doing. The fact that his briefing was aimed at being stuck in 1941—*not* 1943—complicated things, but Deptford was still there. Not being rescued immediately was worrying, but maybe there was some technical explanation for that.

Maybe they needed to choose a different time or place to pull him out. If he had to leave messages in newspapers, maybe it was impossible to pull him out until after he had done so, to avoid the paradox of a rescue prompted by a message he wasn't around to leave. That is, if they found the messages left more than two years after the time they'd be searching.

He spent a cold night under a railway arch near Deptford station, hardly sleeping, constantly on the alert for patrolling police or air raid wardens. There was one improvement from 1941; by this stage of the War the British were heavily into payback, with most of the bombing being conducted over German cities and raids on London now relatively rare. There were no sirens or bombs that night.

When he woke, he was cold and damp, and it was still dark. Unfortunately, it was also still 1943. Jake sat with his back against the rough brickwork of the railway arch and looked out at the rain as the sky paled to gray and the day began. He wondered if he was here to stay. Was that possible? Did the laws of time allow him to live out a life before he was conceived or born? It still seemed unthinkable that he could be lost to his own time, but he had to face the possibility that not having been pulled out yet might mean he never would be. All he could do was make the best of things until the Office got a fix on him.

Jake had always assumed the people running OffTime—the guys on the Eleventh Floor, for whom even Ed Robinson asked how high when they said jump—were people who knew everything they needed to know and had all the angles covered. The life of an OffTime agent was so carefully controlled—the selection process when you were just out of college, the years of training, the way they made sure you lived with other agents and encouraged you to socialize only in OffTime circles. They made you feel special, and trained and rewarded you well. In return, you trusted them when they asked you to do things that would otherwise seem insane, like get zapped ninety years into the past to scare off some crackpots who might want to bump off Winston Churchill.

Jake never questioned the wisdom and competence of the people who had his life in their hands. Sure, he'd been bored at times, as he'd told Robinson. There were times he wondered if there wasn't something better to do with his life. He knew Lew Brockley worried more than he did. For all his hard-bitten exterior, Lew remained a closet idealist. Lew's fascination with history made him feel there was more humanity could be doing with the Darnell system. What a gift to be able to travel back and see the building of the pyramids, to find out for sure what happened to the royal princes in the Tower, to see what treasures were lost when the Library of Alexandria burned.

Jake understood that point of view. It'd be good to live in a world where something like the Darnell Jump could be handed over to historians. But that wasn't the world they lived in and probably never would be. Jake had always had faith in the people at the top. It wasn't their fault that bad people tried to use time travel for bad things. When he stepped naked onto the polished tiles of the Darnell Suite he put his life in their hands, and he had never questioned doing so.

Until now.

Until now, he never expected to be sitting on the cold concrete under a Deptford railway arch, hunched over his knees to keep warm. He watched the rain come down like the backdrop for a black-and-white movie, wondering if he was going to be here for good, like some time-traveling Robinson Crusoe with no way back to his own time—except by living to be 130.

XIII

London, 1943

The room was on the third floor of a terraced house at the north end of Deptford High Street. On one side was a greengrocer shop, on the other was a bomb site—a tidy pile of rubble, from a direct-hit eighteen months earlier. The bomb destroyed one house and left a long crack in the brickwork of its neighbor, through which cold air flowed if Jake held his hand close to the wall. The landlord noticed him looking at the wall when he showed him up to the room.

"Needs a bit of work." He ran a hand back through thin, greasy hair. "But what can you do? The war, eh?"

"It's fine." Jake dropped his bag on the bed.

"Working at the navy yards, did you say?"

"Something like that. Can't say much; you know how it is."

"Oh yeah, 'course," the landlord said. "Keep mum, eh? Is that all your baggage, then?"

"For now. If I need to stay longer, I'll probably bring more," Jake said. "By the way, do you have a phone book I could use?"

"In the hall, by the phone. There's a tin to pay for calls."

After the landlord had clumped back down the bare wooden stairs, Jake lay on the bed and stared up at the paint flaking from the ceiling. He was no more than two hundred yards from the site of the apartment he shared with Hannah in 2040. He could stand up and leave this fleapit and walk home in two minutes.

Well, to be exact, two minutes to walk home and eighty years to wait for his and Hannah's apartment block to be built. In 2040, Deptford was largely rebuilt with several large apartment blocks, one of them owned by OffTime, and a string of lively bars and restaurants along the High Street. In 1943, the

High Street was a shattered string of bomb sites, shops, and tenements with boarded windows.

It was strange settling into life in 1943. Jake still expected to be rescued imminently, constantly awaiting the tell-tale violet light and shimmering nausea of the Darnell Jump. At the same time, he diligently followed the emergency plan no one ever expected to be needed. This room was the first step. It was in the area his briefing required so he could be more easily traced.

The next step was to place his ads. Jake found the addresses of three south London newspapers in the phone book and made a couple of calls. He was too late for today's deadline, but two of the papers promised he could get an ad in before the end of the week if he placed it in person at their offices the next day.

Unable to stay in his room and wait for tomorrow, Jake went out late in the afternoon and traveled into London. Lacking anything better to do, he had the unlikely thought it might help if he spent some time as close as possible to the alley where the May 1941 pick-up was meant to happen. Maybe being near the target area might improve the chance of the Office tech guys getting a fix on him.

At least, he thought so until he got there. The difference from the night of the air raid dissolved his hope. For him, the raid and botched pick-up were only hours before, but the sight of the junction at the north end of London Bridge brought home that for the rest of the world, the night of the raid was more than two years ago.

The Liverpool Victoria insurance building was completely gone, leaving behind a rough patch of uneven ground behind a fence with broken bricks and pieces of timber sticking up from earth colonized by weeds. With no insurance company building, there was no longer any alley beside it. The neighboring building was also gone, the road junction reorganized, with the relatively few cars now obliged to circle round an improvised roundabout made of sandbags.

The sight of the road in front of the bomb sites reminded him of his foolish dash away from his team, drawn by the distress call from someone he assumed must be an OffTime agent. What happened to that guy and what was doing there in the first place? He also thought about Amy Jenkins, whom he'd pulled from the fire that night. He wondered what happened to her after he disappeared into his botched Jump. If he ever got back to 2040, he'd look her up. It would be nice to know she survived the war, so stranding himself in wartime London wouldn't be entirely wasted.

He didn't stay near the pick-up point for long. London in 1943 felt less tense than 1941, and certainly, the fear of invasion must've eased by this stage of the war. Nevertheless, there was, if anything, a more obvious military presence on the streets, and hanging around the same parts of the City for too long would soon attract attention.

He was already conspicuous as a younger man not in uniform. Conscription had been in operation in Britain for more than four years, and although Jake had fake medical documents showing he had a heart condition that exempted him, he couldn't be sure they'd withstand much scrutiny—not least because they were now out of date.

Jake returned to Deptford feeling as if he was suspended in mid-air, unsure if the sensation was that of someone falling or leaping. He sat on his bed, thinking about his options. They were narrow. All he could do was follow the emergency plan. He had a place to stay and tomorrow, he'd start placing his ads. If the first one didn't work, he'd keep doing it to maximize the chances of OffTime researchers spotting one of them in a century's time.

If he wasn't pulled out within a few days he'd need to get a job. The rational part of him still believed OffTime would trace him soon. But he'd need to be working, both to avoid suspicion and give him resources to handle a longer stay.

Next morning, he was up and out early, taking the bus to Camberwell, where he placed a brief advertisement in the following Friday's South London Press. It read, "Jack missing Jill. Time to come home." He stood outside the newspaper office afterward, expecting at any moment the Jump to take him, but nothing happened. Another bus ride took him back to Deptford, where he placed a similar notice in the next day's Greenwich and Lewisham News—still no puff of air and flash of violet light.

Jake pushed thoughts of the future from his mind and pressed on with his plan. Next step—a job. There was no shortage of demand for workers in wartime. Top of the list in his 1941 emergency plan was working as an air raid warden, an ideal occupation for a man of his age who was sadly unfit to join the fighting forces. He quickly discovered that in late 1943, there were still plenty of opportunities in the ARP in Lewisham and Catford; vacancies for unpaid part-time volunteers and, more importantly, opportunities for new trainees to be paid as they learned the job.

Within twenty minutes of walking into the Ministry of Labor office, Jake had the job. He could start the next evening, on the night shift. The speed suited him. He wanted to be busy to take his mind off the future.

The ARP station was on Lewisham High Street. Jake wasn't familiar with the place from his own time. Like other OffTime staff, he and Hannah tended to stay close to their riverside home in Deptford.

In any case, the area had a rough reputation, especially since anti-immigrant riots in the early 2030s burned out a lot of the shops. So, he couldn't compare the 1943 version with 2040. But, however run-down the high street was in 2040, he was sure the main road didn't have a crater thirty feet wide, ringed by a low rope barrier on which was pinned a handwritten notice saying 'Unexploded Bomb—Keep Away.'

He'd been told to report to the ARP station at seven. He had an address on a piece of paper, and it was easy enough to find. The number of vacant spaces created by bombs in what recently were terraces of houses narrowed down the search. A gray-haired man in a shabby tweed jacket sat at a desk inside the door. He looked up when Jake came in.

"I'm guessing you'd be Mister Wesson?"

"That's right." Jake handed him the paper he'd been given at the Labor Ministry. The man took it, wrote something in a large ledger on the desk in front of him and folded the paper into the book.

"I'm Captain Rogers. I run the station. Bit young, aren't you?"

Jake knew what he meant: *why aren't you in the Forces?*

"Not so young," he said. "Army wouldn't have me. Weak heart, they said. I thought six months with the ARP, and maybe they'd give me another chance."

"Well," Rogers said, dismissing the issue. "Let me show you around." He turned and led the way inside. Jake followed him into the interior of the building to the equipment room, where Rogers found him a set of dark overalls.

"These are the largest we've got," he said. "You're the tallest on the station. They don't fit, we're stuck."

"They look fine." The clothes felt heavy and slightly damp. Jake wondered who'd worn them last and where the guy was now.

"And you'll need these." Rogers handed Jake a black steel helmet, shaped like a shallow soup bowl with a flat rim. It had ARP painted on it in large white letters. Rogers also gave him an armband with the same letters on it.

"I'll show you the telephone and wireless later," Rogers said as they walked past the open door to a room containing a desk with an antique-looking radio set on it. "We all get a turn manning the set, so you need to know what to do."

Rogers opened the door to a small canteen, which was unnaturally warm and bright after the rest of the library building. Two middle-aged women were playing chess at a wooden table, each with a mug of tea in front of them. Rogers introduced them as Mrs. Morgan and Mrs. Buckingham.

"Nice to have a young man around the place," Mrs. Morgan said.

"Not as young as all that," Jake said.

"Young enough for us, darling," Mrs. Buckingham said, digging her elbow into the ribs of her companion. They both giggled.

"And that's our Mrs. Farrell." Captain Rogers gestured with his head behind Jake. "But you'll be lucky if she talks to you. She's a quiet one. No danger of loose lips sinking ships there."

Jake looked round. He hadn't noticed her when they entered the room, but a younger woman, maybe mid-to-late twenties, was curled up in an armchair in the corner of the room behind the door. She had a hardback book in her lap, and her head was bent over it, her dark fringe hiding her eyes. She glanced up when Rogers said her name.

Jake recognized her at once. She had dark green eyes, like the sea on a stormy day, slightly sunken in her face, giving her a bruised, sleepless appearance. Her skin was as pale as paper like she'd never been out in daylight, with lips full and red as if she'd eaten cherries. It was Amy Jenkins.

The silence was broken by a faint rustling, followed by a thump as the book slid out of her lap and onto the wooden floor. "Farrell's my married name. You know I don't use it," Amy said to Rogers, with a tone that suggested she'd told him many times. Her eyes remained fixed on Jake, who felt as if the floor was unsteady beneath him.

"Well, well, Mister Wesson," she said. "You don't look any different."

XIV

Amy didn't have a chance to talk to Jacob Wesson until later in the evening when he was given a break after part one of the Captain Rogers Induction Lecture. It was a slow night, and Amy was still in the canteen when Wesson reappeared alone while Rogers made a telephone call downstairs. The chess-playing biddies had disappeared out on patrol.

There was small coal fire burning in the room. It gave little heat, especially with the uniforms hanging in front of the grate, drying on a wire frame. Amy sat in a different seat by now, and Wesson didn't see her at first. He closed the door behind him and, apparently thinking he was alone, something changed in his face and his body—a slump of the shoulders, a softening of the business-like stiffness in his face. There was something vulnerable about him, like a boy who'd lost his mother.

"Do you want a cup of tea?"

Wesson was startled at Amy's voice, rapidly reassembling his outward face. She sat close to the fire, legs folded beneath her on the chair. She yawned and stretched her arms out wide.

"That'd be lovely," Wesson said. "Can you make tea, then?"

"I can do all sorts of things, cheeky bugger."

"I bet you can." He held her gaze. Amy didn't look away, and she was quietly pleased when he had to break the eye contact. She made tea in large white mugs, one of which had a chip out of the rim. She gave that one to Jake, and they sat on either side of the fireplace.

"Funny, you showing up here," Amy said, watching Wesson over the rim of her mug.

"Coincidences just keep happening."

"What have you been doing since... I saw you last?"

"Not much." Jake must've seen the skepticism in her face. "Really, not very much. You'd be surprised."

"I'm sure." There was a soft pop from the fireplace as coal settled in the grate. "Still doing the same work?"

"Kind of. I've got a feeling it might just about be finished."

Neither of them said anything for a while after that. Amy shifted position in her chair, and Captain Rogers' voice faintly carried from elsewhere in the building. He always spoke very loudly on the phone, as if he didn't trust the technology to carry his words over distance.

"What about you?" Jake said. "How have you been? I mean, since. . .?"

"What do you think? Bloody war never ends." Amy was surprised how much it still hurt to be reminded of that last night she saw Wesson, in May of 1941. Thinking about it was like pressing on a bruise. Most days she didn't think about it, but his reappearance dredged up painful memories like rotten leaves from the bottom of an old well.

"That night," Wesson said softly. "In the raid. I'm sorry I had to disappear so suddenly. I couldn't avoid it. I'm glad you made it out all right."

"Well, I made it. Not sure how all right I am." She shook her head. "That bloody night. It was the last of the really big raids. So far. And Christ, they had to make it a truly big one, didn't they? That was the night they got the Tower of London, Parliament, Westminster Abbey. I didn't know a building could go up in flames so fast.

"After you left me," Amy continued, "at that shelter near Cannon Street. It got a direct hit."

"Christ. Really?"

"They told me afterward I was buried thirty feet down," Amy said. "I was still on the stairs near the entrance when we got hit, and I think the stronger walls near the door saved me. They were still standing, although not much else was. They had to dig me out. I remember someone calling down when I was buried, asking me what religion I was."

"And what religion are you?"

Amy looked at him for a few moments. He intended the question to be light-hearted, to lift the mood a little, but she wasn't inclined to play along.

"What religion can anyone be these days? The way the world is."

"You had a lucky escape though."

"Everyone else was killed." Amy kept her eyes on Wesson, but she saw something far beyond him, a long way from this room. "And that building where I worked, where you found me that night. It was bombed after most of the day shift left, so I suppose it could've been worse. But over twenty people were killed."

"I'm sorry."

"The manager of the night shift and all the other staff on the upper floors, all dead. Including the husband I was married to for only a week. I was engaged, married, and a widow all in a year and I wasn't yet twenty-four years old. What religion do you think that would make me?"

"I'm sorry," Jake said again.

"No point being sorry. You just have to get on with it, don't you?" Amy took a deep breath and drank some of her tea. "What about you, Mister Wesson? What have you been doing for the last two endless years of the war?"

"Like I said, surprisingly little. Just getting by, like everyone else."

"You don't look any different," she said. "This bloody war isn't aging you like most of us, anyway."

"Looks can be deceiving."

"Have you had an accident there?" Amy leaned forward, staring at the side of his neck. He had a pink line below his ear as if he'd recently suffered a cut.

"This?" Wesson touched the side of his face. "Oh, just a scratch. Helping a friend move some timber last week." The scratch on Wesson's face reminded Amy of something, but she couldn't place it. She pushed the thought aside.

For her, Wesson showing up at the ARP station felt at first like a painful intrusion. It was as if a ghost from May 1941 had walked in and all at once, images from the terrible night and the endless bitter days after Alfie's death pushed up in her mind like wrecked ships uncovered by a retreating tide. And yet, despite the painful memories stirred by the sight of Wesson, there was something else about him.

She remembered the strange encounter with him on her wedding day and the feeling she had even then that he was a man she could talk to. If she hadn't been in her wedding dress—her wedding underwear, to be honest—this was someone she could've been drawn to.

She could tell he liked her; she'd been used to that in men since she was about thirteen. She'd never had any problem attracting men's attention. But Wesson did more than stare at her legs. She quickly found he spoke to her and listened to her in a way she'd never known from any other man. She felt like he saw her as a full person, not just a woman. He was interested in what she thought and felt.

There was also the breath of mystery clinging to him. Amy didn't know how seriously to take his story on her wedding day, about working undercover. There was nevertheless something unusual about him, and not knowing what it was made Amy want to find out more. Her interest, combined with a new recklessness, emboldened her to get to know Wesson better. After all, no one knew where the war was going or what the future would be like.

Amy had already had the life she grew up for—the wedding and the husband, and the sensible job in an office. Now that was over, like she'd lived one life and was free to find another. Maybe the world would never return to normal. No one even knew if they'd live to see the end of the war, and who could guess what life would be like if they did?

Why not do what you felt like doing?

XV

Hannah Benedict spent the first hours after the return from 1941 at the Darnell Suite with Lew and Nancy, watching the frantic efforts to trace Jake. Ed Robinson called in extra staff until by the end of that day there were eight technicians crowded into the control room—all hunched over touch-screens, conferring in whispers, stepping around Hannah and the others, who could do no more than drink coffee and watch.

Hannah didn't think she'd make it through a single day without knowing what happened to Jake. Surely, she wouldn't have to; how lost could he be when he'd Jumped *somewhere*, and the Office controlled the Jumps? But the day stretched into evening with no trace of him, and Hannah felt as if her head had been pumped full of sand. Tears hung just behind her eyes, but she couldn't cry them out.

Nancy came home with her when they finally gave up for the day. Lew stayed behind at the Suite, dozing on three chairs he'd pushed together. That became the pattern as that first day stretched into two, three, four, and five days without news; they took turns staying at the Darnell Suite, but either Lew or Nancy stayed close to Hannah, afraid she might break if left alone.

Hannah expected Jake's absence to be even harder to bear at home, but strangely she missed him less there than at the Office. It was as if his absence highlighted the way he'd been partially absent from their home for some time, without either of them noticing it.

Everyone expected Jake to be found quickly, but hours stretched into days and then beyond a week. Hannah kept away from Ed Robinson and the other brass, but Nancy reported back to her on a couple of blazing rows in the Darnell Suite, and Lew's almost daily arguments with them over the time it was taking to find Jake. To Hannah, Lew was reassuring. Sure, he said it might take a while to pin Jake down precisely, but it *would* happen. And when it did, they could pull him out from the earliest possible point in the past so this agonizing period of uncertainty would be invisible to him. He'd have very little time alone in the past.

At last, ten endless days after their return from 1941, Ed Robinson summoned the three of them to a meeting. It was the first time any of them had been to his new office on the eleventh floor. Their names were on the list with Security, who waved them into the lift, and they found their passes took them to the normally off-limits eleventh.

"I'm sorry this meeting has taken so long." Robinson waved them into the three seats opposite him. "But I finally I have some news."

"Let me guess, we saved Churchill," Lew said.

"About Jake?" Hannah leaned forward.

"Yes." Robinson took his customary unlit cigar out of the top pocket of his jacket and rolled it between his fingers as he spoke. "It's good news up to a point. But we can't raise our hopes too much just yet."

"We'll try not to get over-excited," Lew said.

"You know I can't afford to worry too much about personal feelings in this job," Robinson said. "But finding Jake is personal for me as well as you. And I'm even more determined to bring him back because of what he means to you, Hannah. You know how close I was to your father..."

"You don't need to say it." Hannah didn't want to think about her father as well as Jake. Tom Benedict was a policeman, originally in Cambridge, where Hannah was born. The family moved around a lot when she was young, eventually settling in south London during the years her father was in the Metropolitan Police. He'd been friendly with the younger Ed Robinson, and no doubt still would be if he hadn't got in the way of a bullet during a shoot-out that ended a siege at the Belgian Embassy. Hannah was fourteen.

"I've known you both a long time."

"I know," Hannah said. "Please, Ed, what can you tell us?"

"You remember how we lost Jake when you all Jumped." Robinson thumbed a mark on the table between them and the wood-effect surface faded out, revealing a screen. It showed the familiar pattern of dots from the night they returned from 1941. One-by-one the dots blinked out. Hannah's eyes felt hot as she saw the last dot go, knowing it showed Jake disappearing from 1941 and into the unknown.

"We can't track people as they Jump through time. We can monitor a specific place and time, and you all have the trackers to make that easier. But it can, in theory, take a long time if you aren't sure where to look."

The screen display between them had changed color. The concentric circles Hannah had seen the day they Jumped from 1941 were back, and a numerical display appeared in the corner. As Hannah watched, the numbers changed rapidly, flicking forward.

"We made a few assumptions," Robinson said. "We were trying to Jump Jake back home, forward in time. That involves a different set of calculations to sending him farther back, so we started by searching between 1941 and the present."

"If he were close to the present, he'd get in touch," Nancy said.

"Exactly," Robinson said. "We assumed he was further back in the past, unable to contact anyone he knows."

"So, have you found him?" Lew said. "Don't keep us in suspense, Ed."

"Let me explain this my way, Lew," Robinson said. "There are things you need to understand."

"I understand we need to get Jake back. What I don't understand is why he isn't here now, if you've found him."

"Lew, let him tell us," Hannah said. Lew shrugged and fell silent.

"Thank you, Hannah," Robinson said. He nodded again at the table between them. The flickering numbers had slowed down. "We started by running sample checks, spread out at weekly intervals, between 1941 and 2010," Robinson said. "We focused on south east London because that's where your emergency briefing told you to stay."

As Robinson spoke, the numbers slowed further and then stopped at 16.35:05.31.1944A. On the screen, just inside the outer circle, was a bright red dot. It pulsed gently.

"Is that—?"

"Yes." Hannah didn't like the serious tone of Robinson's voice. "We've pinpointed Jake in May 1944, in Deptford."

"That's great, isn't it?" Hannah said. "You've found him."

"Why isn't he here now?" Lew added.

Robinson sucked thoughtfully on his cold cigar. He looked like he was trying to find the right words to use to explain to a child that sadly, Santa Claus didn't exist.

"It's a little complicated."

"Hold the front page," Lew said. "Time travel is complicated. But you've found him. Why're we sitting here talking about him when your tracking system shows him on the screen?"

"Here's what you need to know," Robinson said. He stood up from his chair and took a couple of paces back and forth behind his desk, before facing them, arms folded. His cigar sat forgotten on the desk.

"There's no way to dress it up, so I'll just say it. The first problem is that we know Jake is there in May 1944. But we don't know how long he's been there, in his own subjective time."

"What?" Lew said. "Why not just track back?"

"We're doing that, obviously," Robinson said. "But there are limits on how closely we can monitor some parts of the past."

"First I've heard of it," Lew said.

"We don't advertise it," Robinson said. "It isn't an exact science. Some time periods are more opaque than others. And others have been blurred by our activity."

"Meaning what?" Hannah was finding the conversation hard to bear. Why didn't Ed just tell them how and when Jake was coming home?

"When there has already been a Jump to a time or place in the past, it can cause a blurring effect to our instruments. It can make it risky to go there again, and hard to get an accurate fix on it."

"I don't remember that from training," Nancy said.

"The point is, right now, we don't know how much earlier than May 1944 Jake's Jump took him. How long he's been living in the past by then. Obviously, the ideal scenario is to get him out at the earliest possible point."

"Obviously," Lew said.

"We want to rescue him before he's been left too long," Robinson shot Lew an irritated glare. "Just as important, we want to minimize his impact on the past. But knowing where he is in May 1944 doesn't guarantee we can easily locate him two months earlier if he's there."

"But we can't sit around waiting," Hannah said. "If your instruments can't pin him down, why not go back a bit earlier and look for him?"

"Too risky," Robinson said.

"Risky? That's bollocks, Ed," Lew said. "I'd do it today, and I bet I'd get you a dozen volunteers."

"No one doubts your courage, or anyone else's, Agent Brockley. But that isn't the kind of risk I mean. We can't afford to blunder around in the past any more than this incident has already done. If you jump back a few months and miss him, we risk making another patch of the past off-limits, introducing new disturbances on top of any already in play."

"What do you mean, disturbances?" Hannah asked.

"If we can't pinpoint Jake's arrival point, we may have to get him out after he's had to live in the past a while." Robinson sat back in his seat and picked up his cigar again. "That means he'll interact with the world he's in."

"Well? Don't we do that all the time?"

"In very carefully planned ways. Within limits we tightly control."

Hannah thought about the night they Jumped back from 1941 and the chaos of the firebomb raid. She was tempted to ask Robinson what he thought of that as an example of careful planning and tight control.

"Given the uncertainties, I want to know more about what he's been doing and how long he's been there before we try to extract him. It may require some remedial action, but we can't tell yet."

"Send me back, and I'll ask him," Lew said. "I don't get why it has to be so complicated."

"I've explained—"

"No, Ed, you haven't explained," Hannah said. "Lew's right; we could go back right now and talk to Jake. Why don't we do that?"

"He's trying to explain," Nancy cut in. "Why not listen?"

"Don't be such a suck-up, Nancy," Lew said.

"All right!" Robinson was on his feet again. "Let's have some discipline here. Agent Ahmed, I'm glad you've been paying attention, but when I need backup from a junior agent, I'll ask. Don't hold your breath."

"That's harsh, Ed," Lew said. Nancy's face flushed red.

"The same applies to more senior agents, too," Robinson said. "Look, I'll say this, and it doesn't go outside this room. We have reason to believe Jacob Wesson is in a particularly sensitive time and place, which means we need to handle his extraction with great care."

"Sensitive how?" Hannah said.

"I can't say much. It won't surprise you there are some people and events that are crucial for the integrity of the world we know. We keep a careful watch on them, and if there's any hint they could change, we consider intervening. By chance, Jake may be close to one of those points in the past. If things go wrong, especially if we charge in carelessly and certain events happen differently, it may be impossible to retrieve the situation."

"Impossible?" Lew said. "Even with time travel?"

"Yes."

"So, you're talking about something changing with an impact on time travel itself?"

"I can't say."

"I think you just did."

"The point is, I have to insist on this; it's my decision, and I'm playing it cautiously," Robinson said. "There's no doubt we'll bring Jake back. But we take our time and find out as much as possible. When we're sure we know what we're doing, we pull Jake out cleanly and gently from the earliest possible point we can be certain of. Then, when he's back, we debrief him on his activities. If necessary, we put in a team to tidy up."

"Meanwhile, he's left alone a century in the past, in the middle of a war," Hannah said. The thought of Jake alone in the past gave her a cold, tight feeling in her chest. "Thinking we've abandoned him."

"It's unavoidable," Robinson said. "I'm sorry, but it won't be for a minute longer than necessary."

XVI

After that first night at the ARP station, Amy and Jake frequently found themselves together. Both were full-time, among a host of part-time volunteers, and it was inevitable they'd see a lot of each other. Soon, they were working together most nights, often paired up on patrol or working the phone and radio in the office. Amy was pleased. A couple of times, early on, she had a quiet word with Captain Rogers to move her shift to coincide with Jake's. Rogers winked at her but did as she asked. After that, their shifts mostly coincided, as if by magic.

Amy knew she liked Jake and was ready for him to make the kind of move that would put their friendship on a new level. She got the feeling at times, from the way he spoke to her and looked at her, the way he went silent at odd times, that Jacob Wesson felt that way about her too. But days stretched into weeks, and nothing changed. They made each other tea and chatted long into the night on quiet shifts. Amy told Jake the little there was to tell about her life, and Jake said nothing much about his past.

She had the impression something unseen, standing behind Jake, made him hold back, stop himself and change the subject when their conversation got personal. She thought back to that first time they met, more than two years before. She'd been through so much since then, grown up as fast as life allowed. Jacob Wesson, on the other hand, hardly seemed to have changed. When he blundered into her wedding changing room, she had the impression of someone older and more experienced than her. Now the gap was barely noticeable.

Was Wesson really an undercover copper or a spy, or whatever he wanted her to believe? There was certainly something unusual about him, no doubt about it. There was the way he spoke, like he was trying to be casual but not quite pulling it off, and some of the words he used were odd—*okay* this and *okay* that.

Amy had an awful thought—*what if he was a spy, but not the right kind? You were always warned to look out for anything suspicious.* What if Jacob Wesson sounded odd because English wasn't his first language? What if he was German? She didn't believe that, but there was no doubt he was hiding something. It intrigued her.

It was mid-December. They'd worked together for nearly a month. Amy was alone in the ARP canteen when she heard footsteps on the stairs. She glanced at the mirror over the tea urn, brushing her hair back from her eyes. She recognized the footsteps. She bent back over the table where she was working.

"Ah, Miss Jenkins, I presume," Jake said from behind her. "May I make you a drink, or are you full?"

"Always room for tea, Mister Wesson."

"I've got something better," he said. She turned to see him holding a brown bag aloft as if it were a trophy. "I've managed to procure us some coffee."

"I don't drink it." Amy loved the way the room came alive when Jake entered it. She'd been bored, but that was forgotten now.

"You're not alone in that, which is why it isn't on ration," Jake said. "The problem is, it mostly isn't on sale, either. But there seems more of it about now with more Americans over here."

Jake made the drinks and brought the cups to the table Amy was working at—or tables, to be precise since she'd pushed two tables together and covered them with old newspapers. Strips of newspaper were piled at one end, with a jar of water and paintbrushes at the other. She stood upright to take her cup. His hand touched hers as he passed it but nothing showed on his face.

"What're you painting?"

"Paper chains for Christmas," she said. "Oh, yuck!" The coffee was hot and bitter, with a strong taste of charcoal.

"I know," he said. "Coffee, Jim, but not as we know it."

"Who's Jim?"

"Figure of speech," he said. "I've lost track, what with all the fun of the ARP. When's Christmas Day?"

"Saturday," Amy said. "Maybe it'll be the last Christmas of the war."

"We can hope." His face suggested he didn't believe it.

"Have you got any plans for Christmas, Mister Wesson?"

"You can call me Jake," he said. "We're alone, and I won't tell."

"Don't change the subject." Amy knew Jake lived not far from her, down the hill in Deptford, but maybe he had family out of London and was going away. "What're you doing Christmas day?"

"I've volunteered for the night shift here. In case Goering delivers a seasonal surprise."

"So, you're free during the day?" Amy said. "You could come to Christmas lunch with us."

"That's very kind," he said. "But I really couldn't—"

"My mum's been stocking up food for weeks," Amy said. "Someone's got to help us eat it. We've got half a turkey, shared with the neighbors."

"You're very generous, but—"

"You can't be on your own for Christmas. That's settled." Amy surprised herself by placing a finger on Jake's lips to stop him saying more. "Now, you can earn your lunch by picking up that paintbrush and helping me make these paper chains."

XVII

"Could I keep you for a brief word, Hannah?" Ed Robinson's hand was on her arm as Lew and Nancy left his office.

"I didn't want to involve the others in this." Robinson gave her a cool look. "But you may be able to help us speed things up with Jake."

"Just tell me what I need to do."

"There are some things we can do that I can't tell the others about. I can't trust everyone with this." Robinson opened his desk drawer and took out a small plastic card. He pushed it across the desk to Hannah, who picked it up. It had no writing on it, just a silvery surface that rippled with rainbow colors in the light.

"Most people don't even know we have this," Ed said. "We keep it pretty close under wraps."

"What is it?"

"That card will get you into a secure building not far from here. It'll also give you access to a tracking system through which you can see into the past, back to the period Jake Jumped to."

"You can see into the past?" Hannah said. "You mean without going there?"

"That's right. In very limited ways and fairly restricted places."

"How does it work?"

"You know how I am with technical stuff, Hannah. Basically, we can do it wherever we have a special camera in place."

Hannah hardly ever gave a thought to the thousands of cameras on London's streets. Traffic cameras, security cameras, and commercial cameras in every shop doorway to film people on the way in so their browsing and purchasing history could be pulled up from the customer database and the right offers and prices projected to them as they did their shopping.

"But, how many cameras would there be in Wartime London?"

"Well, none." Robinson smiled. "But that doesn't matter. We use the ones we have now."

"What, all the cameras in London, traffic and the rest, they can see into the past?"

"Not all of them are Darnell-enabled. Not even most of them. But quite a few," Robinson said. "The cameras are tiny, practically invisible. The best way I can explain it is that they travel back in time, and return. But really fast, like ten, twenty times a second, so we can get a recording. Anyway, I've set it up so you can go to this facility and help us try to get sightings of Jake in the past. Anything you can add to our knowledge might help us get him back safely."

"Of course," Hannah said, turning the card over in her hand. She supposed she ought to be pleased there were cameras that could peer into the past, anything that helped them do their job, anything that could help get Jake back. But there was something a bit creepy about it.

"There's something else. I need to talk about something a little, ah, delicate," Robinson said. "You know how long I've known Jake. He means a lot to me. But I have to consider every possibility. Have you noticed anything odd about Jake in recent months?"

"What do you mean by odd?"

"Any unusual behavior? You know him better than anyone. Did you notice anything unusual, however trivial it may have seemed at the time?"

"Ed, what're you getting at?"

"When I spoke to Jake about the 1941 mission he seemed distracted like there was something on his mind. It was one of the reasons I wanted him to do the job. I thought he'd benefit from some action, a different challenge."

"He certainly got that."

"I wondered if you'd noticed anything. Whether there was anything he said."

"I don't think so." But Hannah couldn't help thinking of the silences there'd been between her and Jake before they left for 1941. She'd sometimes wondered what Jake saw when his eyes glazed over, and he stared out of the window as they ate their dinner—was there someone else in his thoughts?

"This kind of thing hasn't happened before," Robinson said. "We still don't know why his Jump went wrong. That means we must consider every possibility. We can't rule out that Jake had something to do with it himself."

"Had something to do with what?"

"There's a possibility Jake Jumping to 1943 wasn't an accident."

"What, Jake wanted to send himself to the wrong time? How could he do that? And why risk the chance he might not get back?"

"I don't know," Robinson said. "But you might be able to help us find out."

"That's not what I want to find out, Ed. I want to get him back."

"Take the card," Robinson said. "You're booked in at eleven tomorrow. I've put the data you need on your palmer. We'll talk again after you've learned a bit more."

XVIII

It was a fifteen-minute walk from Jake's lodgings to Amy's house up the hill in Blackheath. On Christmas morning, the streets were still and empty, as if everyone had left the city in the night without telling him.

In truth, Jake often found 1940s London quieter and slower, without the all-enveloping sea of data that characterized the London he was used to. No palmers, no computers, hardly any cars on the road. In 1943, no cameras tracked you as you went, no one knew where you were unless you told them. Hardly anyone had a telephone, and there were few televisions. Even a radio was the kind of luxury many family homes had in only one room, and everyone sat around it and listened as if they were in church and it carried the word of God.

London's wartime streets should've seemed to Jake like a quaint museum, with sandbags on the doorsteps, sticky paper strips on the dirty window panes, and the posters on the sides of buildings—Is Your Journey Really Necessary? and Be Like Dad, Keep Mum. Jake looked at the posters of Churchill with their slogan Let Us Go Forward Together and, in addition to wondering whether he'd really saved the prime minister's life, he couldn't help drawing a contrast with the tone of advertising in 2040, where the message was always you *need* it, you *deserve* it, because you're *special. You. Just you and your friends.* In 2040, the idea of going forward together would've been laughable.

Amy lived with her parents on Dartmouth Row, a side street of small ter-raced houses off the main A2 road toward Kent. As he climbed the hill, Jake remembered coming this way with Hannah in April 1941; nearly three years ago, but to him, it was merely a few weeks in the past. He could've found the right house even if Amy hadn't given him the number. The memory of the younger Amy rushing out of the door of number 10 and colliding with him was fresh in his mind. Some coincidence that she should've bumped into him that day, with them following the precise OffTime schedule so closely.

Amy threw back the door as soon as he knocked. "Happy Christmas!" She took a step back. "My, you've smartened up, Mister Watson."

"Jake."

"Mum, Dad, he's here." Amy tugged him indoors by his arm.

Jake was introduced to Amy's parents, Ethel and William. Mrs. Jenkins gratefully relieved Jake of the Christmas pudding he'd brought, while Amy's father took his coat and sat him at the table with a glass of beer.

"It's so kind of you to have me, Mister and Mrs. Jenkins," Jake said.

"Nonsense!" Ethel said. "When Amy told us you were apart from your family, we couldn't leave you on your own. Anyway," she flicked a sly glance at her daughter, "we were keen to meet you. Amy's told us all about you."

"Mum!"

"The two of you pretty much run that air raid station, I've heard," William said.

"Well, don't tell Captain Rogers." Jake looked around the room. "Great decorations, by the way."

The meal was fantastic. Like so much of the food in wartime London, it was simple, but everything tasted uniquely of itself, unlike the force-grown vegetables and dubiously processed meats of his own time. Jake cleared his plate, to Ethel's obvious pleasure, and accepted a second helping. As they ate, the conversation ranged lightly over the state of the war, food shortages, and whether this was the year it would finally end, now that Germany was so clearly in retreat.

As they talked, Jake had a sense of being gently appraised by Amy's parents, and he wondered what she'd said about him. He knew she liked him, and he liked her, but he was stuck in an emotional limbo a month into his time in 1943. It was a month to him, but OffTime had had a century to trace him and find the best way to pull him out. He'd already placed over twenty newspaper adverts, enough for him to worry his cryptic messages could attract the suspicion of the security services. The fact he was still here a month on was a very bad sign.

There was one difficult moment during lunch. Amy's mother asked about his family. He explained that he had no close relatives living.

"But you'll have some relatives, surely? Cousins, aunts and uncles?"

"Yes, but none in London," Jake said, sticking with the cover story from his briefing. "I've got some cousins, but they're in Ireland."

"Where in Ireland?" Amy's father asked.

"The south west, a village near Killarney."

"We've got family there," William said. "What's the village called?"

"It's years since I was there," Jake said. "It always slips my mind."

"Must be hard to send them a Christmas card."

"I've got it written down somewhere," Jake said. "I haven't been since I was a child."

"I can name some villages," William said. "See if it jogs your memory."

"All right, Dad." Amy came to Jake's rescue. "He didn't come here to meet the Gestapo."

After lunch, they listened to the King's broadcast on the wireless. When Jake left, Amy walked with him part of the way down the hill.

"They liked you," she said.

"You think so? I thought your dad was going to fingerprint me."

"Well, be honest, you don't know much about Ireland, do you?"

Jake said nothing to that, and they continued walking for a couple of minutes. The afternoon was already growing dark, with a sheet of gray cloud above them almost close enough to touch.

"Just tell me this," Amy said at last. She linked her arm through his and kept walking. "I know there are things you're not saying. Maybe you've got good reasons. But I want to know I can trust you. That you're not hiding anything serious."

"It depends on what you mean by serious."

"Well, it'd be serious if you were a German spy."

"True," Jake laughed. "I promise, I'm not a German spy or any kind of spy. It's just that there are things I can't tell you at the moment. Maybe one day I can."

"Very mysterious."

"But I can promise you something." Jake stopped walking and turned to face her, holding both her arms. "There may be things I can't say, but you can trust what I do say. I won't tell you any lies."

"That better be true," Amy said. Her eyes searched his face, and she leaned closer. "I've been let down too much already. I don't need any more of it."

"I won't let you down." Their faces were so close, they were only inches from a kiss. Jake was sure that was what Amy wanted, but something held him back.

"Well, I'd better get home," she said at last. "And you've got to work tonight. Give my love to the Captain." With that, Amy turned and walked back up the hill. Jake watched her go, but she didn't turn around.

XIX

London, 2040

The address Ed Robinson gave Hannah led her to a building next to Vaux-hall Bridge, a reddish-brown dome like a blood blister clinging to the silvery-gray limb of the river. Two parallel lines of lights in the ground ran up to the wall of the dome. Where the blue lights gave out, Hannah stood in front of a curved wall of what looked like a brown-tinted mirror. A red light pulsed gently about five feet off the ground. When she held the card up to the light, there was a soft hum from the wall, and a line appeared, widening as two sections of mirrored wall moved apart, opening a door into the building. Hannah stepped inside, and the door closed behind her.

She was in a small, featureless room. Ahead of her was a steel door with a window in it, and another red-glowing lens beside it. Hannah tried her card again, and there was a flash of violet light and a subtle vibration that made her briefly sway and reach out a hand to the wall for balance. The sensation was unmistakable—she'd just Jumped in time. Hannah remembered the stories she'd heard, about OffTime's secret complex buried deep in the past, and wondered what was now outside the building.

A female voice came from somewhere above her. "Welcome Agent Bene-dict. Please do not be alarmed by our security procedures. Follow the lights to room seventeen. You have one hour and fifty-nine minutes remaining of your authorized session."

Beyond the door, a breadcrumb trail of tiny green lights in the floor led her into the interior of the building and along a corridor for about thirty meters to a door with the number seventeen on it. She saw no other people, nor did she detect any sign there was anyone else in the building. She held her silver card up at the door, and it whispered open. She stepped into a small cubicle without windows. It contained nothing but a plastic chair in front of a desk, on which there was a touch screen.

Hannah sat and touched the screen, which came instantly to life. She took out her palmer and read the instructions Robinson had given her, tapping codes into the keyboard on the screen in front of her. A map of the southern half of England appeared, outlined in blue, with a constellation of tiny white lights scattered across it. The lights indicated places where there was a camera that was past-enabled. The white dots merged in places where there were larger towns and cities. London was a bright blob of light.

Hannah tapped the screen to zoom in, and the lights began to separate. She zeroed in on south-east London until Deptford and Blackheath filled the screen, the lights now strung along the main roads, with a dark patch over the open grass of the heath. Hannah looked again at her palmer, which contained the camera locations Robinson suggested. She started with an address in Deptford High Street. When she touched the camera location on the screen, the map was replaced by a grainy black-and-white street scene. It appeared to be shot from a camera above the entrance to the railway station, facing north up the street. The address she wanted was on the right, next to a fruit and vegetable shop.

At the top of the screen was a row of numbers, showing the time and date—early on the 26th of May, 1944. With her thumb, Hannah stroked the numbers, and the picture ran fast forward. A horse-drawn milk float sped toward the camera, jerking from place to place as it stopped at the curb to make deliveries. Other vehicles raced like ghosts in-and-out of the shot, while people walking along the footpath flicked into view and disappeared. Hannah slowed the picture at 07:50. A man emerged from a door in the building next to the fruit shop and stepped out onto the pavement, buttoning up a long coat.

It was Jake.

Hannah's stomach lurched, and she leaned forward to peer more closely at the screen, tapping the display to freeze the picture. She froze, mesmerized by the sudden sight of him. She'd known he was back in the past, cast away in wartime London, and she'd believed Robinson when he told her Jake was living in Deptford. But believing what you're told was one thing and seeing your lover a century in the past was another.

What was he thinking, standing on the scruffy Deptford street, a few feet from a bombed-out house and just around the corner from the home he'd share with Hannah many years in the future?

She tapped the screen, and the picture moved again. Jake stayed where he was. A banner of steam from his mouth suggested it was still chilly, this early in the morning. He looked away from the camera, up the road as if searching for something. He stuffed his hands deep into his coat pockets and hunched his shoulders.

Then he caught sight of something.

Whatever he saw was out of sight of the camera, but Jake lifted a hand and walked forward. Hannah peered at the screen as if she might get a better view and catch a glimpse of whoever Jake had been waiting for. But she was out of luck; Jake disappeared out of the shot at the bottom of the screen.

Hannah sat back in her chair and gazed at the image of the empty street. Then she rewound the picture a few minutes and watched again. She slowed the replay of the last few seconds, as Jake walked beneath the camera, and froze the picture just before he disappeared. She zoomed in on his face, so it filled the lower part of the screen.

He looked tired, and his hair was longer than when she last saw him. He wasn't looking at the camera, but at whoever was out of the shot beneath it. Hannah stared hard at the darkness of his eyes as if she might see a reflection of whoever he was about to meet.

Do you think of me? Can you feel me watching you?

There was a sketch of a smile on Jake's lips, which were partly open as if he was about to speak. Nothing about him suggested a man marooned in an alien world. He looked calm and relaxed. *And happy*, Hannah thought. The idea reminded her of Ed Robinson's suspicion that Jake might've engineered his own shipwreck in 1944. He looked happy. She didn't know how that made her feel.

She spent ten minutes ranging back in time with the same camera, but she didn't catch any other glimpses of Jake. The second location in her palmer was a view across a busy road, from a camera outside Lewisham Hospital. She tried a time suggested by Robinson, a week earlier than the scene she'd just watched. Early evening, the road was thick with traffic—a couple of double-decker buses crowded with passengers, at least a dozen cars nose to tail, and several men on bicycles.

A stationary bus in the middle of the scene moved away to the right of the screen and Jake was in the middle of the picture, facing the camera as he attempted to cross the road. He wasn't alone. He was part of a group of six or seven people waiting to cross the road, but there was no sign that Jake knew most of them. The exception was the woman who stood next to him.

Hannah saw them cross the road through a gap in the traffic. They were deep in conversation, Jake saying something and gesturing with one hand before the woman replied and they both laughed as they reached the pavement. They disappeared to the left of the screen, leaving Hannah frustrated and wishing there was a control that enabled her to move the camera. Something troubled her about the scene. She rewound it and watched again, slowing the replay so that Jake and his mystery companion appeared to wade through treacle as they crossed the road toward her.

They're too close together.

Jake and the woman were perhaps half a pace closer together than the other people crossing the road. Jake's hand rested briefly on the woman's arm, and she leaned in a little closer to him before they moved apart again. Hannah froze the picture just before they disappeared out of frame. They were walking away to the side of the camera, Jake's hand briefly touching the woman in the small of her back.

Does Ed know about this?

Hannah realized she didn't care what Ed knew. What mattered was what she knew. She ran the recording back another time until she could see Jake and the woman facing the camera. She zoomed in on the woman's face. She looked younger than Jake and Hannah, maybe mid-twenties, although a suggestion of frown lines above her eyes hinted at a young woman who'd known some pain. Unsurprising in the fifth year of the war, Hannah supposed, living in London under nightly threat of German bombing. The woman's hair was dark, although it was impossible to guess the color from the black-and-white picture. There was a hint of girlish freckles across her nose and under her eyes.

Hannah chewed her lip. The reflection of her face on the dark screen overlaid like a pale ghost the frozen image of the woman with Jake in 1944. She studied her own familiar features idly and thought the girl looked plain in comparison. There was something familiar about this girl, but she couldn't place it.

There was one other bit of magic left in the OffTime box of tricks. When Robinson had told her about it, Hannah hadn't thought she'd need it. Now she opened her palmer again and scanned the instructions. A couple of taps on the screen pulled up the function she needed. She zeroed the display on the woman with Jake and pressed once on the desktop to lock in, then ran the scene again from the beginning.

As the scene unrolled, the woman was highlighted by a glowing green line that flowed with her movements, following her as she walked as if she was clothed in an all-covering suit. In the top left corner of the screen, a display appeared. At first it read Possible Matches: 1576. As the scene ran, and the green line tracked the woman's movements, the numbers rapidly counted down. When the woman and Jake walked out of the picture, the display read Possible Matches: 17.

Hannah tapped on the number 17, and a list of names and addresses scrolled down the screen. Fewer than half the entries were in London, enabling her to delete nine. She looked carefully through the remaining eight, and one address stood out—Dartmouth Row, SE10.

Hannah saw on her palmer that a third camera location Robinson had given her was in SE10. She thumbed the screen and navigated to a traffic camera on Shooters Hill Road, looking south across the road and into the end of a small side road. Robinson had, for some reason, also given her a date and time—17:16, 18 May 1944.

Earlier still.

She saw them at once. Jake and the woman again, walking toward the camera from the side road. They were laughing about something and at one point, the young woman put her hand on Jake's arm, and Hannah felt something give way silently inside her. She zeroed in on the woman's face. The luminous line appeared again around her, and the legend on the screen counted down within a couple of seconds to read Possible Matches: 1. With a tap, Hannah pulled up the sole remaining entry:

Amelia Charlotte Jenkins (Farrell m. 7 May 1941, w. 10 May 1941), 10 Dartmouth Row, London SE10.

There was a small asterisk after the name and at the bottom of the screen another asterisk next to the words Project Reset. The words were pale blue and underlined, indicating a hyperlink to another file. Hannah tapped on the link, and a red box appeared in the middle of the screen, containing the words:

ACCESS DENIED

Project Reset

insert access code

Hannah had no idea what Project Reset might be, nor what the access code was. It was probably best not to guess. Someone in OffTime would know if she tried to gain access to a file she shouldn't see. She tapped the corner of the red box, and it disappeared.

She looked again at the close-up shot of the face of Amelia Jenkins, and now she remembered. The long sullen walk she and Jake took from London Bridge to Blackheath the first morning in 1941. The girl bursting out of the small house on Dartmouth Row and bumping into Jake—him helping her up and then gazing after her as she ran off, apparently oblivious to the presence of Hannah beside him. It was the same woman, Hannah was sure of it.

Hannah glanced at the clock on the wall and saw she had ten minutes left. She'd forgotten about searching for any earlier traces of Jake. Next to the listing for Amelia Jenkins was a small tag with the word *'More'* on it. Hannah thumbed the tag and the top half of the screen filled with closely-packed text from OffTime's files on the life of Amelia Jenkins.

Hannah's eyes settled at once on the final words. Her mouth set in a firm line, and she gazed away from the screen at the blank wall as if something important was written there. But of course, the important thing wasn't there; it was on the screen in front of her.

It was also now in her head and nestling like a chip of ice in her heart—the date of Amy Jenkins' death.

XX

London, 1944

It was February 1944, and Jake had now been stuck three months in the past. Off-shift on a rainy Sunday afternoon, he lay on his narrow bed and thought about what to do next.

There'd been no sign OffTime knew where he was or had any way of bringing him home. If they could rescue him, he could think of no reason why they hadn't already done so. Once they knew his location, the obvious thing was to pull him out as early as possible. The fact it hadn't happened yet suggested strongly it wasn't going to happen at all.

He'd begun to believe this was now his life, and he'd never return to his own time. To his surprise, that thought didn't horrify him in the way he'd once have expected. The world of 2040, in many ways, felt less substantial and real than the dirty, battered London of 1944. He missed Lew, Hannah, and the others, but less than he expected. He had a guilty sense of the suffering his disappearance might've caused Hannah, but no great desire to see her.

Before it happened, Jake would've guessed it would be hard to bear, being here in London, nearly five years into the fiercest war the world had seen. These Londoners lived in bomb-damaged houses, ate rationed food and whatever they could grow in their tiny scraps of garden. They barely had enough material to clothe themselves, or coal to heat their drafty homes. There remained the possibility that any night your home could be destroyed and your family killed.

Yet all around him, Jake saw people were working together and doing their best. They lacked a lot of things, but they didn't lack a *purpose*, and that purpose made life worth having... made it valuable. In wartime London, people were all in it together.

Captain Rogers at the ARP told him a story about a young engineer in the bomb disposal squad stationed in Deptford, near the docks. One night, two bombs fell near the church on Deptford Green and didn't explode. This guy was sent to check them out. He found one of the bombs, a fifty-pounder, half-buried in the churchyard. He decided to deal with it himself and dug it out.

He was a strong man, so he picked the bomb out of its hole and decided to carry it to the depot, three hundred yards away. He struggled slowly along the road. Thirty or forty yards short of the depot there was a pub. The man was tired and placed the bomb on the pavement, and then went into the pub and asked for a pint of beer. The landlord sent him packing, telling him he could have a beer for free, but only after he'd taken the bomb away.

Jake thought about this story a lot. He mentioned it to Amy, one evening in the ARP station. They were sitting on either side of the fireplace, sipping tea. Amy didn't understand Jake's surprise.

"What do you expect?" she said. "This is England. Anyone would do it. There's a war, and we're all in it together."

Jake wondered about it now, lying on his bed and listening to fierce rain rattle the window. He came from England too, but he couldn't think of anyone in 2040 who'd lift any fifty-pound weight to help anyone else, let alone a bomb. Could England change so much in less than a century? Wonder piled upon wonder made the life of 2040, objectively, a huge improvement on the 1940s. Yet, he couldn't help feeling that somewhere underneath it all, something vital and important had drained away.

In 1944, people had no money and precious little comfort, and every night strangers tried to kill them from above. No one knew when the war would end, or what the world would be like when it did. Yet there was a concrete sense of everyone pulling together, everyone doing their best and sharing the good and the bad.

Jake came from a world ten times wealthier. He belonged to what Amy would consider an age of miracles, where you spoke to people on the other side of the world and gained access to all the knowledge of the world's libraries through a small machine in your pocket. You extended your life with new organs and limbs grown from your own cells, traveled in time to see the Crucifixion, to meet Cleopatra, or watch Michelangelo at work.

Yet none of these things made people happier. Scientists wiped out small-pox only for fundamentalist nutters to steal a culture from a lab and mail the virus to schools across the country. The slums and rubble of 1940s London were long-replaced by stunning towers of glass and steel, only for disaffected young men to strap bombs to their chests and blow holes in the skyline.

In wartime London, people in the neighborhood soon got to know you and even those who didn't know you acted as if they did. A century later, in Jake's London, you hardly dared walk beyond your street, and you rarely knew anyone even there. Your 'friends' were people you'd never met, whose pictures popped up on your computer screen when you switched it on.

Every new technological miracle simply gave new opportunities to criminals and terrorists. Genetic engineering that might feed a crowded world was used to grow new diseases to sow among enemies. Time travel that could enrich knowledge of humanity's great thinkers or enable the lessons of history to be used to shape a better future was instead used to invent new crimes, such as pre-emptive homicide—interfering with past events so your victim would never be born. Jake didn't know if anyone had yet pulled that off, but he had no doubt people had tried, and maybe one day, he and his fellow agents would fail to stop it.

If he'd returned quickly to 2040, Jake could've pushed these thoughts from his mind. But the longer he spent in this London, the more its simpler way of living came to seem like the right way to live, something people in his own time had lost touch with. Now, he no longer expected to be rescued. He was resigned to living out whatever years remained to him, starting from this time—nearly seventy years before the day he was born. He knew he should've felt worse about this, but he felt oddly happy as if giving up hope of returning to his own time was a liberation rather than a loss.

With this realization came another, one that at last made him sit up from the bed and put on his shoes. He wasn't due to work tonight, but he knew Amy was on duty. He had nothing else to do, and it wouldn't hurt if he showed up and helped out.

After three months working at the ARP station, he found that Amy Jenkins was more in his thoughts than Hannah, with whom he'd lived for nine years.

Maybe he should feel guilty about that, but he didn't. The future he might've had with Hannah had been taken out of his hands. But Amy was right in front of him. They'd become friends, but he'd held back from going further, afraid of the possible consequences.

It was time to start living again.

XXI

London, 2040

Jake was missing for nearly a month when Ed Robinson called Lew Brockley back in. When Lew arrived, Hannah and Nancy were there again. Robinson didn't waste time on preliminaries.

"We're ready to move on Jake," he said. "I want you all in on it."

"Not meaning to be funny, Ed," Lew said. "But if you're ready, why isn't Jake sitting here with us?"

"I told you, this—"

"Please don't say it's complicated."

"Lew, let him speak," Nancy said. "You can make all the wisecracks you want when we've heard the news."

"I said we needed to act cautiously," Robinson went on. "And that's still true. We can't definitively pinpoint Jake earlier than May 1944, but there's evidence that by then, he's been there for a while."

"How long is a while?" Lew said.

"I can't speculate. But the fact he may have been embedded for some time means we need to handle this very carefully. We can't just pull him out without warning. He'll have made connections, found a job, interacted in a thousand ways with people around him. Formed relationships."

Robinson threw a glance at Hannah as he said this. Her head was down, studying her hands in her lap. "So he needs some warning that he's coming back," Lew said. "Someone can go and tip him off."

"That kind of thing," Robinson said. "But a bit more elaborate. We can't take any chances because there's a strong chance he's close to someone who could be very significant. Someone whose timeline we cannot afford to divert."

"Close in what way?" Lew said, ignoring the odd little noise that came from Hannah as if she'd been poked in the ribs. "Living next door? Sharing rides to work?"

"Close enough to have a big influence on a person whose future needs to be undisturbed. The only thing I can tell you is her name; Amelia Jenkins. All you need to know is the three of you need to keep your distance. We want her life disturbed as little as possible."

Lew looked at Nancy, who was watching Hannah. Hannah wouldn't meet anyone's eyes. There was something odd about all this. Lew wondered if Ed had already briefed Hannah.

"Okay, so it's complicated," he said. "I understand. Give me the briefing, and I'm ready to go and help Jake extract himself cleanly."

"That's the plan," Robinson said. "But I can't authorize you going back alone, Lew."

"I won't be alone," Lew said. "I'm going to get Jake and make sure he comes home okay."

"I'm sending the three of you."

"Is that necessary?"

"Well, listen to you," Nancy said. "Real team player."

"It's nothing personal, Nancy," Lew said. "It just seems to me the kind of job we should keep simple. And it's not blowing my own trumpet to say I'm the most experienced."

"Hannah's got as many years as you," Nancy said.

"Hasn't Hannah gone through enough?"

"That's exactly why she'll want to be there," Nancy said. They both looked at Hannah, but her head remained bowed. They could've been talking about the weather for all the interest she showed. "Anyway," Nancy went on, "you were right next to Jake when he went missing. All your experience didn't help much then, did it?"

"All right!" Robinson held up a hand, cutting off Lew's response. "You'll have plenty of time for the team-building conversations. I want you ready to jump tomorrow morning. You'll have full briefing downloads. And there will be a paper pack for Jake. You find him and talk to him. He'll need a bit of time to extract himself. His pack will give him cover stories and suggestions for how he shuts down any loose ends he may have created. Tell him not to overdo it; we can always send in a team to tidy up after him if there's a need for corrections. But it's good if he can get out as cleanly as possible."

"What kind of 'corrections' might be needed?" Nancy asked.

"That's what you need to find out." Robinson stood up, signaling the audience was over. The three of them filed out to the elevator lobby. Hannah still hadn't spoken.

"What's up, Hannah?" Lew asked as the elevator doors opened. "You get to be reunited with your beloved tomorrow. Aren't you pleased?"

Hannah said nothing. She stepped into the elevator.

"You're not worried about this Amelia Jenkins, are you?"

"Fuck off, Lew." Hannah pressed the button. The doors closed, leaving Nancy and Lew on the eleventh floor.

The three of them assembled again the next morning in the Darnell suite. The plan was straightforward enough—Jump into the early evening of Monday, May 15, 1944, in east London. All they had to do was travel down to Deptford and find Jake in his lodgings. After the initial contact, stay close as Jake shuts down as much as possible of the life he'd established in 1944.

That was the only uncertainty; since they didn't yet know how long Jake had been there, they needed some flexibility over the extraction arrangements. If he'd been living in wartime London for two years, it might be tricky.

Lew wondered what Jake thought, as the weeks turned into months with no sign that anyone from his own time knew where he was. It was a terrible place to be, but a part of Lew couldn't help being jealous of his partner. He'd never been idealistic like some of his colleagues. He didn't get excited about OffTime's supposed mission to rid the past of the dangers posed by 2040's many and varied criminals and screw-tops. Leave that to the careerists and true believers in the OffTime ranks. What motivated him was the chance to touch the face of history; to see, feel, and smell the reality of the past, to be close to some of the people who shaped the modern world.

None of them was in the mood to talk before the Jump. Lew moved to the far end of the changing room, away from Nancy and Hannah, and got changed alone. The two women exchanged a look, but frankly, he didn't care what they thought.

It was a long way from the light-hearted mood of their first Jump to April 1941. That had been a month ago, their time, but it felt much longer. Back in the 1940s, three long years of war had passed. Lew wondered how many of them Jake lived through. He was going to have some tales to tell when they got him home.

Lew went first. For some reason, he felt more nervous for this Jump. Maybe it was the thought of what happened to Jake last time out. He stood naked on the tiled floor, his canvas carryall at his feet. Neither Nancy nor Hannah appeared to have any desire to sneak a peek at him unclothed...their loss.

There was a low hum from the generator behind the wall and a tell-tale purple glow. A puff of air in his face and he was gone.

XXII

London, 1944

Amy felt things change one night in March 1944. She and Jake had worked together for nearly four months. The station got reports of incendiaries on Deptford docks, and everyone rushed down there. The Luftwaffe's incendiary bombs were small things, weighing a couple of pounds, but they burned with a brilliant white light and the Germans dropped them in basket loads—sometimes as many as ninety or a hundred over a small area. The trick was to spot where they fell and get them away from the buildings, preferably into the Thames before they could start a fire. Luckily, many of them didn't work.

The raid went on for a couple of hours. They barely had time to breathe, chasing from building to building to kill the fires. A couple of warehouses went up in flames and the ARP wardens had to leave them to the fire brigade. They had dressed for a cold day but soon were soaked in sweat.

Amy became aware she'd lost sight of Jake. On her left, Captain Rogers and two other men were tackling some dud incendiaries. On her right, about fifty yards away, a newspaper warehouse burned fiercely. The heat of the flames warmed her skin even at this distance, like the Devil breathing in her face. There was a fire engine in front of the warehouse, but the fire officers were pulling back, unable to control the blaze.

She held her hand up to her face, shielding her eyes to squint down the street. At the far end of the blazing warehouse, someone was in the road, bent over and moving toward her. A tongue of flame flicked out across the street, trailing a curtain of black smoke, obscuring the person. When the smoke faded away, the figure lay still on the ground.

Amy ran forward, shouting to the firemen. They ignored her, and she kept running, dodging around the fire truck as it reversed away from the flames. Everything moved very slowly. The burning warehouse panted hot breath on the left side of her body. The street ahead of her rippled in the heat haze, and butterfly cinders clung to her uniform, leaving scorch marks. There was a crash from above and fragments of glass and bricks pattered on the road behind her with a sound absurdly reminiscent of summer rain on a greenhouse roof. Each breath sucked fire into her chest.

Jake was lying on his side. There was a small blossom of blood above one eye. Amy put her hand on his chest to check his breathing, which felt regular. There was another crash from the warehouse. The wall above them shivered.

"Jake, get up!" His eyelids fluttered, and his lips mouthed something inaudible. Amy was torn between relief he was alive and despair he didn't look able to get up. "It's not safe. Move!"

Jake's eyes opened and focused briefly on her face. He smiled and said, "It's all lit up behind you."

"That's because the building's on fire. Come on!" She pulled him into a sitting position, then knelt beside him and put his arm around her shoulders and heaved him onto his feet. Keeping his arm across her shoulders, Amy half-pulled, half-guided him away from the burning warehouse. Once they were moving he revived a little, picking up speed as they broke into a ragged trot.

There was another explosion behind them as they reached a low brick wall around a churchyard. Amy pushed Jake against the wall, grabbed his legs and simultaneously lifted and shoved him forward and up. His upper body tipped forward, and he tumbled over the wall and out of sight. Amy threw herself after him. When she hit the damp earth on the other side, she rolled sideways and covered Jake with her own body. At that moment, the side of the warehouse collapsed behind them. A choking cloud of dust and pieces of burning wood came over the wall, but nothing large hit them.

Amy closed her eyes tight against the blizzard of dust and cinders that swept across the churchyard. The collapse of the warehouse seemed to go on for hours, with a loud dying roar, like a hideously large beast sliding to its doom down a steep mountainside. Then there was silence, except for the distant sound of warplanes. The sound was bizarrely comforting, especially in how far away it was.

Amy looked down and saw that Jake was conscious, his face only inches away. His eyes looked straight into hers. Sweat glistened like frost on his forehead and upper lip. In that moment of relief and safety, Amy was startled by how strongly she felt toward him. A few moments earlier she'd feared he'd be killed; only now did she realize how unbearable that loss would be. The surge of feeling for Jake was a rush of fever in her blood.

"On the ground together in a graveyard, Mister Wesson." She was breathless, her words like thin threads in a strong wind. "How romantic."

Jake shifted beneath her, making her suddenly very conscious they were pressed close together.

"If you say so, Mrs. Farrell." His voice was dry and faint like thin paper. "Or is it still Miss Jenkins between you and me?"

"Amy." She studied his face in the flickering light of the nearby fires. "Are you alright?"

"I think so." He shifted position again but made no attempt to get up, and Amy made no move to get off him.

"Do you think they know we're here?" Jake gestured with his eyes, back toward Rogers and the firemen beyond the graveyard wall. "Maybe they think we're buried under the collapsed wall."

"So we could do anything, and no one would ever know," Amy said. Jake's hand pressed gently on the small of her back. She bowed her face closer to his, and he lifted his head. They remained that way for a long moment, their lips an inch apart, until Amy whispered, "Why don't you kiss me?"

He did.

"After all," Jake said. "You saved my life."

"Do you kiss every girl who saves your life?"

"So far, yes."

Amy rolled off him and lay on her back beside him. The grass beneath her felt cool against the burning air above them. She put her head on his chest. Bright cinders circled above them like fireflies in the overheated night sky.

"Do you think this war will ever end?" she asked.

"Who cares?"

XXIII

London, 1944

From then on, Jake spent every shift he could with Amy. The days and nights they weren't working, she let her parents think she was, so that she and Jake could spend time together.

One unusually warm April night, they climbed the wall into Greenwich Park after dark. They sat on the grass near the Observatory, looking over the blacked-out city—a jumble of shadows under an inky moonless sky. The city was so quiet it might've been abandoned, leaving them as the last people here, whispering in the dark as if Hitler might hear them.

"Only one man ever meant anything to me." Amy looked away from Jake, her head a darker patch against the blackness of the sky. Each word a sigh, as her clothing rustled softly in the darkness when she moved.

"I want to mean everything to you," Jake said.

He didn't realize the truth of his words until they left his lips. Speaking it aloud made the fact solidify around him—he didn't want to be parted from Amy. It was as if, all at once, a door opened in front of him where before he hadn't even seen a closed door. In all his years with Hannah, he'd never felt what he did now—Amy was the hinge on which the rest of his life should turn, the prism through which he saw everything else.

This certainty struck him as if it had been beamed into his head from the darkness above, so suddenly and completely he gasped, briefly sucking in air with a sound that made Amy turn to look at him. He put his arm around Amy's shoulders and pulled her toward him. She resisted slightly and then folded into him.

He was in love with a woman who died before he was born. Every second he spent with her, everything he did in this time that wasn't his, risked changing the way the world should be—risked changing history in ways he couldn't predict. Jake found it increasingly hard to care. He felt he was part of history now; what happened in the future was no longer his problem. He couldn't identify the precise moment when he resigned himself to staying in the past. But this moment in the park was when he realized it had happened.

"I want to be everything to you," he said again, hugging Amy close.

"Maybe when the war is over," Amy said.

"What if it never ends?"

"Everything ends."

Everything has ended for me. Except for Amy, who's the beginning.

"You mustn't ever let me down," Amy said after a long silence. "I've been let down too much."

"I won't."

He didn't want this to end; didn't want to leave Amy's time, wanted the war to go on. What if peacetime came and changed everything—took Amy away from him? Could they still be together like this in normal times, if normal times ever came again?

He thought about Hannah. Was she thinking about him? Of course not— she wouldn't be born for another seventy years. But one day she'd think about him, wondering what happened to him when she Jumped back from 1941 without him. She seemed so far away from him now, as did his life with her in 2040. Maybe he should feel guilty about being here with Amy...but how could he? He was as exiled from his old life as it was possible to be.

If he were offered right now a way to be with Hannah again, in truth, he wouldn't take it.

XXIV

London, 1944

The Jump passed without incident, and they got dressed in the backyard of a bombed-out building close to Cannon Street station before taking a train to Deptford. Lew was surprised by the change since their spell here in 1941. Bomb damage was everywhere, with vacant spaces like broken teeth in terraces of housing, but there was a tidier feel to London's streets as if the city had been to the bottom and was on the way back.

The train was full of commuters leaving work in the banking district, and their carriage was lively with conversation and laughter, in contrast with the atmosphere of fear in 1941. The cutting edge of the war moved away to the east when Hitler invaded Russia and Lew sensed that bombing in London had become more sporadic.

They left the train at Deptford and walked down the stone steps to street level. The evening was warm, with at least an hour until the sun went down. At the foot of the stairs, they held back and allowed the commuters to walk away.

"Nancy, can you stay here by the station, watch our backs?" Lew said. "Hannah, come with me. But wait out of sight across the street from Jake's place. If the briefing is right, Jake isn't in there right now. I'll go further up the street and watch for him."

"And you know which way he'll come from, obviously."

Lew ignored Hannah's sarcasm and walked north up Deptford High Street. He glanced across the street as he passed the tall terraced house where Jake supposedly had a room. The curtains were drawn on the upper floor, where the OffTime eggheads claimed Jake was staying.

He reached the corner and looked back. Hannah stood under the railway arch with her hands on her hips, staring after him—not exactly inconspicuous.

Lew walked around the corner, heading toward Greenwich. As mission leader, he had received a more detailed briefing than Nancy and Hannah, especially about what was known of Jake's movements today. There was a good chance he'd return home from this direction, where there was a bus stop.

A bus was at the stop when he turned the corner. As it pulled away, it revealed two people walking toward him. One of them was a woman, dressed in a long, dark coat. The other was Jake. Bingo.

Lew stepped to the side of the pavement and stood out of sight in a narrow passage between two houses. A few seconds later, Jake and the woman walked past. Lew coughed, and Jake glanced his way. He did the kind of double-take normally only seen in cartoons—turning away and then spinning back round to stare at Lew with eyes like two coins and his jaw hanging open like the shovel of a mechanical digger.

Jake brought the woman to a halt with a touch on her arm and said something to her. He ushered her onwards with a hand in the small of her back and walked toward Lew. The woman gave Lew a fierce look before walking away.

"What the hell are you doing here?" Jake stopped a few feet away.

"Pleased to see you too, Jake. I'm well, thanks for asking. How are you?"

"I don't know what to say. It's been so long."

"How long has it been?" Lew asked. "Our genius tech guys couldn't tell."

"Why not?" Jake was shaking his head and blinking repeatedly. He looked like a man who'd just been told he was adopted as a child and was reviewing his life so far. "If they found me, why couldn't they track back?"

"It's a long story. Best explained by Ed Robinson."

"Is he here?"

"Of course not," Lew said. "When we get you home, I mean."

Jake said nothing, giving a half-glance back at the footpath behind him, where the woman had moved out of sight. Lew wondered if she was the mysterious Amelia Jenkins he was supposed to avoid.

"When we all Jumped from 1941, I assume you went home?" Jake said.

"Yes."

"That's good," Jake said. "There were times I wondered if we'd all been scattered and lost. I wondered if I might bump into you, three years older."

"Just you, but now you're found," Lew said. "How long has it been, Jake?"

"I arrived in November 1943."

"Christ! Six months."

"This is a lot to take in." Jake shook his head again as if to clear away confused thoughts. "When I wasn't pulled out, I assumed no one could find me. As time went on, I thought I was here forever."

"You must be pleased to see me."

"I don't know how I feel."

"What if I tell you Hannah and Nancy are waiting to see you?"

"Hannah? Where?"

"She's staking out your new home. Nancy's at the station. We need to get together. Ed's given us a slightly complicated plan. We need to talk you through it."

"Look, Lew," Jake stepped closer and grabbed his arm. "We can't rush this. I've been here months. I need time."

"That's why we've got the complicated plan," Lew said. "It's why we're here to help instead of the tech guys just pulling you out. No one knew how long you'd been here, so there's a plan to cover your tracks."

"Okay," Jake glanced again along the path after the Jenkins woman. "But it's a shock you just appearing from nowhere. I can't just drop everything and go."

"You sound like you're going to miss living in bombed-out London, Jake."

"I'm not saying that," Jake said.

"So, can we get together and agree on the plan? At your place?"

"Of course." Jake closed his eyes, thinking hard. "Listen, Lew, can we start with just me and you? You know where I'm staying? Come there in exactly one hour. Just you."

"Jake, what's the—"

"Don't argue, Lew. Just you, in an hour. Keep Hannah and Nancy away for now."

"What am I supposed to tell Hannah?"

"I don't know! I didn't plan your mission, and I wasn't consulted, remember? Tell Hannah, I don't know, I want to see her properly alone, but you need to brief me first. Tell her I'm not in good shape and can't face seeing everyone together yet. One hour."

With that, Jake turned and ran after the woman he'd been with. Lew walked back into Deptford High Street, dreading the conversation he was about to have with Hannah. He saw Jake on the far side of the road, deep in conversation with the Jenkins girl, leading her away up Evelyn Street.

XXV

London, 1944

It was dark outside when the doorbell chimed, and Jake went down and opened the front door. Hannah stepped inside and hugged him.

"Hannah," he said. "It's you."

"I've been so worried about you."

Jake looked over the top of her head at Lew, who stood a few paces behind her, looking like he was ready to run for it. Lew shrugged in answer to the question he must've seen on Jake's face. Jake hadn't thought he could face Hannah, but now that she was here, he couldn't interpret his feelings. He was pleased to see her, and she felt good in his arms. But there was a lot he didn't want to tell her.

"I thought it was just Lew who—"

"Lew said he thought it should just be the two of you, but I told him where to stuff it," Hannah said. Behind her, Lew shrugged again.

"You'd both better come in," Jake said, pulling himself free of Hannah's arms. "The neighbors will talk."

"It won't take long to cover the work issues," Lew said. "Then I can leave you two for a bit."

"Where's Nancy?" Jake asked over his shoulder as he led them upstairs.

"Sorting out our rooms," Lew said. "We'll need a couple of days."

Jake was conscious of the poverty of his accommodation. The house was badly lit, with thick wallpaper peeling in places and a faint whiff of damp, as if the river ran underneath the building. He led them into his room. Lew took the only chair while Jake sat next to Hannah on the narrow bed. Lew had a shoulder bag, which he held unopened on his lap. The three of them looked at each other in silence for a few moments. After the initial embrace, which surprised Jake with its intensity, Hannah had now pulled back. She watched the side of his face as he spoke to Lew.

"You didn't tell me how long it had been for you. Back up the line."

"About a month since we got back from the 1941 Op. I told Hannah it was six months for you."

"It seemed longer," Jake said. "Until I saw you in the street an hour ago, I had no idea if I'd ever see you or anyone else again."

"We've been frantic," Hannah said.

"Why did my Jump go wrong?"

"According to Ed Robinson, no one has a clue," Lew said.

"When you Jumped," Hannah said. "Was there anything unusual? Did you do anything you don't normally do?"

"Yeah, I accidentally set my watch a hundred years early. Easy mistake to make."

"I was just asking," Hannah said. "No need to be sarcastic."

"It was before my Jump that was odd," Jake said. "When we were all heading for our pick-up point."

"When you got separated from the rest of us?" Lew said.

"There was another agent there," Jake said. "He called for help. Code One."

"Are you sure?" Hannah said. "Who was it?"

"I don't know."

"What happened to him? Or her?" Lew asked.

"It was a man," Jake said. "I ran to help. But he disappeared. I never found him, but by then you'd all Jumped."

None of them spoke for a long moment. Lew shook his head slowly, with a look on his face like a man fretting over the last clue in a crossword puzzle. "Another thing to talk to Ed about, when we're back," he said. "Look, how about we talk business?" He reached into his bag and pulled out a sealed envelope. "Then I'll go find Nancy, and you two can catch up."

The briefing didn't take long. Jake opened the envelope and flicked through the contents. His eye was caught by a page with Amy's photo on it.

"Have you seen this?" He looked up from the papers.

"No," Lew said. "Confidential to you. Ed must've told us a million times how sensitive all this is. We've got our instructions; those are yours. It's all about how you can tie off any loose ends. Cover stories to give people at work, that kind of thing. So there's no fuss when you disappear."

Jake was still leafing through his pack. He saw other familiar names: Captain Rogers, some of the other people at the ARP station, his landlord. "If they knew all this about my life here, I still don't get why they couldn't get me out earlier."

"Maybe that's a conversation we can have with Ed," Lew said. "When you're home. All we know is that there's someone we can't go near. Too risky."

"Who?"

"Someone called Amelia Jenkins," Lew said.

"Amy?" Jake felt Hannah's gaze on the side of his face.

"Ring any bells?" she said. She'd been silent for a while, and her voice sounded too loud in his tiny room.

"Someone I work with." Jake's face was hot as if his guilty thoughts were branded there. "I don't understand what she's done. She's just an ordinary person."

"Something she's done, or will do, or better not do," Lew said. "We don't know. Big secret. Anyway," he spoke more briskly, wrapping up. "We'll be close by, but most of that you'll have to do for yourself. Is that going to be okay?"

"I guess." Jake didn't know what to say. After so long becoming resigned to staying in the 1940s, he struggled to accept he was going back.

"They reckoned three days to cover all the traces, then you Jump back," Lew said. "The pick-up is in there too. But read the pack soon. The ink will fade within a few days. No one wants that falling into the hands of contemporaries."

"Three days?"

"Make the most of it," Lew said. He stood to go. "We'll stay close, but we're not supposed to have too much contact. I'll check that everything's set for the Jump, and we'll go back the same day. It's so good to see you, Jake."

Jake had a small bottle of whisky in his bedside cabinet. After Lew had gone, he poured a measure into a teacup, and he and Hannah took turns to sip it.

"How have you been, Hannah?"

"Not great," she said. "I thought you might be lost forever. Then they found you. I couldn't understand why they couldn't just pull you out."

"Nor can I."

"That was torture. Knowing you were back here, but not knowing how long you'd been here or when you could come home."

"I was pretty sure I wouldn't be coming home. For the first week or two, I expected to be picked up at any moment. But after that—" Jake shrugged.

"How have you coped?"

"Just tried to blend in. I got this place, got a job, kept my head down." Hannah wouldn't meet his eyes. She looked at the wallpaper, the tea cup in her hand, the threadbare carpet—everywhere but his face. "You three turning up like this is a shock."

"I wish we could Jump back now," Hannah said.

"I can understand why not," Jake said. "I've been living here so long. I thought I'd be living the rest of my life here. I've made..." Jake hesitated, groping for the right word. "I've made *adjustments*. I've had to fit in, make connections. I understand why I can't just disappear."

"I wanted Ed to send another team to do the tidying up." Hannah finally looked him in the eye. She sat on the bed, hunched forward as if sheltering from the rain. "I wanted you to come home."

"Hannah, if there are loose ends to tie off, I can see why I'm the obvious one to do the job."

"It's not just a job though, is it? Not for you anymore." Hannah glared at Jake as if she'd just thrown a gauntlet at his feet and was waiting for him to pick it up.

"What do you mean?"

"You know what I mean." Each of Hannah's words sounded like it was weighed and measured before she spoke it. "It's personal, isn't it?"

"I don't know what you're talking about."

"I think you do." Hannah's face was rigid as if coated in transparent plastic. Something stirred behind her eyes, like a shadow rising from the bed of a deep lake. "I know about her, Jake."

"Know about what?"

"Don't fucking play dumb! That woman, Amelia something."

"Amelia?" Jake stared at Hannah, his mind sluggish and empty.

"Oh, for God's sake, Jake! Spare me the little-boy-lost face." Hannah's eyes shone with tears. "You know what I'm talking about. I saw you with her."

"Saw me. How?" It was obvious from the briefing pack that someone downtime knew about his contact with Amy, but Hannah still took him by surprise.

"It doesn't matter. Just tell me the truth, Jake. Don't you owe me that?"

"Okay. Amy." He took a deep breath, like a man about to dive from the high board. "I did get kind of...involved."

"Involved? Is that what they called it in the 1940s? Quaint."

"Look, Hannah, I can understand you being upset—"

"Well, that's something."

"Try to see it from my side," Jake pressed on. "I'm stranded in the past. I have no idea if anyone knows where I am, or if I can ever get back home."

"You didn't wait long to find out."

"Jesus, Hannah. Try it sometime. As far as I knew, I was stuck here forever. I didn't think I'd see you, or anyone I knew, ever again. By the time you were born, I'd be dead."

"I never said it wasn't hard for you."

"I needed to try to make some kind of life. I got a job, somewhere to live. I had to try to fit in."

"So, you screwed this Amelia as a way of fitting in? What a sacrifice for you. And flattering for her."

"It wasn't like that."

"What was it like? Sex with a dead woman. A woman born before your grandmother. Really, I'm interested." Hannah spoke quietly, but she sat with the stillness of an ice sculpture, her upper body rigid, knuckles clenched white on her thighs.

"Look, this isn't the time for this conversation, Hannah." Jake put a hand on her arm. "Maybe we should talk about it when we're back home."

"You're coming home, then?"

"What else can I do?"

"You sound so enthusiastic."

"I'll just do what I have to do here," Jake said. "When we're home, we can talk with clear heads."

"I've had plenty of time on my own to think. Maybe it's you who needs to clear your head. Maybe you've needed to clear your head for a long time now."

"Hannah, I'm sorry about what happened, really I am. I never wanted to hurt you. I just thought I was never coming back." A tear ran down Hannah's nose and dropped silently onto Jake's wrist. "I just need to quit my job, clear the flat, tidy things up with people," he said. "And that's it."

"You'll see her."

"I have to. To make sure there are no loose ends. To finish things off properly. When I come home, it's all over."

Even as he said it, Jake felt himself searching for a way out of his own words, but there was none. It was inevitable that he couldn't see Amy anymore. The heavy, granite weight of history was pulling them apart. When he was born, Amy was probably already dead of old age. There was no future for them. He meant it when he said it would be over between them. But he could also hear in his own voice the second meaning of 'it's all over.'

Tell Hannah you want out. It's cruel not to.

"When you come back, everything will be happy ever after? We'll be back the way we were?" Hannah looked him full in the eye, her cheeks shiny with tears.

"Well..." Jake couldn't meet her eyes. "None of us can predict the future, can we? It's hard enough with the past."

"Do what you must. Why should I worry?" Hannah picked up the teacup and drained the last of the whisky. Her tears had stopped, and her lips were set in a thin line. "It won't matter to Amelia Jenkins what you do."

"What do you mean?"

"Oh, there are things you don't know about your wartime squeeze?"

"Hannah, you don't need to talk like this. I'll do my job. That's it."

"Yes, do your job. That's worked so well up to now." Hannah's eyes glittered like chips of ice, but she had a patch of red on each cheek as if some heat within her was seeping out. "Make the most of it while you can."

"Is there something you're not telling me, Hannah?"

"July 28th, 1944. Mean anything?" Jake couldn't tell if the coldness in her eyes was anger or pity. He shook his head.

"That's when she dies."

Jake stared at Hannah for a long time, running her words over in his mind to try to make sense of them.

"Who dies?" But he knew.

"Amelia Jenkins. Killed by a bomb in July 1944. Don't look so shocked; there's a war going on, you know."

Jake wanted to ask how she knew this, but the words died in his throat. It didn't matter how she knew; she was telling the truth.

"Lucky we're not leaving you with her too long," Hannah said.

XXVI

London, 1944

Amy sat in a high-backed armchair, holding a book. There'd been no sirens that evening, and no sound in the room other than an occasional gasp from the coal fire as it settled.

One of the advantages of an ARP station located in a library was the availability of books to fill a slow night. The book in Amy's hands was a detective novel by an American writer. When she pulled it off the shelf downstairs, earlier in the evening, she thought she might already have read it, but she couldn't be sure. Now she knew for certain; she hadn't read it before. And she wasn't reading it now. Instead, she held it in front of her face, but the words on the page were a blur. All her attention was focused on what she heard downstairs.

The voices had been talking for a while before Amy registered the sound. Once she noticed it, she listened to nothing else, sitting very still with the book on her lap, her head turned slightly toward the door. One voice was the deep growl of Captain Rogers. He was doing more of the talking, although Amy couldn't make out any words, just the rise and fall of his voice.

The other speaker was Jacob Wesson.

Amy's stomach tightened. She'd last seen Jake the night before last, when that strange man appeared, lurking beside the path when she and Jake got off the bus in Deptford. They'd been going to Jake's place. His landlord wouldn't be there until late, he said. Neither of them put it into words, but they both knew how they were going to spend the evening. Amy kept a careful eye on the calendar and was sure the timing was right. That night she could relax, and it was safe for them to do what she knew they both wanted to do.

She'd picked her clothes with care that morning, including the underwear she knew Jake would remember from the time he burst in on her as she prepared for her wedding three years ago. It had been packed away in her drawer since that day, and Amy felt a mixture of sadness for Alfie and excitement about Jake as she took it out and put it on. All day Amy had been unable to prevent her thoughts reaching ahead to the evening, and what they'd do on the narrow bed in his room, leaving the world to continue with its madness beyond the window.

But instead of the evening she'd imagined, this stranger turned up from nowhere, and Jake insisted on speaking to him alone. After they had spoken, Jake walked Amy away from the High Street, and everything changed. Something had come up, he said. She just had to trust him. He would talk to her when he could. Jake had a hunted look in his eyes, like a man who'd lost something, going back over events in his mind, trying to spot where he might've let go of it. When they parted, it was in silence, and Amy sat on the bus conscious of the fancy underwear beneath her dress and frustrated that only she would see them when she undressed.

The sudden appearance of the stranger and Jake's reaction stirred up all Amy's worries about him. Who he really was, where he was from. Whether he was a spy. She'd wondered that night if he'd simply disappear, but now here he was. Amy fought the urge to get up and open the door so she could hear what he was saying to Rogers. It was up to Jake to come to her and explain himself. But what if Rogers didn't tell him she was up here? What if he just said his piece to Rogers and disappeared again?

The conversation downstairs fell quiet, followed quickly by the sound of footsteps on the wooden stairs. Amy shifted position slightly and held her book up in front of her face.

"I guessed you'd be here. I tried your house first."

Amy lowered the book and twisted round in the chair, moving with theatrical slowness. "Well, Mister Wesson, Man of Mystery. Who'd believe it?"

Jake moved closer and stopped four feet away, looking unsure whether to pull up a chair and sit down or leave the room again. He looked tired, and there was something in his face she couldn't read; he looked like a small boy wondering where his mother had gone. Amy had to resist the urge to stand up and sweep him into her arms.

"I'm sorry about the other night, Amy. It was someone I had to talk to. That's all I can say."

"Well, that's all right then. No need for anyone to get upset."

When Amy was angry, a faint hint of an Irish accent entered her voice. She didn't know why this should be; she'd lived in London all her life. Her mother teased her about it. She said Amy's Irish blood was normally diluted by the English, but when she lost her temper, the Irish heated up, spilling into her speech. She heard her Irish voice now. Jake did too, and he frowned.

"I didn't say that," he said. "I'm upset, and I can tell you are too. I had no choice."

"Do you have any choices now?"

Jake looked around the room with a kind of pained restlessness, as if he'd lost something. He didn't seem to know what to do with his hands; they scratched at the material of his trousers, clenched and unclenched.

"I can't stay," he said. "I came to tell Rogers I have to leave the ARP. I need to go away."

Amy felt a cold fist in her chest. "Go away, why?"

"I can't really say."

"Where?"

"Amy, I—"

"You can't really say. I know. More of this secret-service nonsense. I thought we were finished with that."

"Can I see you tomorrow?" Jake said. "Somewhere alone. I need to talk to you."

"If you're sure you've got time. I don't want to get in the way; you're obviously busy."

"Amy, please. This is hard enough for me, without you making it worse."

"Well pardon me. I hate to make it hard for you. Have you thought about me?"

"All the time," he whispered. "I think about you all the time."

The obvious misery in his voice softened Amy's anger, and she said, "I can meet you tomorrow. Take me for pie and mash." A thought came to Amy so suddenly and fully formed she was sure it must be visible on her face. To cover up, she dropped the book and made a fuss of picking it up. "Manzi's in the

High Street is always good," she said. "Just down the road from your place. Unless you've moved out."

"Not yet."

They agreed on a time, and a moment later Jake was gone. Amy sat and stared at the cold fireplace as his steps faded down to the ground floor, and his kiss dried on her lips.

XXVII

London, 1944

Amy stepped back behind the stone pillar beside the church entrance when she saw Jake leave the house. He crossed the street and disappeared around the corner.

She stepped out from her hiding place and walked along Deptford High Street to Jake's lodging house. It was midway through the morning, under a cotton blue May sky. Further down the street the fruit and vegetable market was doing its usual brisk trade, but up this end there were few people around, and no one took any notice of her as she stepped up to the front door of the tall, terraced house and knocked on the door.

It was answered by the landlord, a skinny fiftyish man in a grubby dressing gown worn over gray shirt and trousers. A hand-rolled cigarette clung to his lower lip. His eyes crawled all over Amy as she explained what she wanted.

"Mister Wesson's out," he said. "What did you say you wanted him for, love?"

"ARP business."

"Oh yeah. That what you call it?" He leered at her. "I've seen you before. Been stepping out together, eh?"

"He told me he'd be here. I've got something for him." Amy gestured with her hand, which held a cloth shopping bag. It contained two library books, but the landlord didn't need to know that.

"Leave it with me. I'll see he gets it."

"Well, that's it, you see." She smiled sweetly at him. "I really need to give this to him myself. It's personal. Maybe I could just wait in the room for a bit."

"Well—"

"I'd be so grateful." Amy cocked her head to one side and gave her best girlish and winning expression.

"Come on then." He stood aside.

Amy didn't hesitate, walking in and continuing up the stairs before he could change his mind. She was conscious of his gaze on the back of her legs as she went. Maybe it'd be good if Jake did come back soon.

The landlord opened the door to Jake's room and stood back, giving his hand a swipe through his greasy hair. Amy walked in. She'd been here before, but it was very different now. Every surface was clear, and the door to the wardrobe hung open, revealing empty hangers and cleared shelves. A canvas carryall was on the bed, packed and ready to go, while a cardboard box on the floor was half-filled with bundled clothing and shoes.

"You knew he was moving out, of course." Jake's landlord watched Amy's face like a bookie giving her the odds.

"'Course," Amy said. "I'm helping him move."

"My name's George, by the way. Like the King."

"Amy."

The last time Amy was here, Jake had a row of pictures stuck on the wall above the bed; postcards of London views; the Tower of London, Big Ben, a tram. Now the wall was empty. The only picture left was a small black-and-white photograph of Jake and Amy, wedged into the frame of the mirror above the tiny washbasin.

The picture had been taken one afternoon the previous week, when they had a few hours free and went to London Zoo. A photographer at the gates snapped everyone as they went in and you could buy the picture on your way out for a shilling. Amy thought it was too expensive, but Jake insisted on buying it. The two of them were walking toward the camera, Amy's arm hooked through Jake's. They both noticed the photographer a moment before he took the picture, and the print caught their different reactions. Amy grinned theatrically at the camera, while Jake turned partly away, with his face only visible in profile, his hand slightly raised in front of him.

Amy had previously thought Jake was turning to her in the picture, striking a pose of affection, cuddling in for the camera. Looking at it now, she realized he could just as easily have been turning away from the lens, trying to hide his face. She wondered why the photo was the only thing he'd left on display. Was he taking it with him, or leaving it behind?

She sat on the edge of the bed, taking care to position herself centrally to limit the room for George to join her. She smiled up at him. "Don't suppose there's any chance of a cup of tea, George, is there?"

He hesitated, but in the end, his trace of good manners got the better of him and he nodded before turning for the stairs.

"I'll put the kettle on."

"You're a darling," Amy called after him. "Little bit of milk, just one sugar."

She listened to his steps recede down the uncarpeted stairs and into the back of the house. After standing up and tiptoeing to the door, she leaned out to listen. There was a faint sound of cups rattling and a cupboard door being closed, far down in the interior. She moved back into the room and squatted down beside the box on the floor. This was the stuff Jake was leaving behind. Beneath the clothes, which included his ARP jacket and some shoes, were a few old newspapers and a couple of tattered books. There was nothing of any personal significance or value. Amy pushed things back roughly the way she found them and turned her attention to the carryall on the bed.

There was less inside than she expected—a large, white cotton shirt and some clean underwear; a wallet; a cloth-bound notebook; and a blue folder made of a strange, smooth material, light as paper but rigid. Amy picked up the folder. It had a flap that folded over the top, keeping the contents inside. She pulled it open and flicked through the papers inside. Most pages were covered with closely printed text. She rubbed a finger lightly over the words, unsure how the pages were printed. They didn't seem to be typed, and the ink didn't smudge.

Nothing written on the pages made much sense. They seemed to be a disjointed set of dates, times and descriptions of London locations. She recognized some of them—a few places in Blackheath and Deptford, and a couple of addresses in the City. Leafing through more pages, Amy found something more interesting. A series of sheets of paper contained pictures as well as words. The first had a photograph of George, the landlord, somehow printed on the top half of the page in full color. Amy had never seen a color photograph, although she'd heard it was possible. Nor had she ever seen a picture reproduced so clearly on a printed page—far superior to anything you saw in the newspapers.

The picture of George looked as if it had been taken from outside the house, while he stood on the doorstep in his dressing gown. He didn't look like he was aware of the camera pointed at him. Beneath the photo were two paragraphs of close text, which Amy scanned quickly. They gave a potted biography of George, including full name and date of birth, and his nearest living relative— a brother in Stratford. A couple of sentences caught Amy's eye. *Scotland naval posting cover story. No details. Forwarding address—post office, Oban.'*

Other pages had similar photographs with written instructions beneath them. Some of the photos showed buildings—she recognized a view of the north end of London Bridge, not far from Bank station. Others showed people, some of them unknown to her, but others familiar. Captain Rogers was photographed in the entrance to the ARP station. Beneath that page, Amy found another that made her grip the paper so tightly she could see tiny vibrations on its surface.

It was a page about her.

Her photograph was a head and shoulders shot, in color like the others, taken from an angle that suggested the photographer was slightly above her. Amy stared at the picture for some time, trying to work out where and when it was taken. Which was difficult because the focus was so tight on her face that little could be seen behind her.

She looked very young. With a shock, Amy realized the photo was taken on her wedding day. She remembered the moment; she was smiling for the cameras, and out of shot she knew Alfie stood beside her, grinning fit to burst. It was a mystery who took the photo. So far as she could tell, it was taken from an angle above the heads of her wedding guests, and some way behind them. All she remembered of that part of the heath was open grass stretching away to the road. A couple of hundred yards away and beyond the road was a row of tall townhouses, but they were surely too far away for the mystery cameraman to have been there.

Amy read the words beneath her picture. As with George, there was some basic biographical information and then, *'Scotland naval story. No address details—offer to write. Obituary notice Glasgow Herald 30 June, backup team to send anonymously.'*

There were footsteps on the stairs. In the last few seconds before George returned, Amy flicked open the small notebook. On the first page Jake had written, *'Pick-up Friday 19 May 1944—21.00. St. Mary at Hill, off Lower Thames Street. In position 20.45, no later than 21.15.'* Out of time, Amy slipped the papers back into their folder and closed the carryall. When George came into the room, she was sitting where he'd left her on the bed, gazing idly at a crack high up on the wall, humming a Vera Lynn tune.

"Couldn't find no biscuits," George said as he put a tin tray on the bedside table. He handed her a steaming mug of tea.

"You're such a darling." Amy took a sip of the tea and then put the mug back on the tray. "Do you know what? I've got some things I need to do. Maybe I won't wait." She stood up, smoothing her skirt down over her knees. "Thanks for the tea, George. I'll see myself out. Next time, I'll bring you some biscuits."

With that, she left the speechless landlord in Jake's room, skipped down the stairs and left the house. She still had an hour until her lunch with Jake. She had no idea how that conversation would go. She'd always been aware there was something odd about Jake. But had he been spying all long? It didn't make sense; what possible reason was there for anyone to spy on her, George, and Captain Rogers?

XXVIII

London, 1944

Amy was in Manzi's, sitting on a long oak bench at a table facing the window, with a cup of tea and a slice of bread. She watched Jake approach in the street outside. He looked worried, a kind of frozen stiffness in his face. He caught sight of her through the steamy window of the pie shop and flashed a smile, but it instantly subsided again into that blank expression.

"Right on time," Amy said as he slipped onto the bench across the table from her. "I always liked that about you."

"I have a thing about time."

It was early, and the only other customers were a group of three men in railway-worker uniforms down the far end of the narrow restaurant. The pie and mash shop was a local institution, and it looked as if it hadn't been redecorated since Queen Victoria died. The floor was bare boards, worn smooth by years of customers' shoes, and layered in sawdust. The walls were tiled in black and white.

A boy of about fifteen approached their table. He wore a white apron that looked like it could do with a wash. He took their orders for pie and mash and went back to the kitchen.

"So," Amy said. "You've got things to say."

"Yes." Jake looked so miserable Amy wanted to reach a hand across the table and comfort him. But she held back; she was, after all, angry with him.

"You might as well say what you've got to say, Jake. I'm all grown up and a widow already. I can cope."

"I have to go away." Jake's shoulders slumped wearily. "I always knew it was possible, but I didn't know when."

"Where?"

"I can't give the details, I—"

"It wouldn't be Scotland, would it? Not Oban, by any chance?"

"Well, yes." He frowned. "It is Scotland, actually."

"I'll miss you, obviously," Amy said. "But I'll write. Give me the address."

"I haven't got the address yet. I'll have to send it." Jake's frown deepened. This obviously wasn't going the way he planned.

They were interrupted by the boy returning with two large plates, which he placed heavily on the Formica tabletop, dumping knives and forks next to them with a clatter. Amy took a fork and skimmed up a small piece of lumpy mashed potato. She dipped it in the lake of green parsley sauce that drowned the food.

"How long will you be gone?"

"Not too long, I hope. I can let you know."

"Make sure you write. After everything I've been through in this war, I don't need you to disappear, and all I see is some anonymous death notice in a few weeks' time. That'd be too cruel, wouldn't it?"

"Yes." Jake had a faintly puzzled expression on his face, as if he'd mislaid his part of the conversation and didn't know how to get back on track. "Amy, I—"

"Don't say anything else."

"Why not?"

"I don't want to hear it. Whatever you say, I won't believe it so just save your breath."

Neither of them spoke for a long time. Amy ate some of her lunch, but the pie crust was like cardboard, and the mashed potato was barely warm. Jake stared at her emptily like a boy who'd just seen his puppy run over. At last, Amy put her cutlery down and sat with her face in her hands, elbows on the table. When Jake's hand touched her wrist, she couldn't prevent a sob wrenching itself out of her chest. In an instant, her cheeks were wet with tears.

"Amy, I'm really sorry. If there was anything I could do."

"Just leave it." She shrugged his hand away. "Don't say anything else. I don't want any more lies. I trusted you, and you treat me like this."

"I haven't lied to you."

"Oh, come on!" The serving boy behind the counter looked across at them when Amy raised her voice. "It's always been obvious there were things you weren't telling me, but I thought in time you'd be honest. But you've just been using me."

"That's not true."

"It's not fair," Amy said. "You knew how it was with me. If you never planned to stick around, you shouldn't have gotten involved."

"I wanted to stay," Jake said. He rubbed his eyes with his hands, wincing as if he was in pain. "Everything I said to you, everything I've done, was sincere. I thought I could stay, but I can't. I can't stay here."

"Why not?"

"I can't say."

"Two days ago, everything was different," Amy said. "Why the sudden change? Was it that guy who turned up? New orders from Himmler?"

"Amy, it's nothing like that."

"So, you're not going to giving me any of that undercover bollocks again?"

"Amy, please believe me." Jake spread his hands palms-up on the table top. "If there were another way, I'd do it."

"I trusted you," Amy said again. "Like no other man. I thought when the war was over, we could be together."

"I thought so too," Jake said flatly. "If there was anything else I could do…."

"I just don't get it," Amy said. "What aren't you telling me? Is there someone else? Have you got a wife somewhere?"

"It isn't that," Jake said. "I just don't belong here. I can't stay."

"Oh, this is pointless!" Amy stood up. "Do you know how pathetic you sound? Just do what you want. I give up." She gave him no time to respond but walked out of the restaurant.

Outside, the sun was high in the bleached blue sky, but none of its heat reached the ground, just the joyless light of another day of the war. Amy glanced back through the window as she walked away. Jake still sat at the table, head sunk in his hands.

XXIX

London, 1944

Jacob Wesson left Cannon Street station and walked toward London Bridge. The ground sloped down to the north bank of the Thames, empty of boats this far upstream. The bag in his right hand bumped against his thigh as he walked. He'd considered dumping the carryall after he left Deptford; he needed nothing in it, but some things came from 2040, so the rules said they should go back. Everything in its proper place and time was the OffTime way.

In his early weeks marooned in the past, Jake had fantasized about the chances of rescue. He'd dreamed of Lew or another agent popping up to take him home. Those thoughts came less frequently as time passed, but when he finally saw Lew signaling to him from that alleyway, it was a shock to find he didn't want his friend and partner to be there. If there'd been anyone to ask him during most of those long months stranded in the 1940s, he would've said he was desperate to go home. To resume the life he knew in the world that made him.

The sight of Lew waiting for him beside the path threw up two almost instant realizations. The first was that Amy had changed everything; she'd made him forget 2040, OffTime, and the life he'd led for thirty years. She made him feel that London in 1944 was the right place for him, so the prospect of staying and living out his life there no longer seemed so forbidding.

The second thought came instantly behind the first. It was the realization that his own time couldn't let him go. He was deluded if he thought that a man from the future could be left in peace to live a life decades before even his parents were born. OffTime had tracked him down, and he was a fool if he thought anything he'd done was hidden from them. And a bigger fool if he thought he'd be left alone to drift away into a quiet life with Amy in the 1940s and 50s. OffTime had a hook in him and they always would. Now, they were reeling him in. He felt broken inside at the thought of leaving Amy, but he saw no alternative.

He reached the wide road junction before the bridge. The offices and shops on this side of the Thames were closed for the weekend, and there were few people around. St. Mary at Hill was a narrow side road off the north side of Lower Thames Street. Jake glanced at it as he walked past. There was no one in sight and no sign of activity in the low terrace of houses on the west side of the street. Jake noted the mouth of a narrow passage between houses, which might be a good place for his pick-up. Most of the east side of the passage was a bomb site, fenced off with a couple of strands of thin wire nailed to wooden posts.

Jake was early, so he continued walking east rather than hanging around in the target road, risking suspicion. He planned to get in position just before the pick-up, stand as far out of sight as possible, and strip for his usual naked Jump.

Unbidden, the thought of taking his clothes off brought with it another: the memory of Amy Jenkins walking out of Manzi's yesterday. Jake considered going after her but stayed to pay the bill and then walked back to his room. He'd lain for a couple of hours on his bed and stared, unseeing, at the ceiling. Later, after dark, he'd set out to walk up to Blackheath, thinking he'd knock on her door and talk to her one last time. He hadn't known what he'd say but the thought of never seeing her again, of her angry departure from lunch being their final moment, was unbearable.

It took him fifteen minutes to walk up Shooters Hill and with every step his resolution drained away. He walked onto Dartmouth Row, continued past the unseeing front door of Amy's house, and without pausing walked back down to Deptford. His head felt like it was pumped full of cold liquid and if he squeezed his eyes shut too tight, the pressure might cause it to leak from his skull.

What could he say to her anyway? *Forgive me, Amy. We can't stay together because I won't even be born for sixty years. And even if I stayed all I could do is watch you get blown up in a few months' time.*

Or maybe he'd get blown up with her. Perhaps then he wouldn't be born at all. Maybe, all things considered, that wouldn't be such a bad thing.

A few hundred yards past St. Mary at Hill, Jake looked at his watch. Eight forty-five, time to get in position. The sun had now set, and shadows pooled in doorways and between buildings. He walked briskly back the way he'd come, slipped onto the side road and made his way to the narrow passage he'd seen earlier.

He dropped his bag beside him in the shadows, pulled off his shoes and socks, and removed his clothes. The evening was too chilly for hanging around naked in the street, and Jake was glad he wouldn't have long to wait before the Jump. Just before he removed his underpants, Jake glanced behind him at a faint sound.

Amy stood ten yards away.

"Jake, what're you doing?" She stared wide-eyed at his bare chest.

"Amy, stay away." Jake glanced around in panic. There was nowhere he could go, no way to get out of her sight in the next few seconds. "You shouldn't be here."

"And you should be? What're you doing? You'll get arrested."

"Amy, please, you've got to go." Jake felt trapped. Seeing her cracked the resolution that had brought him this far. His longing to be with her surged up within him, making him sway where he stood as if dizzy. He looked frantically around. What if he ran out of the alley and away from the pick-up point? Could he get far enough away to miss the Jump? Could he stay in the 1940s with Amy?

There was a brief flicker of purple light in the dark passageway, telling Jake it was already too late. The air crackled with electricity. The hair on his arms stood erect, and there were goose bumps down his legs. The pick-up was coming within seconds.

Amy would see him Jump.

"Amy, I'm sorry for everything." He edged further back into the alley, seeking some scrap of shadow. "Just remember, I love you."

There was a soft popping noise and a flare of purple light. Jake turned away from her and crouched down. She shouted something, and there was a scraping noise behind him. A puff of warm air in his face made him flinch, and at the same moment, he felt something strike him in the back and slide around his right shoulder. Something else pressed against his waist on his left side.

Everything lurched sideways, and Jake was suddenly on his knees in the Darnell Suite, the bright lights hurting his eyes. His stomach spasmed, but he swallowed hard and kept everything down. There was a momentary pressure on his arm, and then it fell away, and someone moaned, followed by a scraping of something on the hard floor. With a faint pop, Jake's bag appeared in front of him. He ignored it and turned to look behind him, searching for the source of the moaning.

Amy Jenkins lay on her side behind him, doubled over in a fetal position. She looked as if she might be unconscious, her eyes closed and a puddle of vomit on the floor in front of her.

Jake stayed on his knees for what felt like an endless frozen moment. He was so still that, in the end, he became acutely conscious of the one part of him that still seemed to have the power of movement; his rapidly blinking eyes as he stared at Amy on the floor. His blood roared in his ears, and there was a taste of metal in his dry mouth.

This was impossible. No one could Jump into their future, or so Jake had always been told.

But the proof was at his feet. Amy Jenkins was in 2040 with him.

PART III

Extract from Sunday Times Magazine, 21 May 2024

Man Out Of Time: The German Scientist Creating a New Window on the Past

…*three months ago, the world woke up to the astonishing news that scientists in Geneva had stumbled on a discovery so big that most of the world's heads are still spinning from trying to understand it. No one has yet been back to shake hands with Julius Caesar, but the announcement that travel into the past was not only theoretically possible, but had already been happening for over a year to particles in the CERN large collider, caused a sensation.*

In all the fuss, surprisingly little attention has been given to the man experts say is responsible for the breakthrough—Axel Darnell, the shy and softly spoken head of the basic research section at CERN.

Born of an American father and German mother in 1959, in the city of Koblenz in what was then West Germany, Darnell's career, so far, can hardly have prepared him for the global fame that has burst upon him. He spent twenty years teaching and researching particle physics at universities in Germany, France, and the United States. He came to Geneva in 2013 and spent the last decade laboring in comfortable obscurity. Unnoticed by the non-geek world, his research covered the strange behavior of particles that seemed, in some conditions, to disappear completely, only to return a short time later, subtly changed. Meanwhile, other apparently identical particles seemed to appear from nowhere and then disappear again.

Darnell proved the particles were changing in a way that could only be accounted for by time—they were getting older faster than anyone could explain. He set up the key experiment that showed that both sets of mystery particles were the same. The particles were disappearing a week into the past and then coming back a few minutes later, having aged more in the past than the time elapsed since they went away.

They were traveling in time, and in a way that made it possible that other larger objects could do the same. And not just objects—scientists tell us that there is no reason why living things, even human beings, cannot travel in time.

What of the man at the eye of this storm? Darnell lives a simple life, in a second-floor apartment in an elegant Geneva building. He is unmarried, a widower since his wife died of cancer seven years ago. He has two sons, neither of whom has followed their father into the family business of nuclear physics.

Darnell's early life was also unexceptional. Indeed, Darnell himself made a joke of his unremarkable upbringing in one of his few recorded interviews, given to a physics journal ten years ago. For those without the right scientific training, it can be hard to tell, but experts suggest that his words contain what scientists might recognize as physics jokes.

"Even the most unusual life," he said, "is completely unexciting compared with the extraordinary activities of the building blocks of matter. I can say this especially, as someone who has had the most unexciting life imaginable. The most interesting thing about my life is the fact that I was born at all because the chances of my parents meeting were so slim. My father had never been to Koblenz before the day he met my mother, and he probably would not have come back if they had not met.

"Their meeting was pure chance; my mother was learning English, and her regular teacher had fallen ill. She had the morning free and tried to find a substitute teacher. She went to an address someone gave her in the center of the city, but had no luck and thought her day was wasted. She walked down to the Rhine and stopped for coffee in a small place with a view of the river.

"She was about to leave when my father approached her. He was on a day's leave from his airbase near Cologne. He asked my mother if she knew where he could find a German teacher. Right here, she said. Years later she told me that she was so bold only because she thought she could get some English practice for free.

"There was no reason for my parents to meet, and probably any other day their meeting would have led nowhere. Even on this day, five minutes later and my mother would have left the café. So," the world's most famous physicist

said, no doubt with a twinkle in his eye, "even my dull life illustrates the random nature of the universe and the importance of chance."

XXXI

London, 2040

There was a flicker of violet light as Amy grabbed Jake. The world lurched sideways, and she fell to the ground, groaning as her internal organs tried to force their way out of her body. She lay on her side, hands clutching her stomach. The skin on her arms prickled and a film of sweat covered her face. When she again became aware of her surroundings, Amy lay on a smooth, warm floor. The light was too bright, making her eyes hurt even behind her squeezed eyelids.

"Shit!" Jake's voice was very close. Amy wanted to say something in response, but it took all her concentration to keep her insides where they belonged. She had nothing spare to operate her mouth. She felt Jake's hand on the back of her neck. His touch was surprisingly gentle, and even through her pain, Amy felt pleasure in his concern for her.

"Amy, it'll feel awful for a while, but you won't die."

Pity. That might feel better.

"I'm going to get you out of here," Jake said. Amy tried to respond but her words were drowned by a convulsive cough, and she vomited green fluid onto the floor. It left a burning sensation in her mouth. Jake moved away, and she opened her eyes to him standing in front of a wide metal door. It had three colored lights above it and no handle.

Jake spoke to the wall. "Agent Wesson returning from uptime. This is classified. Repeat, deep classified. I need assistance."

He used a voice Amy hadn't heard from him before—authoritative, older than he looked. Maybe he really was a spy.

There was a moment's dead air, and then a voice came from somewhere. "Jake, it's Lew. We're your welcoming committee. I'll open up."

"Lew, wait. Who else is there?"

"Me and Hannah."

"Look, I need you in here and only you. This is deep cover. Just you and me, no one else."

"Sure," the other voice said. "Lucky it's a slow day."

Jake pressed something on the wall again and stepped back. He then crouched over Amy, leaning close to whisper. "Amy, don't say anything, just listen."

No problem there; if she tried to speak there'd be more green bile to deal with.

"You have to trust me and do exactly as I say. We're in a place that'll seem very strange to you. I can explain everything later, but now I need to get you out of here and somewhere safe."

This floor feels safe. If I keep my mouth closed.

"I need to move you away from this door." Jake took hold of her beneath her arms. Amy groaned as he lifted her, but clamped her mouth shut when she saw the alarm in his eyes. Jake pulled her half to her feet, and she tried to get her legs under her, but they still wouldn't move. Her stomach lurched painfully, and she tasted acid at the back of her mouth. Jake settled for dragging her backward to the side of the room, putting her in a corner, with her view of the door partly blocked by a low metal cabinet. He returned to the center of the room and bent over his bag, pulling out clothes.

There was a low hiss as the door slid to the side and a man stepped in. He was older than Jake, maybe mid-to-late thirties, tall and thin, with dark hair receding a little on his forehead. Amy recognized him as the one who called to Jake from the bushes that night a few days ago. He was followed by a woman, about Jake's age, with short hair.

"Fuck!" Jake said, as the woman stepped into the room behind the man, who was presumably the Lew Jake had just spoken to.

"Pleased to see you too, darling," she said.

Lew held out some clothes. "Thought you'd need something more up-to-date to wear. What's up, Jake?"

Jake held his finger to his lips and glanced upwards as if someone was above them listening. Then he gestured with his eyes to where Amy lay on the floor. The man and woman turned and saw her.

"Woah!" Lew said.

"You've got to be kidding," the woman said.

"Say nothing," Jake said, giving them both a fierce glare.

"But, what the fuck—"

"Hannah, you either help or else just get the fuck out of here."

There was a tense silence as Jake put on the clothes Lew had brought in. They looked strange, a blue shirt with no collar, made of a very thin material, and white trousers that were very baggy at the hips but tapered sharply in at the ankles. Amy had no idea where you'd get material like that, in such quantity, in wartime London.

Jake gestured Lew over to where Amy lay. Hannah remained by the door, arms folded and her face looking like she'd just been slapped. Amy felt slightly better; instead of simply wishing she was dead, she could now contemplate staying alive unless death was particularly painless. She'd probably be fine if she could just hug the floor for a few more hours, occasionally spewing green chunks. Jake bent over her.

"Amy, we have to move." He spoke very quietly and close to her ear. "Don't speak, and hang on to us." Amy wanted to object, but it seemed easier to go with the flow. Jake took one arm, and Lew took the other as they lifted her to her feet between them, putting her arms round their shoulders.

"Where are we going?" Lew said.

"Don't know," Jake said. "Can we get out of here without meeting anyone?"

"I know the security guy. I can call ahead."

"Are you serious?" Hannah said. "What're you doing?"

"This was a complete accident," Jake said. "We can sort it out, but I need your help."

They walked Amy to the door, and Jake pressed something. He tensed as the door slid open again, but all it revealed was an empty room—some kind of changing area, with low benches and lockers, and a damp smell. They moved quickly and stopped at the next door, which looked more normal to Amy, with an actual door handle at waist height. Lew kept hold of her, while Jake stepped away and searched through lockers. Hannah went with him, and they began an urgent, whispered conversation, which Amy couldn't make out.

Where is this place?

The walls and the furniture were made of a material Amy hadn't seen before, smooth like metal but dull rather than shiny. There was very little wood, even in the flooring. *A secret bunker? Something used by the military?* Amy had heard rumors about underground shelters and government buildings. Some people said there were vast tunnels under London, where the politicians and the royal family could hide when the city was attacked.

Lew shifted and pulled something out of his pocket, a small box with rounded edges, about half the size of a tobacco tin, but made of something else, like a soft, colored glass. He held this up to his face, and Amy was startled to hear a voice come from it.

"Kumar," the voice said. "No picture."

"Not today, Bassi. It's Lew Brockley here."

"Well, thanks for sparing me the visual of your ugly mug, Mister Brockley."

"Bassi, I need a favor." Lew glanced sideways at Jake, who was back at Amy's side, ripping open a small package he'd taken from a locker. Amy felt her stomach flutter ominously again. "And I need it off the books."

"Depends what it is."

"I'm just in from a mission," Lew said. "Deep cover, *really* deep. I need out of the Suite quick and no audience. Got to get straight to debrief."

"Why wasn't I told in advance?"

"Come on, Bas. Sometimes things come up in the field and plans change. You know how good the back-room prep can be."

"Tell me about it. What do you need?"

"Four of us, straight out to street level from the Jump Suite. I'll come and do the paperwork later."

"Okay. Take a right out of the changing room and then the stairs on the left."

"You're a diamond." Lew slipped the speaking box into a pocket.

"Just a minute," Jake said. He pulled up the sleeve of Amy's jacket and before she could move, stuck a needle in her arm. It might've hurt if she wasn't already in pain all over her body. "This'll help," he said. He dropped the empty syringe on the floor.

Lew opened the door, and they dragged Amy along a featureless corridor to another door. This door didn't slide like the others; Lew kicked it open, and they went rapidly down some metal stairs and along a further corridor. Amy was vaguely conscious that the woman, Hannah, followed behind, but she didn't speak. Amy concentrated on keeping her mouth clamped shut, and avoiding any unnecessary movement of her limbs, which felt like they were made of wet cardboard.

Everything was bright and featureless, with white light from all around without any visible light bulbs. They stopped in front of another door with a row of numbered buttons on the frame. Lew took out the box he spoke into and pressed it against a metal patch beneath the buttons. A green light flickered above it, and the door clicked and moved partly open. A puff of wind came through the small gap, bringing an odd smell, like a crowded room with no windows.

"I really don't think we should be doing this," Hannah said. Jake and Lew ignored her.

"Ready?" Lew said. Amy felt Jake nod beside her. At that moment, her stomach clenched again, and she coughed a pellet of gray vomit the size of her thumbnail onto Lew's chest.

"Christ!"

"Sorry."

"Wow, she speaks." Lew looked across at Jake. "Where to, Maestro?"

"I don't know. Away from here, then decide what to do."

"Great plan," Hannah said.

"Nancy Ahmed lives in Shoreditch."

"Okay."

They stepped through the door and let it slam behind them.

XXXII

London, 2040

The smell was the first thing that struck her. They were out in the open—Amy could see a gray sky above, like a high, painted ceiling—but the air tasted old and full of chemicals, like the atmosphere in a bus garage. They were on a narrow street, with a high wall behind them. In front, across the street, a wall of glass rose like a mirrored cliff. Amy lifted her head and felt dizzy as she looked up in search of the top of the building. The glass changed color as it rose from the street, fading into clouds above. A low whine drew her attention back to street level, and she looked to the right.

"Bus?" Lew asked.

"No," Jake said. "Walk a bit then let's see."

"Bit conspicuous with Cinderella here," Hannah said.

"Nobody likes a moaner, Hannah," Lew said.

"Shut up, Lew. Some of us have careers that might be worth saving."

"If you don't want to help, just walk away," Jake said. "We'll sort this without you."

The whining noise came from a tall red vehicle approaching along the street. It looked a bit like a double-decker bus, but taller, with three rows of windows. The whole of the front was glass, and Amy could see people sitting behind it. No one looked their way as the vehicle swept past them.

It's got no wheels.

There was nothing holding the bus up, and Amy could see most of the way underneath it. Her stomach quivered again. Surely there was nothing left to come up. They moved again, crossing the street and hurrying along the pavement to a path that ran down the side of the tall glass building. Hannah stayed with them, having made her unsuccessful protest. Amy's feet were beginning to get back with the program and she could now take some of her own weight.

"Just a minute," she said, calling them to a halt when they were away from the road. "I can walk."

"It speaks again," Lew said. He let her arm drop, and she leaned against Jake. Lew wiped at his chest with his sleeve, muttering under his breath.

"How are you feeling?" Jake said.

"Still alive. Just not sure if that's better than being dead."

"You'll be all right. The injection should be working soon. We'll get there quicker if you can walk. Then you can rest."

"Jake, where are we?"

"London."

"No, really. Where are we?" He'd obviously gone crazy. This was no place Amy had ever been, and she'd lived in London all her life. "How did we get here? There was a light and then—"

"I'll explain," he said. "Later."

They walked on, Jake supporting Amy round her waist, Lew walking ahead, Hannah following sullenly behind. They came to another street and turned right, moving slightly downhill. One side of the street was taken up by what appeared to be shops. They had wide glass fronts, and people moved in-and-out, some of them carrying packages. They walked past a store with a window full of tiny objects, some of them like the box Lew spoke into.

A woman appeared from nowhere in front of them. "Good to see you, Mister Wesson," she said, in a voice that came from somewhere to the left of her mouth. "Isn't it time you upgraded your palmer? I've got some attractive deals." She gave a wiggle, showing a fat expanse of cleavage down her blouse. Jake ignored the woman and walked straight at her, pulling Amy on with him. Amy flinched away from the collision, but the woman was gone as suddenly as she appeared.

"Who was that? Where did she—" Amy looked all around, but there was no sign of the woman.

"Just an advert," Jake said. "Come on. Look away, Lew. Cut down the iris scans."

"They don't bother with me," Lew said. "Not married, don't spend enough money."

They passed through a more crowded area. No one made much effort to leave space to pass on the pavement and Amy couldn't tell who was real and who was like the woman Jake had walked through. A couple of times her shoulder bumped people as they passed. One young man shoved her back, hissing "Eat shit, sister." Jake spun her quickly away from the man, and Hannah stepped between them, holding up a wallet.

"OffTime. Take a walk."

"Chill, Darlin'," the man said, holding his hands up, palms out and backing away. "I'm history." He smirked and stepped away, disappearing into the crowd.

"Thanks, Hannah," Jake said. Hannah shrugged, and they moved on. Amy was coming to her senses enough to wonder about Lew and Hannah. It was obvious they knew Jake well. The three of them acted with remarkably little communication, as if each knew what the other thought. Lew, while older than Jake, deferred to the younger man, content to follow his lead. She wasn't sure how Hannah fit in. She looked like she wanted to punch Jake.

They turned onto a narrower street. The buildings looked older here, some of them made of brick instead of steel or glass. The road opened into a small square, and Amy caught a glimpse of water between buildings. It was a river, lead-colored under the dull sky, about as wide as the Thames. In the middle of the square was a raised platform of dirty stone. A thin, round column rose high above it, with a metal globe on the top.

"Wait a minute," Amy said. "I recognize that."

"Well, yeah," Jake said. "It's been there a long time. What is it, Lew?"

"The Monument. Built after the Great Fire."

"But that's in London," Amy said. "Close to where I worked."

"What did I tell you?"

"How did it get here?"

"You'll work it out," Jake said. "Come on, we can take a tube from here."

He steered her toward an opening at the side of the square, and they stepped onto a metal staircase. As their feet touched it, the steps moved slowly downwards, and Amy screamed in surprise. Jake held her arm tight. Her stomach lurched again, before subsiding. Her head was starting to ache fiercely like there was a cold metal spike lodged behind her eyes.

At the bottom of the stairs, Jake lifted her onto solid ground and they walked through a tunnel and into an open hallway. This was familiar ground to Amy; it was like the London Underground platforms she was used to, except cleaner and more brightly lit. Instead of posters on the walls there was a bewildering display of moving pictures, like a wall full of small cinema screens.

The train was different too, whirring out of the tunnel on a blast of warm air. Like the bus, it had no wheels, and it bobbed very slightly up and down when it pulled to a stop and the doors slid open. Amy hesitated, but Jake and Lew ushered her inside and steered her to a seat. They sat to either side of her. Hannah remained standing in front of Jake.

"Jake, this is insane," she said. "You can't do this."

"I told you," he said. "I don't know how she got here. We just need time to think it through."

"We have to tell Ed."

"Not yet."

This train was much quieter and smoother than the tube trains Amy was used to, rocking gently from side-to-side as it sped away into the tunnel. Jake turned away from Hannah and spoke to Amy, "Feeling any better?"

"A bit," Amy said. "I don't know what happened."

"I'm not sure either. You must've grabbed me as I Jumped and we both came downtime. But it isn't your downtime. It shouldn't have happened."

"I don't know what you're talking about. Where are we going?"

"To a friend's place. She lives in Shoreditch."

"There's a Shoreditch—"

"In London. I know."

Shoreditch was the second stop. Lew led them off the train and up to the surface. Jake and Amy followed, Hannah still trailing behind. Amy was now able to walk almost unaided, and her nausea receded to a dull background queasiness. She even managed to step on and off the moving stairs without falling over, although Jake kept a tight grip on her arm.

They emerged at street level as it began to rain, fat drops of oily water that left greasy marks on the sleeves of Amy's blouse. The air was thick and warm. The street was very different here—the buildings older, dirtier, and largely brick and stone. Further away, there was an impossible backdrop of towering spires of metal and glass—some of them piercing the low cloud cover like needles in a ball of wool.

Lew didn't allow them to stop to admire the view but hurried them on. He and Jake glanced behind them a few times as if worried they might be observed. Hannah just plodded at their heels, occasionally shaking her head as if unable to believe what she was seeing.

"This is it." Lew led them onto a side street and stopped in front of a narrow, five-story block. "Top floor." He nodded at a row of buttons beside the entrance. They had labels next to them, and the top one said Ahmed.

"How did you know, Lew?"

"I'm a sociable guy." Lew spread his hands in a gesture of innocence. "But you'd better ring, Jake. She won't let me in."

"Why doesn't she live in an OffTime block?" Jake said, as he stepped forward and pressed the button.

"Ask her. Good thing for us she doesn't."

There was a crackling noise from a metal box below the call buttons, and a woman's voice said, "Hello?"

"Nancy, it's Jacob Wesson. I'm here with Hannah and Lew."

"Jake. You're back."

"Nancy, did you join the Office for excitement and adventure?"

"No."

"Me neither," Jake said. "But sometimes you can't avoid it. Can we come in? We need your help."

There was a loud click, and the door opened.

XXXIII

Lewis Brockley was impressed with the way Nancy coped with the four of them walking through her door. Hannah marched in first without speaking and went to sit in a chair by the window. She was followed by Lew and Jake, supporting Amy between them.

Lew suspected that Nancy recognized Amy straight away, and was maybe calculating the possible consequences for her career, but to her credit she said nothing and moved on swiftly. She instantly took charge of Amy. Jake's wartime sweetheart looked like she'd been running on adrenalin and memories of when the world made sense. Lew thought she'd perked up a bit on the Tube, perhaps with the help of the Timesickness shot, but now they'd stopped moving she looked ready to drop.

"Lew, get us all a drink," Nancy said, nodding at her kitchen. "Come on, my dear, I've got some towels and clean clothes in here."

Jake stood in the middle of the main room, uncertain whether to follow Nancy and Amy into the bathroom or sit with Hannah, who was chewing the back of her thumb and looking out of Nancy's picture window at the sky darkening behind the skyscrapers of the financial district. As he filled Nancy's coffee machine, Lew listened to Nancy and Amy talking quietly beyond the bathroom door. There were no voices from the room behind him, where Hannah and Jake were.

As he brought cups and a coffee jug to the table, Nancy came back into the room alone. She walked into the kitchen and returned with a bottle of wine and four glasses on a tray. "You all look like you need something stronger than coffee," she said. "I know I do." The sound of Nancy removing the cork and pouring the wine was unnaturally loud in the tense silence. Hannah still hadn't turned back from the window, and Jake was slumped in a chair, staring at his hands.

"She's exhausted," Nancy said, handing Jake a glass. "I told her we'd be right outside the door and she fell asleep in seconds."

"Thanks, Nancy."

Nancy took a mouthful of her wine and swallowed audibly. "I've gotta say, Jake, you're a man of surprises."

"I didn't plan this."

"Surprises even to yourself."

"It's not a joke, Nancy."

"Sure isn't. What happened? I've got some of it from Amy, but maybe you should tell me what's going on. I assume Hannah and Lew know."

"Don't include me in this," Hannah said. "I'm here under protest."

"I'm just asking you to help, Hannah," Jake turned on her. "But nobody's pointing a gun at you. If you want to leave, you can."

"Yeah? Maybe you want me to go downtown and let Ed Robinson know what's happening."

"Hannah, I want you to stay," Nancy said. "We're a team, and we should decide what to do together."

"Tell that to the team captain here."

Nancy turned to Jake again. "Please, Jake, tell me what's happened."

"Amy's from 1940s London."

"Really, you think?"

"Do you want me to tell you or not?" Jake glared at Nancy.

Lew decided to watch and listen. He knew people sometimes thought of him as unsophisticated. But when he chose to, he could pull back and make himself unobtrusive, focus hard on picking up every detail of the situation. It came in handy on missions, when blending in with the background and soaking up every clue in the surroundings was a valuable skill. He leaned back in his chair, letting Nancy and Jake share most of the eye contact, watched by Hannah.

"I met her briefly when we were all in 1941," Jake said. "She got married in the church while Lew and I were chasing those guys in the park."

"Romantic," Nancy said.

"Her husband died in that air raid the night we Jumped back. Or you Jumped back. I ended up in 1943."

"Where you found her again."

"I didn't find her. I was stuck in the past. For all I knew, I was going to be there until I died. She was working in the same ARP station."

"Coincidence."

"Yes. Coincidence. I was there for six months. I didn't know if I'd ever get back here. I got friendly with her. Too friendly, I guess."

Lew sipped his wine, watching Hannah, who was staring out of the window again. It was obvious she already knew about Jake's involvement with the girl from the past. Nor was it a surprise to Lew; sometimes you just have to see two people together. There'd been something about the way Jake and this girl walked along that told him they were connected. He'd seen it at once when they found Jake in 1944, and Lew couldn't help feeling a small squeak of jealousy.

"I followed the plan you gave me," Jake was saying. "I gave her the cover story and told her I was going away. I thought that was the end of it. She must've followed me up to London, to the pick-up. I didn't see her until I was just about to Jump."

"But how did she get here, Jake?" Nancy asked. "This is her future."

"I don't know. I felt her grab me just as the Jump happened. Then we were in the Darnell Suite."

"Bit of a shock for her."

"It was a shock for me."

"I thought it was impossible," Nancy said, "to Jump into the future."

"That's what I've always heard." Jake put his wine down and rubbed his temples with his fingertips. He looked dog-tired. "That's what the Office always said."

"Maybe they don't know what they're talking about," Lew said.

"Or they tell lies," Jake said.

"Oh, for fuck's sake!" Hannah sat forward abruptly. "Why don't we talk about the real issue that's staring us all in the face? I don't know why she's here or how it happened. What I do know is that we can't brush it under the carpet. We need to tell the Office."

"You may be right, Hannah," Lew said. "We might need to do that. But let's just think things through before we rush to judgment."

Nancy was obviously not listening to Hannah. Typical of the new recruit, she was still thinking about the time travel issues. "Maybe you can travel ahead so long as you're not personally present in that part of the future," she said, speaking like she was trying the words out to hear what they sounded like. "If you met your future self it could cause paradoxes. So maybe, you can only go ahead beyond your own lifespan. Amy couldn't be still alive now, she'd be, what, over a hundred and ten."

"She's not alive now," Jake said. "She dies in July 1944."

Nancy and Lew glanced at each other at precisely the same moment and then looked at the closed door, behind which Amy slept. Hannah didn't move.

"That's not why she's here," Jake said. "I didn't bring her deliberately if that's what you're thinking."

"Of course we're not," Nancy said.

Of course we are.

"Even if I wanted to do that, which I didn't, I had no idea it was possible."

"Does she know?" Lew said. "About her death?"

"No, and you can't tell her. Not yet, anyway."

"How does she die?" Nancy asked.

"There's a war on back there, you know. People got killed."

"Are you sure? I mean, how do you know?"

"I told him." All three of them turned at the sound of Hannah's voice. She held her wine glass in front of her like a communion cup.

"What?" Nancy said. "How did you know?"

"Ed Robinson let me do some research," she said. "While Jake was still back there."

"Woah!" Lew said, holding his hands up, palms out. "I'm not getting this. Ed was mad keen to tell us that we had to take great care with Amy. None of us was meant to meet her. She was the reason they got their knickers in a twist about pulling Jake out of 1944 without being sure we'd covered his tracks."

"But why?" Jake said. "I can't think of anything that makes Amy so important. And if she's going to die in a couple of months anyway..."

He broke off and looked at the door behind which Amy was presumably sleeping off her time sickness, and recovering from the exhaustion of doing what none of them had ever heard of anyone doing before—Jumping into the future nearly a century beyond her own death.

"That's obviously the point, isn't it?" Hannah said. "It's her death that's important for some reason."

"But why?"

"Does it matter why? The point is, you've done exactly what Ed was afraid of. If she's here, she won't die when she should."

"Can I ask something, Jake?" Lew said. "We're involved now, so we need to know what we're dealing with."

"Isn't it obvious what we're dealing with?" Hannah said. "Jake's just put a bomb under time."

"Let's not be over-dramatic, Hannah," Lew said. He drained his wine and put the glass down with a firm gesture. "Jake, when you found Amy had Jumped with you, why did you want to get her out of the Suite without anyone knowing?"

"Partly for her," Jake said. "I didn't know what they'd do with her."

"Aren't they more likely than you to know the right thing to do?" Hannah said. "You don't have a clue, do you?"

"I know what they'd do," Lew said. "They'd send her back."

"Is that safe?" Nancy said. "Now she knows about us, now she's been to the future."

"It doesn't sound like she's got very long to do anything with the knowledge." Lew saw Jake wince at his bluntness. "Trust me, they'd send her back."

"I don't know," Jake said. "But I can't trust them anymore. Something's not right about all this—our mission in 1941, the agent calling to me during the air raid, getting dumped in 1943 for months, and now this. If they lied about the possibility of traveling forward, what else are they hiding?

"And I had another reason for hiding her," Jake went on. "I admit I panicked a bit. If the Office knew she came with me, they'd think exactly what you suspected. They'd think I brought her here on purpose, trying to save her from the bomb in 1944. It wouldn't matter what I said, that's how it'd look to them."

"I guess," Nancy said.

"No need to guess. That's how it would be."

"Never mind what OffTime might do, Jake, what're you planning, now that we've got Amy out of the Suite and tucked her up in Nancy's bed? What are we going to do with her?"

"Right now, I can only think of one option." Jake's pale face betrayed his misery. "We'll have to do what you think the Office would do."

"Really?"

"What else can we do? How can she stay here? We have to take her back."

None of them said it, but Lew would've bet the same words were in all their minds.

To her death.

XXXIV

London, 2040

Hannah made Jake sleep in the spare bedroom. He didn't mind. Right now, he had no idea how to navigate his way back to where they'd been in their relationship, nor did he know whether it was a journey he wanted to make. All he could think was to get through the next couple of days, do what had to be done with Amy, and then see where the pieces fell.

He woke early, from a dream of burning buildings and guns clattering like dry bones hammering on a tree trunk, bright flashes cutting through the thick darkness, rain sweeping like tattered curtains across flat fields of mud. The dream dissolved and Jake thought, *It's an air raid.* He sat up.

He found Hannah in the kitchen, making breakfast. "I've made you a smoothie," she said, with a forced brightness. "Lots of antioxidants. Help you detox after all that primitive food."

"Thanks." Jake looked at the glass on the table. The liquid in it was viscous and blue-green like a slug had fallen into the blender. "I'll get breakfast on the way in. I'm seeing Ed early."

"So you said last night."

"I'll keep you out of it, don't worry."

"That's not what I'm worried about, Jake. It's you and what you've done. What you still might do."

"I didn't plan things this way, Hannah. I don't know how many times I've said it. We'll sort things out. Trust me."

"I'm trying, Jake. But you don't look like a man who can trust himself."

"I'm fine."

In truth, he wasn't fine. He was tired from deep inside, so tired his bones felt hollowed out and filled with mercury. His eyelids scraped across his eyeballs every time he blinked, and his head felt heavy as if it contained a chunk of concrete. He wondered if he might be ill. Could he have picked up some infection in 1944? That didn't seem likely—he was up to date with his shots before they Jumped to 1941 and they were meant to last a year. Maybe the way he felt was linked, in some way, with too many Jumps and too long spent in the past? You never got to hear anything definite, but there were rumors that too much time travel could cause stress and psychological problems.

He left Hannah at home and walked to the tube station. Instead of going straight to the Office, he took a detour to Shoreditch and went to Nancy's home. She buzzed him in without comment, and he took the elevator. The doors opened on the fifth floor and he was almost knocked over by Amy throwing herself into his arms.

"Oh, Jake," she said, her head buried in his chest. "What's happened? What's going on?"

"It's okay," he said. She felt so thin and fragile in his arms. He could've picked her up and carried her into Nancy's apartment without difficulty. "Come on, let's go back in and talk."

Amy sat next to him on Nancy's sofa. She already looked much better than the day before. After the Jump from 1944, as they'd dragged her through east London, she'd looked as if her face was made of pale wax, and moved like someone frightened her limbs might break if anything touched them. She remained very pale, but there was now a hint of pinkness in her cheeks and a gleam in her eyes where before there had been the dullness of a dog waiting to be kicked.

She held his hand as they talked. He saw Nancy's raised eyebrow at that, as she served them coffee. Nancy had her windows open, and a tepid breeze came in, carrying a smell of baking bread from the bagel shops on Brick Lane—one of the things that hadn't changed since Amy's London.

"Is it true, Jake?" Amy said. "Nancy told me you're all from the future. A hundred years."

"Yes, it's true."

"I just can't believe it," she looked from him to Nancy and back, her eyes wide. "We were in London, I followed you to that alley."

"We're still in London."

"Nancy told me, but it's not my London, it's like another world." Amy squeezed his hand. "But it's too much to take in. I feel like I'll wake in a minute and find I dreamed it."

"That would simplify things," Nancy said, smiling over the top of her coffee cup.

"Nancy's been fantastic," Amy said. "Last night, I just wanted to die before my head exploded. She looked after me so well."

"You certainly look a lot better than when we dragged you in here," Jake said.

"At least some things make sense in a way they didn't before," Amy said. "I always knew there was something odd about you."

"Many of his friends would agree," Nancy said.

"He has friends? Seriously, Jake, I never thought you were a spy, but there was always something unusual about the way you spoke; I couldn't place the accent. And then you came and went without warning. The night my husband died, you saved me from the fire and got me to that shelter, and then I turned around and you were just gone."

There was something distant in Amy's face, as she watched some unseen reel of memory in her head.

"And that time you disappeared for over two years, when I saw you again you looked *exactly* the same, like you hadn't gotten any older. The night you pulled me away from the bomb site I noticed a scratch on your face. It was fresh, some bits of dried blood were smudged across your left cheek. When I saw you again, two and a half years later, you had a mark on that same cheek, like you scratched it a couple of days earlier.

"Anyway," Amy said. "There had to be some explanation for all that. And when I found you stripping in a back alley, well, it was almost a relief to end up here. Other explanations for that could've been worse."

"I was so worried about you last night, Amy."

"Don't worry; one thing about living through a war, you just learn to get on with things. Inside, I'm terrified. I'm just glad I don't still feel the way I did last night. I thought my guts were turning inside out."

"It's quite common. It's why we—"

"Strip, I know. Nancy told me. Spoiled all the romance of the moment I caught you in your underpants in the street."

"Funny idea of romance."

"Maybe it's the Irish in me."

None of them spoke for a long moment, sipping their coffee to fill the gap in conversation. Jake broke the silence first.

"Amy, I can't stay. I just came to say there are some things I have to do today. If it's okay, can I leave you here until later, when I can get back? Nancy, if you don't mind."

"If you have to, Jake," Amy said. "But I'm frightened. I don't know what's outside that door. I wouldn't know how to buy a loaf of bread here on my own."

"Of course, the whole thing is a shock. I can't imagine how it must be for you. But we'll look after you. I just need to sort some things out today."

"I can't stay here, can I?" Amy said. "You'll be able to take me home?"

"That's what I need to sort out," Jake said. Nancy watched him, and he avoided her eyes.

When Jake left, Nancy followed him to the elevator and came with him to the ground floor. "She needs to know the truth, Jake."

"I know," he said. "Just let her get over the shock of being here first. Then we'll think about how to tackle everything else."

"It isn't fair. We've got to tell her the truth, and she has to have some say in what happens."

"I don't need a lecture, Nancy," Jake said. "I'm going to talk to Ed Robinson, and then I'll be clearer where we stand. Let's get together tonight and decide what's next. Could you get Lew over?"

"I will. And Hannah?"

"If you must."

XXXV

As he traveled into the Office on the tube, Jake felt weighed down with tiredness, like he could sink into his seat. On top of that, he had a strange confusion in his feelings. On one level, it was remarkable how swiftly he returned to normal life after six months in the past; the hiss of the train doors, the subdued whine of the engine as the train pulled away from the station, the carriage full of silent passengers all connected to headphones and looking at the screens of their palmers, no one meeting the eyes of anyone else. This was how it'd always been, and Jake slipped back into the routine like an eel released into a river.

Yet at the same time, he could've been a visitor from another world. He carried the heavy secret of Amy's illicit arrival in 2040. And his own time was now alien to him. Why didn't anyone talk, like they did on the crowded buses in 1944? His fellow passengers looked fat and well-nourished, but somehow pale and anxious as if any unplanned encounter in a public place was a threat to be avoided.

The contrast was striking with the skinny people of 1944, who survived on vegetables grown in their own back gardens, who took care to share the limited rations around and shared jokes in the bread lines, all while expecting explosives to fall from the sky daily. Those people faced danger, but at least they had the comfort of knowing who the enemy was, far away in Europe, and they could trust the people in their own city. No wall-mounted cameras panned to follow them as they walked away from the railway station.

He was grateful he didn't encounter anyone he knew as he entered the OffTime building. He went straight to his meeting with Ed Robinson and found him already in a meeting pod on the ninth floor. It had a view of the park, reminding Jake of his conversation with Robinson in a similar room before the mission to 1941. It was early spring now, and a couple of young men played lazily with a hover disc, setting it in flight toward each other and sending it ducking and weaving with their gestures.

"Jake, good to see you." Robinson stood up when Jake entered the room, coming around the table and shaking his hand heartily, clapping him on the shoulder with his other hand. "Sit down, son, sit down."

Jake sat, and Robinson resumed his seat across the table. He thumbed the surface in front of him and the windows frosted over, shutting out the park. Robinson had two thin folders in front of him. Jake noticed his name was printed on both. One of them was the usual boring olive-green color OffTime used for its limited paper files, but the other was a dark red Jake hadn't seen before. It had the word RESET stamped on it. Robinson noticed Jake's glance at the folders and casually moved them, so the green one covered the red.

"I was so relieved when I heard you checked back in last night," Robinson said. "We've been frantic about you."

"I was pretty frantic myself."

"Of course."

"I'm grateful for everything you've done," Jake said. "And the guys at Darnell, obviously."

"Maybe you could talk to Lew Brockley. He's still angry with them for losing you in the first place."

"Well, I wondered about that."

"We'll get to the bottom of that, trust me." Robinson spread his hands in a magisterial gesture. "I've set up a full debrief for you. We'll need to get as much detail as we can on what you went through."

Jake kept his face blank. He wondered how much Robinson knew. Lew said the Office was nervous about Jake's impact on the past. Something about Amy had them worried.

"But I wanted to talk to you first," Robinson went on. He plucked a fat cigar out of his shirt pocket and rolled it between his fingers as he spoke. "I've never had an agent go through something like this."

"Do you know why my Jump went wrong? Why I went to 1943 instead of back here?"

"That's a question, all right. The guys are working on it." Robinson gazed intently at the cigar in his hand as if the answer might be there.

"Could it have had something to do with the air raid that night?"

"It shouldn't. It's not like the Germans were using electromagnetic pulses, is it? They were just dropping old-style explosives."

"You ever been in an air raid, Ed?"

"I've been lots of places, Jake."

Ed's answer sounded like something a politician might say, Jake thought—avoiding the question, avoiding denial. When did Ed start talking to him like a politician? Had he always spoken this way, or was it something you picked up as you got more senior in the organization?

"Ed, was there another team back there?" Jake asked. "In 1941?"

"I think I'd know about it if there was." Robinson frowned at him. "Why do you ask?"

"The night of the Jump, I missed it because there was someone there," Jake said. "In the middle of the air raid, he called a Code One, shouted to me from down the street. I went to help, but he was gone."

"Are you sure?"

"I think I'd know," Jake said. "I wouldn't risk missing a return Jump without a good reason."

"Of course," Robinson said. "I'll look into it. Leave it to me. But tell me how you're feeling. After what you've been through, I wanted to see how you were. Before the de-briefers get ahold of you."

"I'm okay."

"Just what I expected you to say. But six months is a long time to spend in the field."

"It wasn't so bad."

"I'm impressed you managed to keep your cover all that time."

"Good training, I guess."

"How do you think you left things? In 1944, I mean. Living there that long, I assume there might be some, ah, loose ends we might need to tie off."

"I had a good briefing," Jake said. "I did what it said, used the cover stories."

"Do you think it worked?"

"I can't see why not."

"What about Amelia Jenkins?" Robinson appeared casual, looking down at his hands on the desk, but Jake felt the air between them go still.

"What about her?"

"Was the briefing okay for that, ah, entanglement?"

"It was difficult," Jake said. "But I did it."

It felt strange, holding things back from Ed. Jake had always trusted the older man, but something was different now. The guilty secret he was holding about Amy was part of it. As he sat opposite Ed, Jake was constantly on the point of confessing what happened, but something kept him from doing so. Maybe it was the way things had gone wrong with his trip into the past that shook his confidence in the Office. Once, he would've had no hesitation in trusting anything the organization told him or did with him. He didn't feel like that now.

"Did Lew or Hannah say anything about her, about the Jenkins girl?" Robinson was rolling the cigar between his fingers again. Sometimes Jake wished he'd just light the thing and smoke it. Maybe it'd set off the fire alarm and sprinklers, but anything had to be better than watching the man torture himself like this.

"Just that you were anxious about her," Jake said. "That she was important in some way. I didn't get it."

"I can't say much," Robinson said. "We monitor a lot of people and events in the past. Sometimes, we get indications that there's a changing probability of something happening differently. We do our best to make sure key events don't go off track."

"Fine," Jake said. "But what's Amy got to do with that? Hannah told me she dies in July 1944."

"*Died*," Robinson said. "It was nearly a century ago."

"Sure, but I left her in May 1944. What's the big thing she did in the next two months?"

"She died." Robinson's eyes on Jake were dull stones. "And we couldn't afford anything to interfere with that."

"Why not?"

"I can't tell you. I'm sorry if this all sounds cold-blooded, but remember this all happened a century ago. We're not causing Amelia Jenkins' death, the Germans did that. But it's our duty to head off the risk of history being interrupted. If Jenkins had lived, it could've been very destabilizing, in ways that are hard to predict but potentially disastrous. I'd expect any of our agents to do anything they could to make sure that didn't happen."

XXXVI

London, 2040

After his meeting with Robinson, Jake took the glass-walled elevator down to the OffTime entrance. The camera above the entrance moved soundlessly to follow him as he walked out into the crowded street. Jake resisted the urge to wave at it.

By concealing Amy's presence in 2040 from Robinson, Jake had taken a step he couldn't pull back from. Until the meeting itself, he thought he might tell all. Yesterday, once he got over the shock of Amy coming to 2040, he'd thought maybe it was a lucky accident. Perhaps she could stay, and by staying avoid her death in 1944. He and Amy had Jumped forward from May 1944. Amy was due to be killed by the German flying bomb in July. After that, she was lost to history—no more life to live and no more impact to be made on other people and the world around her. No new husband, no children, nothing. How much difference would it make if Amy didn't live out those two months in 1944? How serious could it be?

At first, in the Darnell Suite, his only thought was to get Amy away before she was discovered. Later, he thought he might've acted too hastily. Maybe this was the answer, this accident of Amy Jumping into his time, leapfrogging her impending death. What if he owned up to the authorities and talked to Ed? Amy's presence in 2040 couldn't damage the future from here on out because that was unwritten and unknown. Surely Robinson would see how little risk there was in Amy missing a few weeks of her obscure existence in 1944 London. Jake could even argue that sending her back, now that she knew about OffTime and the visitors from 2040, was the bigger risk.

This spasm of optimism soon died. The OffTime brass was paranoid about any interference in the past—except their own, of course. Everything they did was focused on keeping the course of history running the way they thought it should. Robinson would argue that any number of Amy's actions in those miss-ing months could be significant. She worked as an air-raid warden; what if she was meant to be there in June 1944 to pull someone from a burning building? And if she wasn't, maybe someone died who shouldn't have.

As he spoke to Robinson, Jake realized there was no honest conversation with him that would lead to Amy being left free to stay in his time. And frankly, even if the Office agreed to it, Jake no longer trusted them to keep their word. Too much had gone wrong. There was the screw-up over his Jump back from 1941, and the length of time they left him in the past. Even before that, there was something odd about their mission in 1941, their fruitless chase after that guy Kav and his cronies. One minute they were a serious threat, the next they escaped from Jake and Lew in Greenwich and no one was interested in them anymore.

OffTime was telling lies. They said it wasn't possible to Jump into the fu-ture, but here was Amy. It was hard to believe no one at OffTime knew it was possible, and if they knew but kept it from their agents, you had to wonder what else they concealed.

Jake left the Office and took the tube south of the river. On the way, he checked his palmer for the exact address he needed. He emerged from the tube station in a place called Ladywell. He had to walk half a mile from the station to the cemetery, and it was palpable how the road moved down the income scale as he went along it. It was a refugee district, and Jake passed several men in loose-fitting tunics and baggy trousers, some with lengthy beards. They stared at him as he walked past, but no one spoke to him. A man sitting in a doorway twenty yards away looked up and waved a bottle in Jake's direction.

A lot of shop fronts were boarded up, sometimes with makeshift tables set up in front of them, covered with piles of fruit and scabby-looking vegetables. Jake didn't stop. It felt like the kind of area he only saw on the evening HD—a place you heard about when some illiterate Yemeni kid got on a hoverbus with explosives strapped to his calves, or the locals set up a roadblock to protest an obscure outrage in their equally obscure country of origin.

Hardly anyone walked around London these days. It was easier and safer to travel on the tube, for those who didn't have the money or the influence to get a city driving permit. People stuck to the places they knew. The stories in the news about street crime didn't help: lurid tales about people who'd kill you for your organs, the gangs who stole small children to sell into slavery in the new caliphates of southern Europe. In the 1940s, all you had to worry about was Hitler dropping bombs on you from the air—and even when that happened, you got a warning from the air-raid sirens.

Jake almost missed the cemetery. The houses and shops faded out, replaced by a ragged wall of trees and shrubs, backed by bent iron railings and sheets of particleboard. A barred iron gate sat between two stone columns. There was a sheet of wood fixed to the gate behind the bars, blocking off the view inside. A sign said the cemetery was closed. Jake glanced behind him, then reached up and pulled himself quickly up the gate and dropped down on the other side. Someone shouted in the street behind him, but he ignored it.

The shabby confusion of the street disappeared, and Jake found himself in a secret garden looking out across an expanse of rough grass and trees, with a chaotic broken-toothed jumble of gravestones. There was a derelict brick cottage to his right, beside the gate, its windows smashed and vacant. A statue of an angel stood in front of it, her stonework stained and mossy, face buried in her hands.

A broad avenue ran away in front of him between tall trees and rows of stone mausoleums. Jake walked along it, reading the words carved into the gravestones as he went. Some were too old and weathered to be legible, but the further he walked from the gate the clearer they became. A warm breeze swayed bushes around Jake as he walked, and a small bird chirped anxiously in a tree above. Jake wondered when he'd last heard a bird in London. Maybe they all hung out in the cemeteries.

Jake took a side path, which ran between stone crosses partly obscured by bushes. He found what he was looking for at the end of the path, where a clump of rhododendrons screened the cemetery wall. In among the bushes was a group of stones bearing dates from the 1930s and 1940s. Many of them were broken and eroded, peeping here and there from the undergrowth as if the graveyard were slowly sinking.

A flat granite stone, speckled with moss, bore two names. The first inscription was carved into the stone, and the letters overlaid with lead: *"Alfred Thomas Farrell. Called to rest May 10, 1941, aged 26. Not lost but gone before."*

Beneath that, in a plainer script, were the words: *"Amelia Charlotte, born Jenkins, beloved wife of the above. Killed by German flying bomb, July 28, 1944. Though she dies, yet does she live."*

Jake read the words on the stone several times. He couldn't make himself accept their connection with the Amy Jenkins he knew. All he could think about was Amy in another graveyard, incandescently alive, lying on top of him the night of the fire raid on Deptford, her face lit with the amber glow of the burning warehouse—that night was only weeks ago. The same Amy kissed him only hours earlier today. It was impossible to believe she could be here, below the ground in front of him, almost a century dead.

A small sound behind him—a brush of grass on clothing, a scratch of shoe on a gravel path. Jake turned, fearing he'd been followed by someone from the seedy high street, perhaps to be robbed. Ten yards away, Nancy and Amy stood watching him.

"Nancy? What are you—" Jake's first thought was to block their view of the gravestone. He stepped toward them, positioning himself in Amy's eye line. He was too late, she was already looking past him, recognition lighting up her face.

"I thought I knew this place," she said. "That's Alfie's grave."

"We shouldn't be here," Jake said. He shot Nancy an angry glare and stood in front of Amy. "Come on, let's go." But Amy shrugged him aside and walked closer to the headstone.

"This really is the future, isn't it? It's Alfie's grave, but really old." She stopped and bent down to read. "There's more writing on it. Oh!" Her hand went to her mouth, and she swayed slightly as she straightened up and turned back toward Jake. Her eyes glistened with tears.

"Amy, I'm so sorry," he said. He held his arms out to her, but she seemed so far away. She looked at him as if he'd just let her go, and she was falling from a cliff. "I didn't know how to tell you." He took her in his arms before she fell. Her breath came in ragged gasps against his chest. He looked over the top of her head at Nancy, who still stood where he'd first seen her.

"Great work, Nancy."

"You couldn't keep it from her."

"But not like this," he said.

Amy's labored breathing sounded unnaturally loud in the quiet cemetery. Jake's face felt rigid like a mask, and his eyes were hot and gritty. They stood this way, like new monuments in the old graveyard, for several minutes, before they walked in silence back through the cemetery, to climb over the gate and return to the modern world, where Jake once thought he belonged.

Jake kept his arm around Amy most of the journey back to Shoreditch. She barely spoke, and her eyes were glassy as if she'd been sedated. As if the shock of landing in this alien future wasn't enough, she'd now seen her own grave. It was hard to think of anything more that could be done to test her psychological resources. Jake was seriously worried she'd have some kind of breakdown.

Only once did she rouse herself, when they were on a brief bus ride to the tube station. The ride took them down another shabby high street. Amy looked out at the boarded-up buildings, some with metal grilles over windows and doors, the rubbish piled on the pavements, picked over by ragged children.

"Is it like this because we lost the war?"

"No," Jake said. "We won."

Back at Nancy's, Amy rejected Jake's attempts to talk and said she needed to lie down, alone, for a while. Jake followed her into the bedroom.

"We'll get through this," he whispered, conscious of Nancy just outside the door. "I won't let anything happen to you."

"It's happened, hasn't it," Amy said. "What can you do?"

"I'll think of something. Get some rest. When Lew gets here, we'll think of something."

"There's nothing you can do, is there?"

"There has to be."

XXXVII

As arranged, Lew met the other three members of the 1941 team back at Nancy's apartment at six. He sat in an armchair by the window holding a beer. Hannah sat opposite him, saying little but with a face like an approaching stormfront. Jake leaned against the window frame behind Hannah's chair, presumably so she couldn't constantly spear him with her angry gaze. Nancy and Amy sat next to each other on a short sofa.

"I've ordered Chinese," Nancy said. "Should be here soon."

"Chinese what?" Amy asked. Hannah rolled her eyes, and Lew had the feeling this was going to be a long evening.

"Food," Nancy said. "Don't worry, you'll like it."

Jake left his position behind Hannah and hesitated for a moment before perching on the arm of the sofa next to Nancy, where he could see everyone. "Well, let's talk," he said. He looked like he'd just lost a winning lottery ticket. "I'll start."

"Great," Hannah said. "I've been looking forward to hearing the plan."

"First, I spoke to Ed Robinson," Jake said, ignoring her interruption. "So far as I can tell, he doesn't know about Amy being here."

"Yet," Hannah said.

"Second, Lew and Hannah, you need to know that Amy knows what's meant to happen in July 1944."

"Shit!" Lew said.

"How?" Hannah asked.

"She's seen her grave," Jake said. "Nancy took her there."

Nancy was denied the chance to comment by the sound of her buzzer signaling the delivery of their food. Jake and Lew got everyone drinks from the kitchen and Nancy deposited the take-out and plates on the coffee table between Hannah's and Lew's seats. As they helped themselves to food, Lew watched Amy closely. He couldn't imagine how she was handling everything she'd been through in the last thirty-six hours.

"We need to agree what we do," Jake said at last when they were all sitting again.

"It's obvious," Hannah said. "We hand the problem over to the Office."

"That's one option," Jake said. "Personally, I don't trust them. If there's a way to solve this ourselves, we should."

"What about other options?" Nancy said. "Could Amy stay here without the Office finding out?"

"Yeah, she can live with you, Nancy," Lew said.

"Even if you forget about the consequences of taking her out of her own time," Hannah said. "Which you shouldn't. How long would it be before the authorities got wind of it?"

"There's another option," Lew said. "If we agree Amy should go back to her own time, we can take her ourselves."

"How can we do that?" Jake asked.

"Same way we do any other Jump," Lew said.

"But what about the security, the cameras, the record-keeping?"

"You just need the right people on shift," Lew said.

"You're kidding."

"No," Lew said. "If we decide to do it, I can arrange it."

Amy watched the conversation, turning her head from one speaker to another, occasionally pushing a piece of Chinese food around her plate. She looked unconvinced it was actual food.

Lew thought finding out the date of their death would put anyone off their dinner.

"Are there any other options?" Jake asked. When no one spoke, he went on. "Everything we've thought of so far has one drawback. Taking Amy home ourselves or letting the Office send her back, they both end up the same. Trying to hide her here would probably end the same way too; if she's discovered, they'll send her back. All three choices end up with her back in London, where we know a bomb went off in July 1944."

"There's nothing we can do about that," Hannah said. She glanced briefly at Amy. "I'm sorry, but what happened has happened. We shouldn't try to change it, and if you've seen a grave doesn't that tell us that we aren't changing it?"

"Excuse me," Amy said quietly, staring down at her hands in her lap.

"There's another way," Jake said. "If Lew is right, and we can arrange a Jump off the books, we could take Amy somewhere out of reach of the bomb."

"Oh, come on!" Hannah slammed her fork down on her plate. "Are you crazy? Isn't it bad enough you've brought her here? Isn't that risking enough damage already?"

"I'm just thinking through the options," Jake said. "Before we decide, we should consider every alternative."

"Excuse me," Amy said again.

"Oh, so what alternative are you thinking of? Maybe you want to take your wartime girlfriend for a stay in the Swinging Sixties, hang out with the Beatles?"

"Excuse me!" Amy thumped her plate down hard on Nancy's table. They all fell silent and stared at her. "Can I say something, please?" Amy said. "Or do I just have to sit here while you argue about me?"

"Go ahead," Lew said.

"Thank you," Amy said. She looked at them one by one, her gaze resting last on Hannah. "I'm sorry, I know who the others are here, but I don't think we've met properly, Hannah."

"I'm Jake's partner."

"You're married?"

"Kind of," Jake said. "People can have partner contracts. They last a few years." Hannah shot him a cold look. Lew suspected she would've liked to shoot a lot more.

"So not exactly till death us do part?" Amy said.

"Are you married?" Hannah said.

"Widowed. Thanks for asking," Amy said. "Look, I don't understand most of what you're talking about. I still think I'm going to wake up and find myself back home. I would think this was all a dream if I thought my brain could come up with something so weird."

"We all feel like that sometimes," Lew said. "And we live here."

"You need to know this wasn't Jake's fault," Amy said, looking hard at Hannah. "I followed him and found him just before it happened. If I hadn't interfered, he would've come back on his own, just as planned. And we wouldn't have this mess."

Hannah glanced at Jake. He was looking out of the window as if searching the skyline for places he'd rather be.

"Anyway, the thing is," Amy went on. "I don't belong here, and I can't live here. I'm terrified just thinking about what's outside the door. If I stayed, Nancy or someone else would have to hold my hand forever. When you were talking just now, you said one thing I understood. You said it, Lew. You said you could send me back. If you can do that, then that's what I want."

"But, Amy—" Jake's attention was fully back in the room now. He stared at Amy in dismay.

"I know," she said. "I saw it. But I can't stay here. I'll take my chances with Hitler's bombs. He hasn't got me yet."

Her words reminded Lew of Captain Oates on the famous Scott Antarctic expedition, setting off into a blizzard, saying, 'I may be some time,' and sacrificing himself to save his companions. Very Twentieth Century British. The thing was, the words she'd seen on the grave suggested Hitler's bombs did get her. Lew suspected she knew that.

"Could we really do it?" Jake asked Lew at last.

"Yes," Lew said. "I'll make some calls. It may take a day or two."

"We should tell Ed," Hannah said.

"No way. Drop it, Hannah," Jake said. "You've got what you want. We take Amy home, but we do it my way. The minute we involve the Office, it'll get complicated."

"And it isn't complicated already?"

"Jake's right," Nancy said, speaking for the first time in ages, stepping down at last from the fence. "There's no point making it worse. If Lew can fix it, I say we should do as Amy wants."

"So that's Amy and three of the team," Lew said. "What do you say, Hannah?"

Hannah looked from one face to another. She had a deep frown line on her forehead that Lew couldn't remember seeing before, and her mouth was thin and tight like a small worm. "Okay," she said. "Do it your way."

XXXVIII

London, 2040

Lew left to make the arrangements. Hannah also left, to go home Jake hoped, rather than to run to Ed Robinson. Jake took Amy out for a short walk. "At least I'll have one nice memory of 2040," she said.

"We won't go far," Jake said. "Stay close and close your eyes if I tell you. There are cameras and iris scanners everywhere."

"Brick Lane and east of there should be all right," Nancy said. "I'll wait for Lew."

Outside in the street, Amy took Jake's arm, and he steered her east toward Brick Lane. "Let's just go a little way." Amy was leaning heavily on Jake's arm as if she'd sink to her knees without his support. "You must still be tired."

They fell silent for a while as they walked south along the market street. In contrast with the financial district to the west and the towers of Canary Wharf to the east, many of the buildings along the Lane still had their original Victorian brick facades. That wasn't universally true; there were places, especially on the western side, where new steel and plastic buildings had gone up, walling off the Lane from the area around Aldgate.

"Are you sure about going back?" Jake said at last.

"I don't see what choice I have. I can't stay here."

"What if you gave it a bit longer? You might not find it as hard as you think." Even as he said it, Jake knew he was whistling in the wind. It was surprising Amy hadn't been discovered yet. His chances of keeping her hidden much longer were tiny, even if she wanted to stay.

"It's not going to work, is it, Jake?" Amy said. "And I don't want to stay here. Although it can't be harder than coping with some of the things I've had to deal with."

Brick Lane had been the scene of violent riots in 2034 when anti-poverty protests got out of hand. Several streets had been completely burnt out, and Aldgate became the first part of London to be sealed off by the police. Jake noticed Amy looking closely at the five-meter high plastisteel wall along one section of the street. They both fell silent as they walked past a gated checkpoint. Two armed policemen stood in front. Jake couldn't tell through their dark visors whether they watched him and Amy pass.

"The future doesn't exactly seem like Paradise," Amy said. "I've been watching that television thing, the HD? There was some fighting in Croydon."

"Some riots," Jake said. "But it's just illegals. Can't get work, but it's hard to deport them. It's always trouble."

"These soldiers, Nancy said they were police, but they were huge, covered in this silvery armor, helmets and all. They were shooting people."

"Croydon's an illegal zone. They're not allowed to get out."

"I can't believe you've got parts of London that people can't leave."

"They weren't really shooting them." Jake shrugged. "They use stun guns."

"Oh, great."

"Of course, I forget," Jake said. "You come from a time when policemen wore pointy hats, told you the time, and rode bicycles."

"And helped old ladies across the road, don't forget."

"Yeah, remind me again how safe it felt in the 1940s. What with the Germans dropping bombs on us every night."

Jake could've punched himself in the face for mentioning bombing. They walked a bit further without talking. Amy looked down at her feet on the cobbled pavement. Jake was thinking of the words on her gravestone. He would've bet she was too.

"At least you knew who was trying to bomb you," Amy said at last. "We didn't get people living in London—English people—killing themselves to blow up buildings in their own city, like that one."

She pointed at a gap between two low buildings and Jake followed her gesture to see what she was talking about. At first, he didn't get it, but then realized she was pointing at the distant Shanghai Bank building, with the chunk missing from its silhouette, like King Kong had taken a bite out of it.

"Come on, Amy, you get lone nutters anywhere. Except in your time, they were running most of Europe."

"No one in my London could've done that."

By now they'd reached the south end of Brick Lane. They stopped walking, and Jake took Amy's hands in his as he took a step backward, drawing her with him into the doorway of a boarded-up shop. For a few moments, they were sheltered from the view of anyone on the street, except those passing directly in front of them.

"Amy, are you sure about this?" he said. "Whatever you decide, I'll back you."

"I have to go back. You know that."

"Even if, I mean, even though you know—"

"Even though I'm supposed to die, you mean?" The strain of the past two days was painfully visible on her face. She was as pale as paper, and there were smudges like ink stains beneath her eyes. "Do I really have any choice? That grave was a hundred years old. If I were meant to stay here, it wouldn't exist, would it?"

"I don't know."

"Well, if you don't know, what chance do I have?" Amy rubbed her eyes with the back of a hand. "July 28th. Maybe I'll just have to spend the whole day in a shelter."

"We can do better than that," Jake said.

"What do you mean, 'we'? It's not your name on the gravestone."

"Maybe it doesn't have to be yours." Jake accepted that he couldn't keep Amy in 2040. She'd have to go back to her own time. But that didn't mean he had to send her to her death.

"I've seen it. It's my name."

"I'll take you home," Jake said. Amy's hands were still in his, and she stood very close to him in the sheltered doorway. Jake noticed standing this close, Amy was shorter than she seemed. He brushed a coppery strand of hair away from her face and looked into her green eyes. "But Amy, I'm coming with you."

They were in each other's arms, and Jake didn't know whether he moved toward Amy or she to him. They simply came together like two magnets. Jake hadn't known he was going to say those words until they were out but, all at once, it was clear to him there was no future in which he could bear to lose her.

"I'm so glad." Amy's voice was muffled against his chest. She turned her face up to his again and tears brimmed in her eyes. "I thought you were going to abandon me."

"Never." He'd never said anything he meant more. "You can't say a word about this to anyone. No one must know. But I'm going to stay with you. Whatever happens."

XXXIX

London, 2040

Lew arrived at Nancy's building at four-twenty in the morning. Amy and Nancy were already waiting on the doorstep. It was dark, and the air was cold. Amy clutched a thin jacket closed at the neck, her shoulders hunched.

"Ready?"

"As we'll ever be," Nancy said.

"Nancy persuaded me to wear this," Amy said, gesturing down at her clothes: loose-fitting jogging pants and what looked like a baggy sweat-shirt under the jacket. "So I can strip off quickly."

"I'll look forward to that."

"Lew, behave," Nancy said. "She only has eyes for Jake."

"I'll do anything to avoid feeling that sick again." Amy nodded to a small bag on the step at her feet. "You can send my old clothes through after me?"

"That's the plan."

"There's a plan? Wow."

They fell silent at the sound of footsteps as two figures appeared from around the corner and walked toward them in the shadows, quickly revealing themselves as Jake and Hannah. Jake carried a canvas carryall that looked surprisingly large and heavy for the short trip they'd planned. Hannah carried nothing, apart from a facial expression that could turn milk into yogurt.

The five of them stood awkwardly for a few seconds, no one knowing what to say. Lew saw a look pass between Jake and Amy, but neither of them spoke, and Jake remained standing close to Hannah. Lew didn't think he'd ever seen two people stand so close together and look so far apart. The space between them looked like it'd freeze oil.

"Ready?" Lew said. "Bassi starts his shift at five. He reckons we'll be clear until six-thirty, but he can't guarantee anything after that when the Suite gets busier."

They set off. The streets were very clear this early, and the walk to Monument took only twenty-five minutes. Lew led the way, with Nancy and Amy behind him and the unhappy couple bringing up the rear. When they approached the high external wall of the Darnell Suite, Lew gestured for the others to wait and went forward alone. He found the door they'd fled through two days earlier but held back from it. Instead, he stepped back into the shelter of a doorway across the street. He took out his palmer and messaged Bassi, then watched the door across the way.

A couple of minutes passed before he heard a muffled click, and the secure door swung inward a few inches. Bassi's dark, bearded face appeared in the gap. Lew whistled, and Bassi spotted him. Lew held up two fingers—two minutes— and walked quickly to the street corner and beckoned the others forward. They kept their faces down to avoid cameras as they walked through the door and into the OffTime complex.

"Security's a bit feeble round here, Bassi," Lew said. "Somebody ought to make a report."

"I can do that for you if you like, Brockley." Bassi was in his forties, with flecks of gray in his beard like ash blown from a distant fire. Some of the Black and Asian staff at OffTime resented the limitations the business placed on their job prospects. For obvious reasons, there were large swathes of Britain's past that it was tricky for them to visit on field missions. Nancy Ahmed got clearance for missions back beyond the 1960s, despite her Gujarati grandmother, because she was pale-skinned. The restrictions confined guys like Bassi to less glamorous back-office roles, and some of them could be chippy about it. Not Bassi, though, whom Lew had known since his first days in training.

"Maybe we'll let it go this time, Agent Bassi." Lew shook his hand. "Thanks. I owe you one."

"You owe me more than one, man. When do I ever get to collect? That's what I'm wondering."

"Surely virtue is its own reward."

"That's what he always says," Bassi said, turning to the others. "Hey, Mister Wesson and Miss Benedict, you in on this too?"

"You never saw us," Lew said.

"Oh man, how I wish that were true. Now, better get busy." Bassi's face was instantly serious. He gestured along the narrow passageway, and they started walking. "Turn right and up the stairs. We've got maybe twenty minutes. I've got Johnny Sanders in the Control Room. He won't notice anything."

"You sure?" Jake said.

"I told him to concentrate really hard on not noticing anything."

"What about cameras?"

"Routine maintenance." Bassi winked.

They walked in single file up the concrete steps and turned left at the top. Bassi ushered them along the corridor to a door at the end, which Lew opened for everyone to step through and into the changing room next to the Jump Room. Lew caught sight of the tight expression on Amy's face. No doubt she remembered her previous visit here, and how bad she'd felt at the time.

"Lew." Jake stepped close and spoke softly. "I can't believe how easily we're getting in here. How can the security be so sloppy?"

"The right people are on duty, and they know us."

"But it can't be this easy. Otherwise, agents would be tempted to travel back in time off the books."

Lew held Jake's gaze and raised an eyebrow. Jake's eyes widened.

"You're kidding me," Jake said. Lew shook his head. "Have you ever…"

"Once. But I know guys who've done five or six trips under the counter."

"Christ, Lew."

Jake sounded shocked, which Lew found interesting. He assumed anyone who'd been with the Office as long as Jake would know what went on.

"What about the risks?" Jake said.

"Do you think there's more risk with a trip I plan myself than something planned by the back-office geniuses who dumped you in 1943?"

"Where did you go?" Jake asked. "The time you did it."

"Maybe it's best to ask me no questions."

"Have you ever wondered?" Jake said. "I mean about where someone could make the biggest impact. If you really wanted to change history, what would be the place to go?"

"Why would you want to?"

"I wouldn't," Jake said. "But if you did. I guess saving Churchill's life was something, although it didn't change the result of the war."

Lew said, "I've always thought, if you wanted to be mischievous, you could stop Axel Darnell's parent's from meeting. It was a fluke apparently."

"So, no Darnell, no time travel?" Jake said. "But quite a paradox—using time travel to change things, so time travel doesn't happen?"

"I'm not recommending it. Right everyone." Lew raised his voice. "Let's move. Jake and me in there, Amy get changed here. Nancy, can you help her?"

"It's my privilege to serve." Nancy gave him a sarcastic smile.

Jake and Lew stripped off and waited by the door to the Jump Suite. Amy reappeared in a shapeless cotton robe. Nancy gave her a brief hug and pushed her gently toward Jake. Hannah stood back, her arms folded and a stiff expression on her face. Amy gave Jake a thin smile, and Lew opened the door into the Jump room. He palmed a message to Bassi, who should by now be back in the control room. A message came back at once—*Go. Two minutes.*

"We'll be back as soon as we're sure we've got Amy back where she should be," Lew said. He noticed Jake take a half step toward Hannah but she gave him a fierce glare, and he turned away to join Lew. The three of them went into the room, and Lew closed the door behind them. They walked to the center of the room, and Jake took Amy's arm and made sure she stood on the correct mark on the floor. Jake stood closer to Amy now that they were out of Hannah's sight. He leaned close, his hand on her arm, and spoke in her ear, too quietly for Lew to hear.

"Come on. You can say your goodbyes uptime. Get on your mark."

Jake stood in his position, three feet from Amy, and placed his heavy bag and hers away to the side.

The Jump went perfectly. There was a pop, and Jake faded out in a purple glow, followed quickly by Amy. Almost at once there was another soft pop, and Lew stumbled slightly to one side. He put out a hand to steady himself, and it met a damp brick wall that lurched into existence six inches in front of him.

He sniffed the air—they were back in wartime London.

XL

London, 1944

Lew turned to see Amy on her hands and knees behind him. Jake helped her to her feet. Her face was the color of bleached linen. She forced a thin smile.

"Gets better every time, doesn't it?" she said.

"Wait till the novelty wears off."

With a sound like someone tapping on wet cardboard, Jake and Amy's bags flicked into existence on the ground. The three of them got dressed, before Jake picked up the bags, one in each hand.

"We should go," he said.

"Go where?" Lew said. "Get Amy on her way, and we go back straight away. That's the plan."

"Change of plan, Lew. Sorry."

"What do you mean, change of plan? Come on, Jake, you can't do this to me. I'm out on a limb for you here."

"I know that, Lew. I'm really grateful. I'm not going to cause trouble for you, but I need a few hours here."

"We agreed we'd bring Amy back and make sure she was safely home. That's it. Then you and I go back home, and we leave it there."

"Come on, Lew, you knew I wasn't going to do that." Jake put the bags down again and spread his arms wide in a gesture of sincerity that made Lew want to punch him. "Didn't you wonder why I brought a bag?"

Lew had no answer to that. He may not have admitted it to himself, but Jake's treachery was predictable.

"You go back as planned," Jake said. "I'll follow tomorrow."

"Maybe it's not that easy to set up these Jumps off the books. Think about that, Einstein?"

"I'll just have to take that chance."

"It's not just you taking a chance, is it?"

"Lew, whatever happens, I'll take as much of the blame as I can."

"Big of you."

It was Amy who broke the tension. She stepped forward and placed a hand softly on Lew's arm.

"Jake couldn't have a better friend than you, Lew." There was a musical undertone to her voice, which broke through sometimes when she was angry or spoke softly like this. "I'm glad I got the chance to meet you. We would've been lost without you."

Lew blinked and turned away. He could face down Jake, but he was putty with a good-looking woman. Amy's sudden tenderness was overwhelming, and he was pierced by the thought that she really didn't have much to thank him for. He'd returned her to 1944 so she could die the way History wanted.

"No point standing around arguing," he said. "Do what you must. I'll do what I can to bring you back tomorrow without a full welcoming committee. But no guarantees."

Jake picked up the bags again, and the three of them moved to the end of the alley and peered out into Lower Thames Street. It was deserted, and nothing moved on the steely surface of the river beyond.

"Looks like we arrived as planned," Jake said. "Early morning."

"Yeah. Maybe it'll even be the day we planned." Which was Saturday, May 20, 1944. London was still at war, but the center of the fighting had long moved away. In Italy, Allied troops had just beaten the Germans at Monte Cassino. In two weeks' time, on June 6th, the Allies would invade Normandy. The invasion would prompt the Germans to unleash their new weapon, bringing the war back to London with a new Blitz from the V-I flying bomb—including, in July 1944, the one with Amy's name on it.

"I'll walk with you a bit," Lew said. "Then turn back, so I'm here for the pick-up." The deal with Bassi was a pick-up forty-five minutes after they arrived, now only half an hour away.

They walked along Lower Thames Street. The only sound was the shrill squawking of gulls over the river. Lew didn't know what to say. He'd never see Amy again, and he now understood why Jake got so entangled with her. He also couldn't help feeling that this parting with Jake was significant too. He didn't know what his partner planned, but instinctively, he didn't like it. Jake's bag was too heavy, his mood too light.

They walked onto London Bridge and stopped halfway across. Jake and Amy leaned back against the concrete wall and Lew stood in front of them. A cool breeze whipped up whitecaps on the surface of the Thames below.

"I better turn back here." He shook hands with Jake and attempted to do the same with Amy, but she surprised him by stepping forward and seizing him in a fierce hug. His throat tightened, and he coughed and blinked rapidly when Amy, at last, let him go. He punched Jake weakly on the chest.

"You take care. Both of you."

"It's my middle name," Jake said.

"Not the story I heard."

He watched them as they walked away along the bridge. Two barrage balloons attached to the southern end of the bridge stood guard, like sentinels welcoming Jake and Amy into a new world. At first, Jake walked beside Amy with a bag in each hand. After a few minutes, they stopped, and Amy took her bag from him. They resumed walking, hand-in-hand.

Into their future, into the past.

PART IV

XLI

London Evening News, Thursday 22nd June 1944

London Evening News, Thursday 22nd June 1944
Mystery Punter Scoops £30,000 As Long-Shot Umiddad Takes Gold Cup

Only the bookies win. That may usually be true, but one lucky punter at Ascot would dispute it after Umiddad won the Ascot Gold Cup at the mouth-watering odds of 30-1. Few punters gave the four-year-old the slimmest chance of victory, yet the horse romped home in an impressive four minutes and eighteen seconds, over two miles and four furlongs, accompanied by the sound of betting slips being torn up in the grandstand.

If that wasn't surprising enough, word quickly spread that a London man staked £1,000 on the outsider mere minutes before the race began, so late that the starting odds were not affected. A spokesman for Ladbrokes declined to comment.

Earlier, cheering crowds greeted the King and Queen Elizabeth as they took a short break from official duties to visit Ascot and watch the King's horse, Kasbah, run in the Gold Cup. Sadly for His Majesty, but of course not for the mysterious London man who is now £30,000 richer, his own horse pulled up two furlongs out, leaving the field to Umiddad.

XLII

London, 1944

With Amy's help, Jake found a new room in Blackheath, in the basement of a four-story house on Kidbrooke Road. He intended to stay there for only a few days before moving somewhere more permanent, but he needed an initial base. The room had a gas ring, and the first thing Jake did was put the kettle on.

"We haven't got any tea yet," Amy said.

"It's not for a drink," he said. "I need you to help me with something."

Amy watched him as he opened his bag and took out a tube of antiseptic cream, a large cotton dressing pad, and a sharp knife. He began to unbutton his shirt.

"What are you doing?"

"We have to stop them tracking me." He poured boiling water into a cup and put the blade of the knife in it. He dropped his shirt and sat on the bed, turning his back to Amy, reaching up as far behind his back as he could with his left hand. "Between my shoulder blades, near my finger, can you see?"

"You've got a scar," Amy said, leaning close. "And there's a lump."

"Touch it."

Amy did so. "There's something under the skin."

"You've got to cut it out."

"You're joking."

"You have to. They can track me with it."

"They didn't do much of a job tracking you last time," Amy said. "You were here for months."

"I don't think they were trying very hard," Jake said. "We can't rely on it again. They'll know when and where to look."

"I can't do it," Amy said.

"Please Amy, you have to. I can't reach it." He picked up the knife and handed it to her, handle first. "Come on, you've done worse things in the ARP."

Amy took the knife as Jake turned away. He removed the belt from his trousers and gripped it in his teeth. He couldn't prevent himself flinching as the blade pressed against his skin.

"Keep still if I'm going to do this," Amy hissed.

Jake bit down on the belt and dug his fingers into his thigh. Amy pressed harder and pulled the knife down between his shoulder blades, before scraping across. The first cut hurt surprisingly little as if she was only scratching the skin. The second cut released a lightning bolt of pain up his neck, and Jake growled into the leather belt in his mouth, twisting away from the knife.

"Just keep still!" Amy stabbed him again, and Jake tasted acid in his throat. He closed his eyes and wedged his arm beneath him to stay upright. Something warm and wet ran down his back. "There," Amy said at last. She stood up and dropped the knife in the sink.

"Don't lose the tracker," Jake gasped. "We need it." He handed her the dressing pad, and she taped it to his wounded back. She took his face in her hands and wiped the tears from his cheeks.

"Don't ask me to do anything else like that," she said.

"Don't worry. It's all great from now on."

"Until I get blown up," she said.

"I've got a plan for that."

The first part of Jake's plan was accomplished that evening when he traveled back into London alone. He had the canvas bag he'd brought from 2040. It now contained only the bloodstained knife and the tracker Amy cut from his back. He didn't linger long in the alley where they'd arrived after Jumping from the future. The pick-up promised by Lew wasn't scheduled for nearly twelve hours, but he didn't want any accidents. He wedged the bag into a narrow gap between the alley wall and a pile of wooden pallets that looked as if they'd been there for months.

The second step in his plan was more difficult. Part of the problem was Amy herself. She spent the first night back in 1944 at her parents' house and met Jake again the next morning. He tried to persuade her that they should leave London—move as far away as possible; Scotland, Cornwall, Jake didn't mind where—just a long way from London.

"I can't just leave my family," Amy protested.

They were in Greenwich Park, outside the Observatory. It was a sunny morning and the slope below them, stretching down to the Maritime Museum and the river beyond, was crowded with people sitting on the grass. A small group of boys further away, where the ground levelled out, were playing football. Jake and Amy leaned on the railing in front of the statue of General Wolfe. The sun was warm on their necks, casting short shadows down the grassy slope in front of their feet.

"You don't have to leave anyone. You can stay in touch. But we need to make it harder for anyone to find us."

"You think they'll come after us?"

"I'm sure they will."

OffTime would quickly find out what he'd done, despite Lew's cover-up attempts. Once they knew he'd gone uptime, they could make a good guess what he might do. It was unthinkable that they wouldn't try to stop him. Slicing out the tracking chip made it harder for the Office to trace him, and the fact he hadn't already been intercepted or pulled out was a good sign. But it was clearly not impossible for them to track him down; they'd discover, at least approximately, the time he'd come back to, and they'd guess who he was with, even if Hannah and the others kept quiet. His chances were much better if he could persuade Amy to go into hiding with him, at least until the date of her death passed. That was the crucial thing—keeping her away from Lewisham High Street on July 28th.

"They're bound to try to find me," he said. "Take me back."

"And they'll want me to die on time."

"They like things tidy," Jake said. "But it's nothing personal, and maybe they won't worry too much about one fewer casualty in a war."

Jake hadn't told Amy about the importance people like Ed Robinson attached to her dying as planned. He wasn't sure how seriously she took the 28th of July. She'd experienced years of bombing and survived. At times, she appeared to think she could dodge the bomb by being extra careful on the day.

In addition, London's fear of bombing had eased by this time in the war. Jake thought Amy might take the threat more seriously again once Hitler sent his flying bombs, but no one knew about those yet.

"If it were just me, I'd probably give them the slip," Jake said. "There's not much at this time to lead them to me. The problem is you, Amy. They know your address, family connections, friends—all those things are on record. They can find you unless we make a change."

"But I can't just cut off all contact with my family and friends."

Hitler's V-1 will cut it off soon enough if you don't.

"It won't be all contact," he said. "We just need to be careful until the end of July. After that, it'll be easier."

In the end, she saw the sense of what Jake said. They agreed he'd find new accommodations in the area, using a new identity. Amy wouldn't, despite his arguments in favor of it, move in with him and pose as his wife. But she'd spend nights with him when she could.

In the meantime, she quit her ARP job and moved out of her parents' house. She'd stay for a short time with a school friend in Greenwich, while she found rooms for the summer. Jake assured her that money wasn't an issue—he'd pay. Before leaving 2040, he'd checked the historical records of some horse races in 1944, and anticipated a few profitable bets.

Jake knew the set-up wasn't ideal. OffTime would find it easier to locate Amy than him. He'd simply have to be careful and vigilant in the hope that when the time came, he'd have a chance to intervene. They'd also take a holiday, spend a couple of weeks by the sea, maybe in the north or Wales.

Ideally, in late July.

XLIII

London, 1944

After a few days in his rented room, Jake found a new home. The house was a four-story mansion overlooking Blackheath. Stone steps led up to the front door, which was sheltered by an overhanging balcony. Jake glanced up at the balcony as he approached. Two wicker chairs sat behind wrought-iron railings. It looked a pleasant spot to sit with a beer.

Jake rang the bell and the tall wooden door opened within seconds. A woman of about sixty stood there, wearing a pale blue housecoat and peering at him over the top of tiny spectacles.

"Mrs. Downing?"

"That's right, dear." The woman's voice sounded marinated in cigarettes and sweet tea. "You must be Mister Jackson. You're early."

"Time and tide, Mrs. Downing." Jake gave his new landlady a cheesy grin.

She led him inside and up to the first floor. As he'd hoped, his flat had the balcony. He didn't know how long he'd be staying, but there was no harm in enjoying a little comfort, insofar as 1944 London offered it. The flat had a bedroom and large reception room with a view over the heath.

Mrs. Downing made a great fuss of showing him the self-contained bathroom and toilet, and the small kitchen. Everything was clean, and the ceilings were high with tall windows, filling the rooms with bright, almost antiseptic light. Even so, there was still the faint whiff of damp that seemed a feature of almost every room in 1940s London.

"I hope you'll find it comfortable, Mister Jackson," the woman said as he dropped his small case inside the door. There was very little in it, but it seemed sensible to show up at his new lodgings with some luggage. "The previous tenant was such a gentleman. I didn't think I'd have to let the rooms again so soon." She ran her hand absently down her skirt as if smoothing out creases.

"He was an army colonel, and his regiment was moved south. Very hush-hush, of course. You're not with the Forces, Mister Jackson?"

"Wish I was." Jake tapped his chest. "It's the tubes. Otherwise, nothing would stop me. Runs in the family."

Mrs. Downing's mouth tightened, and the ghost of a frown flickered on her brow. She wasn't sure whether it was the chest problem that ran in his family or some kind of military career. Jake thought it was best to keep her guessing.

"Very nicely kept, Mrs. Downing," he said. "You can always tell with military training. Unless it's your own good housekeeping, of course."

"You do what you can, don't you, dear?"

"I'll get unpacked straight away," Jake said. "Then I have some business I must see to." He put his bags down on the patterned rug in front of the balcony and pulled out the fat leather wallet he'd bought after his trip to the races. "The deposit and first month's rent, I think you said?"

All interest in Jake's military career, or lack of it, was wiped from the woman's face by the sight of the notes he peeled from the thick roll in his wallet. The money disappeared into the deep pocket of Mrs. Downing's housecoat.

"I'll let you settle in," she said. "I'll slip the receipt under the door later."

Her slippers slapped on bare wooden treads as she walked downstairs. Jake left his bags on the floor and opened the balcony windows. They moved stiffly, as if reluctant to be opened. It didn't look as if the virtuous colonel used the balcony much. No doubt he was far too busy winning the war to waste time sipping tea in wicker chairs. Jake lowered himself gently into one of them, which creaked theatrically beneath him. He put his feet up on the other chair and sat for a few moments gazing out over the sunlit grass of Blackheath.

The view was nice, but the most important thing was that the flat was close to Amy; she was moving into a rented room a quarter of a mile away. Jake leaned back, lifting his face to the warmth of the sun. He closed his eyes for a moment, opened them again, and surveyed the heath once more. At least, sitting here, there was a good view of anyone approaching the house. Maybe he and Amy could while away the days on Jake's balcony, keeping watch for OffTime agents and flying bombs.

The thought sent his gaze to the far side of the heath, where a long row of cream-colored houses marked the top of the ridge that, on its far side, descended through woods and progressively less wealthy homes into Lewisham. Down there was the street where history said Amy Jenkins met her death, a little over a mile from where he now sat.

Jake pictured the street market on Friday, July 28, 1944—now only weeks away. Women carrying shopping bags loaded with potatoes and carrots, small children clinging to their skirts as trams and buses thundered past. Amy often visited the market. It was close to the ARP station, and several times a week she picked up vegetables for her mother. It was all too easy to picture her in the High Street as the bomb fell from a pitiless blue sky.

Keeping Amy away from Lewisham High Street on the 28th was the most important thing. Afterward, there'd be less to worry about. They'd work something out. With Amy still alive on the 29th, anything was possible.

✦✦✦

Settled in his new home, Jake soon began to feel events accelerate toward the day he feared. After a week, he hoped he'd given OffTime the slip. If they found him, they'd surely intervene as early as possible. The fact he and Amy had been undisturbed for a week gave him hope.

On the morning of Tuesday, June 6th, London felt febrile and excited, on the edge of hysteria. You could see it in the eyes of strangers in the street as they scanned your face, as if they thought you might have news, or might want to hear their news. Walking through New Cross, he and Amy listened to laughter from a crowded bus that passed them and, as it waited at a busy junction, someone inside the vehicle struck up a song and within seconds the whole bus was singing "Roll Out the Barrel." They discovered the cause of the excitement when a woman in her twenties dashed from a shop doorway and, before Jake could react, grabbed him and kissed him full on the lips.

"Isn't it great?" She let him go and stood back. "Isn't it just the best news?"

"What is?" Amy said.

"Haven't you heard? It's been on the wireless and everything. We've invaded. Our boys and the Yanks are in France. Hitler's on the run."

Of course. As soon as she said it, Jake realized. This was the day Europe had been waiting for, the event hanging unseen and unspoken in England's air all spring. British and American troops had, at last, landed in northern France. Jake knew that despite fierce fighting, within a few days they'd break out and advance south toward Paris. The war was racing to a conclusion.

A few days later the buzz bombs started, as Jake knew they would. There'd been rumors for some time of Hitler's secret weapons, and now that his troops faced final defeat, he used them. Jake was surprised how soon he saw his first one. He was on Blackheath, and two men stood in front of the church pointing at the eastern sky.

There was the noise of an engine, and a small plane slid across the sky. It had short wings, and he couldn't see any propellers. There was a line of dark smoke behind it. The engine noise grew louder, into a throaty roar, and then the smoke cut off and the noise stopped. The front of the strange plane dipped, and it glided downwards in a wide arc. It flew over the heads of Jake and the two men, about a hundred feet up, and disappeared over the top of some houses on Shooters Hill.

The world lurched sideways, and Jake was thrown to the grass. There was a loud explosion beyond the houses, and a thick column of smoke rolled upwards into the sky.

It was as if Amy's death had announced itself. The clock was ticking toward the 28th of July.

XLIV

In the days after Jake disappeared, there were new faces at the Office, some of them in uniforms Lew didn't recognize. A bunch of top brass showed up the day after he slipped back into 2040 when Jake failed to return—a couple of sixtyish men, with unseasonal tans and hair like the pelt of a white mink, accompanied by younger, slab-faced men who looked too big for the OffTime reception hall.

The newcomers stood around with a kind of disciplined casualness, leaning on the marble walls, all looking in different directions with eyes that flicked from place to place. The younger ones looked like they were constantly resisting the urge to flex their biceps. They weren't in reception for long but were quickly ushered into the express lift and disappeared, so the canteen wisdom said, up to the eleventh floor.

So far as Lew could tell, his involvement and that of Nancy and Hannah in Jacob Wesson's disappearance remained a secret. He doubted they could remain free of suspicion forever. Someone would talk. But for the moment, no one bothered to ask him what he knew, and no one seemed to know that Amy Jenkins had been in 2040, and had stayed at Nancy's place for forty-eight hours before Jake flitted with her back into the past.

So far as he knew.

But Hannah had spoken hardly a word to him or Nancy since the day of the Jump. And he knew very well how close she'd always been to Ed Robinson. Lew knew Robinson a long time himself and always got on well enough with him. But Ed was management, and Lew was unsure which side of the line Ed Robinson stood when it came to choices between Jake's welfare and the rulebook. For Lew, the choice was simple, and the rulebook was complicated.

He met Hannah and Nancy at Hannah's apartment on the third day after his return from 1944. Nancy was last to arrive. She came straight from work. When she arrived, Hannah and Lew sat on the balcony, drinking red wine and looking out over the silver ribbon of the river. Lew was glad to see Nancy. Hannah had barely spoken.

"Want some wine, Nancy?" Hannah wiggled the bottle in her hand.

"No thanks. Bit early for me."

"Not something we could say about you, Nancy," Lew said.

"Sorry. I thought I could get away at four," Nancy said. "I was just about to leave when I noticed some action in the Jump Suite. I bumped into a guy I know, just back from a Jump."

"Oh yeah?"

"Not what you're thinking, Lew Brockley. Just a guy I trained with. I see him occasionally when our old group gets together."

"Nice. Did you chew over old times?"

"No. I saw this guy—Kurt, German father—as he came out of the Suite. Barely recognized him, he looked so exhausted. I was just passing but got involved in helping the medics. One of the guys with Kurt was ill, not time-sick; Kurt said he was wounded on their mission. Gunshot."

"Christ! Where'd they go?"

"That's just it," Nancy said. "Kurt wouldn't tell me much. He said the mission was classified."

"Aren't they all."

"He really meant it. I could see he thought he'd said too much, even with the little he did tell me."

"Which was?"

"He said they'd been in 1944. July 1944."

"Looking for Jake?" Hannah said. At the mention of the date, she tore her eyes away from the contemplation of her wine glass and turned to Nancy. "We should've known about that."

"Not looking for Jake. Kurt didn't know anything about him. He said they'd traveled to the coast and crossed over to Belgium. Said it was a nightmare, the south coast crawling with American and British troops, and the fighting in northern France."

"Belgium? What were they doing there?" Lew said.

"Kurt said they had to wear German uniforms—he made a joke of it. He now knew why the Germans lost the war; the quality of their uniforms by 1944 was so low they must've just felt like giving up."

"But why were they there?" Hannah said.

"He wouldn't tell me. I got him on his own for a few minutes while the medics were dealing with his mate. I told him Jake was in 1944 and he had to tell me if he knew anything that could help us. But he just shrugged, said he was working on a different project, something called Reset, and he wasn't allowed to talk about it. But nothing to do with Jake."

"Reset?" Hannah stared at Nancy with obvious confusion.

"That's what he said. Why, have you heard of it?"

"I saw it written somewhere," Hannah said.

Lew watched Hannah, who stared out over the Thames with a face carved from ice. The word *reset* rang no bells with him, but something in what Nancy said meant something to Hannah, he was sure of it.

Outside, the wind drew shifting parallel lines on the surface of the river. Lew took a sip of his wine and wondered what Jake was doing right now. But what a stupid thought that was. If he didn't return from 1944 then at that moment, in 2040, he was long dead and Amy Jenkins with him. It was a strange thought, Jake dying of old age years before Lew even met him. Lew wondered if when he died, he thought it was all worth it, throwing away his life in the twenty-first century to live a secret life in the dead years before he was born.

With the woman he loved, of course.

Maybe that could explain anything. Lew hoped he thought it was worth it. That Amy was worth it, the woman he broke Hannah's heart for. What would it be like—the long years in hiding, living an invented life, never knowing whether OffTime would find him and drag him back home? While world events around him took a predictable course, everything happening just like in the history books and no surprises, trying to feign interest when Apollo 11 lands on the moon.

He should say one small step for a man. Oh, he did? What a coincidence.

Lew genuinely didn't know what to hope for. On one level, he was sure it'd be better to find Jake and persuade him to come back to his own time. That was the safest and tidiest solution. On the other hand, he didn't want him forced to return against his will. If the guy wanted to stay with Amy, let him. He knew there were good reasons to worry about people doing things in history that history said they shouldn't do. But really, wasn't that what OffTime did all the time? And if it were so bad for Jake to disappear into the 1940s, wouldn't any bad effects have already happened? If the past was different, would anyone know?

"One other thing was odd," Nancy said. "I asked Kurt who else was on his mission. He wouldn't say much—it was all too secret and important. But he did mention the name of the team leader; a new guy called Kavanagh."

"Kavanagh? Did you see this guy?"

"No. Kurt said he hadn't Jumped downtime yet. Kurt said he was tall, bald with a beard. When I said I didn't know him, Kurt clammed up. He seemed a bit worried when I asked more questions like he'd already said too much and regretted it."

Kavanagh. Lew thought immediately of the bald man they chased in 1941, the one whose buddy referred to him as Kav. He also thought about Jake's conviction that there was an unknown agent there in May 1941 when they Jumped back during the air raid...someone who distracted Jake with a distress call and then disappeared.

Hannah was still gazing out over the river as if Nancy and he weren't there. Lew said, "Hannah, you know what Jake's planning to do, don't you?"

"No. It turns out there's a lot I don't know about him."

"Come on, Hannah. What's your best guess?"

"It's that woman, isn't it? It's obvious."

"What's obvious?"

"He's infatuated with her. He wants them to be together. He thinks he can save her, and damn the consequences."

"That simple?"

"Probably. Why, what do you think?" There were pink flecks of color in Hannah's cheeks, above the slight bulge of tight jaw muscles.

"You were the one who told Jake about her death," Lew said. "What exactly was this research that Ed got you to do?"

"I'm not supposed to tell you."

"Hannah," Nancy said. "We're trying to think what we can do for Jake. Don't you want to help?"

"He doesn't want us to do anything," Hannah said. "He wants to be lost."

"Why do you think that?"

"Isn't it obvious? He wants to save her from the bomb that's meant to kill her."

"Do you think that's possible?"

"Go and check her grave and see if he succeeded. The Office will stop him."

"If they know what he's planning." Lew watched Hannah's face. "They didn't show much urgency last time he was missing."

"Not this time. Ed—" She caught herself and stopped, her cheeks flushing brighter red.

"What about Ed? What've you told him?"

"He would've found out anyway," Hannah said, her head bowed.

"Does he know Amy was here, in 2040?" Nancy asked. Hannah nodded without looking up.

"And he knows about her death," Lew said. "So, he'll assume Jake will try to save her."

"Maybe not," Hannah said. "Maybe Ed will think Jake hasn't completely lost touch with reality. Maybe he'll believe Jake wouldn't do something so selfish, so reckless."

"Yeah, right."

"Maybe Ed can't do anything. Maybe there's nothing anyone can do."

"What else did you tell him?"

"That's it. I'm not sure how much was news to him. Maybe the Office already knew."

"Maybe." Lew looked out over the river, wondering what to do next. A low barge was passing, pushing laboriously upstream against the ebbing tide. A cold wind came off the water, and Nancy suppressed a shiver.

"Maybe a lot of things aren't news to guys like Robinson," Lew said at last.

"What do you mean?" Nancy said.

"There's something off about this whole thing. Something wrong. Ever since we Jumped back to 1941 too much has gone wrong. I'm wondering how much of it was accidental."

"You sound like Jake," Hannah said.

"That doesn't make me wrong."

"I don't understand," Nancy said. She glanced at Hannah, who stared out across the Thames.

"I don't understand either," he said. On Hannah's cheeks, two shiny lines trailed down from her eyes. "But I'm going to find out. I think it's time I talked to Ed Robinson."

XLV

"I wondered when I might see you, Agent Brockley." Ed Robinson sat behind the desk when Lew walked in. "What can I do for you?"

"I want to be part of the team that goes after Jacob Wesson." Lew took a seat across from Robinson. "I can help."

"How do you know there's a team? And you don't think he's had enough of your help?"

Lew wasn't sure from Hannah's remarks exactly how much Robinson knew. So far, no one had taken any action against him for his part in Amy's spell in 2040, or her secret return. There must be a reason why the Office was holding off tackling him on it. Being optimistic, maybe they hadn't got the proof, and he could still get away with it. Even if Robinson and the rest of the Brass knew exactly what had gone on, there was no sense confirming anything.

"He's had as much help as he wanted," Lew said. "He's my partner. If he wants more, I can only find that out by finding him."

"And you think you can find him when no one else can?"

"I don't know. How close is anyone else to finding him?"

Robinson gave him a fish-eyed look. "How long have you been with the Office, Lewis? Must be what, fifteen years now?"

"Closer to twenty, if you count the time with the Met."

"That's right. You joined straight from school. Unusual these days."

"There's a few of us."

"When you've got your twenty years, Lew, what're your plans? Plenty of openings in private security once you cash in your pension here."

"I haven't thought about it."

"Can't stay on field service forever."

"Maybe not."

"Ever thought about a management position here? Openings sometimes come up on the eleventh floor."

Lew decided not to share with Robinson his views on the openings on the eleventh. They usually began with the letter 'A' and featured the word 'hole.'

"Ed, I really appreciate your interest in my career, but I thought we were talking about Jacob Wesson."

"What makes you think we're not? I'm just saying, there are opportunities for someone with your experience and ability, Lew. But to get to a certain level, you have to deal with tough choices. You have to be trusted, show loyalty."

"My loyalty can't be in doubt."

Robinson didn't answer for a while, just held his gaze. Lew could guess what he was thinking: was it loyalty to the organization, or the loyalty you felt to your partner on a mission? Was Robinson telling him he might soon have to choose between Jake and the Office?

"All I'm saying is when you want to think about your next career move, talk to me. I've been where you are, Lew. I can guide you."

"I appreciate that, Ed. But right now, I'm just thinking about Jake."

"Believe me, I'm thinking about him too." Robinson leaned forward, thumbing the screen on his desk. It was angled up toward him, hidden from Lew. "You know how much Jake means to me. I've known him and Hannah for a long time. But he's presenting us with one of the tough choices I'm talking about."

"Have you found him?"

"He hasn't really been lost, has he? He Jumped to June 1944."

"Are you sure?"

"You tell me, Lew. Maybe you know more about it than I do."

Robinson watched him without expression. Lew thought that when there was nothing helpful to say, it was usually best not to say it. Instead, he shifted the conversation on. "If you know where he is, why not track him?"

"He's proving quite resourceful."

"What do you mean?"

"We had him on a trace and tried to pull him back, but all we got was his bag. It was almost empty."

"But if they had Jake on a trace, how come only his bag came back?"

"His bag was nearly empty, but not quite," Robinson said. "Inside, we found some briefing notes and a knife. There was blood on it and blood smeared inside the bag. Hannah Benedict has confirmed the knife came from their kitchen. Their sharpest knife, she says."

"I don't understand."

"And his tracking chip," Robinson said. "That's what they had a trace on. It wasn't Jake, just the chip."

"He cut it out?" If Lew weren't so upset himself, he would've enjoyed the look of disgust on Robinson's face. Nothing normally surprised him, a man who'd seen and done everything in his years in the service. But Jake found a way to shock him.

"He sent it back in the bag," Robinson confirmed. "Resourceful, like I said."

"So we can't find him?"

"I wouldn't say that. He doesn't have his tracking chip anymore, but we know where Amelia Jenkins was living in June 1944. It's a fair guess Jake isn't far away."

"Send me to bring him back."

"Why you?"

"He trusts me. He may listen to me more than someone else."

"That might depend on what you say."

"What do you think I should say?"

"Let me turn that around, Lew. What do you think should happen? You know the situation, I think. What should Jake do?"

"I guess that depends on the answer to other questions," Lew said. "What harm would it do if he does what he wants and stays with Amy? And why should Jake trust us, after everything that's happened?"

"There's no precedent for someone with Jake's knowledge living in the 1940s. He could have all sorts of impacts on the fabric of known history. We can't risk it."

"But it's happened," Lew said. "It was a hundred years ago. He knows the risks, and he'd have the sense to keep his profile low, stay away from situations where he might have an influence."

"Trying to prevent Jenkins dying in a V-I attack." Robinson fixed him with a cold stare. "Someone who was meant to be dead would instead be alive for God knows how long. You call that low profile?"

"I don't get it, Ed," Lew said. "Hannah said she found out about Amy's death somehow. Has that changed? I'm sure you've checked."

"You're being naïve."

"Really? Jake's gone back. Whatever he was going to do, he has already done many years ago. Has it caused a disaster? Even if he managed to save Amy from the bomb, how much harm could it do?"

"Come on, Lew," Robinson said. "You know all this as well as I do. If things haven't changed, it's because of the action we still might take. Of course, our current reality is based on what actually happened. But time travel introduces an uncertainty principle. It's always conceivable that someone might travel back in time and take some action, so there's always a possibility that things could've happened differently."

"Okay, but Jake's gone. Whatever action he's taken has happened, long ago."

"Yes, but so has any action we may yet take, in our future, but involving travel into the past."

"It's all a bit circular," Lew said. "Why are you so determined to make sure Amy Jenkins died? Was she really so important?"

Robinson stared at him for a long time and then thumbed the desk screen. Lew could see the man's weariness, hanging on him like a damp overcoat. He'd never given much thought to what Robinson and the rest of the Brass did all day up on the top floors. Meetings and sending dull memos to each other was his guess. All at once, he saw the weight that someone like Robinson carried. Every day, he and people like him were making choices with consequences almost impossible to imagine. Not just the future of the world was in their hands, but the past too.

"This is classified," Robinson said. "But you need to know what we're dealing with. We don't advertise this, but the Office regularly monitors key events and significant individuals. We dip in-and-out of the past, making sure that neither our own activities nor any illegal time travel Jumps are damaging important pillars of known history."

"How do you do that?"

"I'm not going into the details. It takes a lot of time and effort, and it isn't an exact science. But by monitoring certain fixed points in history, we can get a decent fix on the consequences of specific changes."

"What's the fix on Amy Jenkins?"

"Nothing is certain. We're talking about probabilities." Robinson leaned back in his seat, staring up at the ceiling. "Because of the uncertainty introduced by time travel, the reality we experience is based on probabilities. Britain could've lost the war in 1941, let's say if someone assassinated Churchill."

"I thought we stopped that," Lew said. "In any case, we didn't lose even with him dead."

"Let's say that in 1941 there was a 10% chance that it could happen that way, that he could die," Robinson went on, ignoring Lew. "Looking back now, we know that didn't happen. The 90% chance came through, and History is what it is."

"But, imagine someone from the future interferes in some way that affects 1941," Robinson went on. "And we get an indication that the probability has risen to 30% or higher. As seen from 1941, looking forward, nothing's changed; history is still intact, but we might start to worry, and perhaps step in to take corrective action."

"But if we failed," Lew said. "The probability might rise further. What if it tips over into being likely?"

"Events might actually change," Robinson said. "In 2040, we wouldn't know. The new reality would be our history, unless we could connect an unauthorized Jump to the event, as with the Churchill assassination. For most past events, even with the destabilizing existence of the Darnell Jump, the probabilities of things happening differently remain vanishingly small. And many minor events wouldn't cause disaster if they changed. But we monitor the events and people we identify as fundamental to the integrity of our world."

"I can't see how Amy Jenkins fits that description," Lew said. "Nice though she was."

"We can't be certain, but if Amelia Jenkins survived the war, she could've met someone in 1949. Someone we wouldn't want her to meet."

"Joseph Stalin?"

"Very funny. But meeting Stalin would be better than the risk we identified. After all, Stalin died in 1953, and most of his impact on history happened before 1949. As I said, this is all about probabilities, but we identified a chance that a living Amy Jenkins would meet an American airman posted to England. If they met, our psych evaluation suggests a chance they'd become involved and marry. His name was Frank Darnell. Axel Darnell's father."

"Wasn't Axel Darnell's mother German?"

"That's right," Robinson said. "His father was posted to Germany after a tour in England. He met Heidi Kastelein in 1952, in western Germany. The Darnell everyone has heard of, Axel Darnell the man who discovered time travel, was born in Germany in 1959."

"You think if Amy didn't die, she could've got together with Darnell's father?"

"That's the risk." Robinson spread his hands, palms upward on the desk, the very image of sincerity. "As I said, it's only probabilities, but if Darnell senior weren't in Germany in 1952, he wouldn't have met Heidi Kastelein. No marriage to Heidi, no little Darnell in 1959."

"No Darnell Jump."

"Exactly."

Lew thought about that for a while, as Ed watched him. "But it doesn't make sense," he said at last. "If there's no Darnell Jump then we can't go back to the 1940s to start with. Jake wouldn't meet Amy, and he couldn't save her from the V-1. Amy meeting Darnell's father and diverting him from meeting the mother would make the sequence of events that led up to that impossible."

"That's what paradox means. I don't make the rules, Lew. I just try to enforce them."

"But it can't happen like that. Never mind paradox, even on a basic human level, I can't see it playing out like that. If Jake saves Amy, he stays with her. They're taking a big risk to be together. She won't be making eyes at some American pilot a few years down the line."

"I assume that not long ago you would've been just as certain that Jake wouldn't get involved with a woman from the past."

"That's different. Jake was stranded in the 1940s. For all he knew, he was there for the rest of his life. Even if I'm wrong, and Amy Jenkins got involved with Darnell, like I said, preventing Axel Darnell being born would prevent time travel happening, and that would prevent Jake going back to save Amy from the bomb in 1944. It just can't happen like that."

"We can't afford to take the risk," Robinson said. "What I've told you is one strand of events that have a significant probability, based on what we know. There are others, some less damaging. But the fact remains that allowing anyone to interfere in a way that left Amelia Jenkins alive, beyond the lifespan she really had, would be dangerous."

"But it's so cold-blooded, sentencing Amy to death."

"We didn't kill her," Robinson said. "Amy Jenkins died in the war as a result of German bombing, just like thousands of other Londoners.

"What about Jake?"

"We need him back here and away from Amy Jenkins. He won't be able to go on any more missions, but apart from that, I'll do what I can to protect him. I don't blame him for what's happened."

Yeah, right.

Lew could tell from the way Robinson spoke he assumed he'd won him over. In truth, Lew had no answer to what he'd heard. He thought of Jake and Amy as he last saw them, walking away hand in hand across London Bridge. They looked so innocent. Although Jake said he'd Jump back to 2040 the next day, Lew had known Jake would try to save Amy from her looming death— one look at Jake's eyes when he was with Amy told you that. There was no way he could step back and let the German bomb take her.

Lew had known Jake for a long time, and all those years he assumed Jake and Hannah would stay together. They seemed as close and permanent as any couple he knew. But he never saw Jake look at Hannah the way he looked at Amy Jenkins. Jake's feelings for the woman from the 1940s glowed in every gesture: the way he put his hand lightly on Amy's arm as they spoke, the way he reached up and gently brushed a strand of hair out of her eyes as she spoke to him—the way she let him do it.

He didn't doubt that Jake would try to prevent Amy dying under that bomb. If he were with her in 1944, it'd be impossible for him not to act on his knowledge of her fate. Despite what Robinson said, Lew still didn't know how he felt about that, didn't know whether he'd want to stop Jake or not. Part of him wished he could love a woman enough to feel the way Jake obviously felt— determined to save her and damn the consequences.

Nor was he sure he entirely bought Robinson's scare story about the future of the world depending on Amy Jenkins dying and staying dead. Jake reached a place where he was prepared to risk everything, like Samson pulling down the temple because he couldn't stand aside and let Amy die. Lew simply couldn't believe that if Jake saved her, Amy would be fluttering her eyelashes at Darnell's father only five years later—and if she did, so what? Even if what Robinson said was true, there was a subversive voice within Lew that whispered that maybe a world without the Darnell Process might not be a complete disaster.

One thing was certain, he couldn't stand aside and let this play out without him. Jacob Wesson was his partner and friend. If OffTime hadn't finished with him, if they were determined to reach back to the 1940s and interfere again, then he had to be on the team that went.

"I understand what you're saying, Ed," he said at last. He kept his voice flat and emotionless so that neither of them knew how far he was telling the truth. "You can count on me to do the right thing. Tell me how I can help."

XLVI

London, July 1944

Late on a July afternoon, as he drank tea on his balcony, Jake heard a noise like a small motorbike. A few miles to the east, a wooded hill filled most of the horizon. What looked like a small airplane came over the top of the hill, heading straight toward Jake. As it came nearer, he saw it had very small wings, and there were flames showing at the rear.

The V-1 attacks, which now came almost daily, had brought the Blitz back to London in a new form. Britain fought the Luftwaffe to a stalemate in 1941, but to Londoners it felt as if the Nazi terror from the air had gone into hiding for three years, licking its wounds and producing a bastard mutant offspring in the form of the new pilotless planes.

People called them doodlebugs, and during June and July, they seemed to fall everywhere. Air-raid wardens didn't know what to do—there was no point nagging people about the blackout; the bombs came in broad daylight to plunge blindly from a clear blue sky, and it didn't matter whether you showed a light or not. The combination of massive explosive power and the arbitrary nature of their impacts made them the most terrifying element of London's war.

In Jake, they stirred a strange mixture of anxiety and complacency. The complacency arose from his knowledge that the bomb he needed to fear, for Amy's sake, wouldn't arrive until the end of July. The anxiety arose from the realization he had no such guarantees about bombs that might threaten him.

He put down his tea and leaned forward in his chair, wondering whether he should go inside and take cover. The bomb maintained its chillingly straight path above him. Jake wondered at what point he could relax, when it would be past any chance of falling on him. The bombs were unpredictable; when their engines cut out, they fell quickly, but not always in a direction consistent with their path under power. He'd heard of them spiraling wildly as they fell, with no chance of anyone on the ground knowing which way to run.

The doodlebug moved out of sight above the roof, and its engine cut out with shocking suddenness. After a few seconds, there was a loud explosion behind the house. The windows rattled, and Jake's teacup slid to one side on the small table beside him. Jake sat back in his seat and exhaled loudly, wondering how long he'd been holding his breath.

It would've been better if he and Amy could've left London entirely. But at such a nervous phase of the war, she refused to go too far from her parents. In early July, she took a temporary job in the Deptford shipyard. It was still too close to Lewisham for Jake's comfort, but at least she was no longer working with the ARP, and consequently had little reason to visit Lewisham High Street. Amy agreed to Jake's proposal that they should go away to the coast for ten days, covering the 28th of July. He booked them separate rooms in a small hotel in Bournemouth, from Saturday, July 22nd.

He lived in constant expectation of OffTime finding him, but nothing happened and the days crawled past without incident until Jake received a letter on July 17th. It was postmarked Bournemouth. He tore it open to find it was from the manager of the Excelsior Hotel.

Dear Mister Jackson,

I apologize for the short notice, but I fear I must alter the reservation you made with us for two rooms from Saturday, July 22nd. As I may have mentioned to you on the telephone, some of our rooms were requisitioned earlier in the summer for the armed forces. I was assured that they would be released by now, but I have discovered today that your rooms will not be free in time...

The letter went on to offer Jake his deposit back, or he could move the booking to the following week, starting on Saturday, July 29th. Jake contemplated simply bundling Amy on a train to Scotland. When he calmed down, he phoned the hotel and shifted the reservation to the 29th of July. Of course, in order to take the holiday starting that day, there remained the problem of keeping Amy away from the V-I the day before.

"Maybe we should just travel to Bournemouth on that Friday," Jake said. "See if we can find a place for one night."

They were walking up Shooters Hill, after Amy's work shift had finished for the day, making their way back to Jake's place. Amy looked tired and pale after her day in the warehouses, but the low evening sun put strands of gold in her hair and Jake thought he'd never seen anyone so beautiful. They walked close together and occasionally Amy's arm brushed his, making the side of his body tingle with the anticipation of closing the door of his flat behind them.

"I've got a better idea for a free day," Amy said. "I'll take you on a trip for a change."

"Where?"

"How about a surprise?"

"On one condition," Jake said. "It's away from London, and we leave early. You know why."

"That's two conditions. But I promise."

Amy was true to her word, and when the morning of July 28th arrived, they were up early and on a train to Victoria Station before eight in the morning. Jake glanced out of the train as they pulled out of Lewisham. In less than two hours, a ton of German high explosive would fall from the sky among the busy market stalls. Fifty-one deaths would make it the worst flying bomb explosion of the war.

Fifty, Jake thought, as the train rattled away from the scene of Amy's death postponed. *Only fifty dead now.*

Should he feel something about the fact that he'd altered the course of history? Shouldn't it feel important, momentous, that the train was moving them, every second, further away from the possibility of events happening the way history said they should? At 9:41, when the V-I exploded in the crowded market, after hitting the roof of an air-raid shelter outside Marks and Spencer, Amy wouldn't be there.

Jake knew because he'd looked it up before they Jumped to 1944, that the bomb would devastate the market and destroy shops more than a quarter of a mile from the impact site. In addition to the people killed, more than a hundred were seriously injured, and hundreds more were hurt less badly. The destruction, as always in these events, was arbitrary; he'd read about one market stallholder who survived unharmed while those around him perished because he fell down a drain whose cover had been left open for some water repairs. But otherwise, it was total destruction—market shoppers, people in the Post Office, and the basement café of Woolworths, people on passing buses. The blast reached up and down the street, and in an instant ripped hundreds of lives apart.

But not Amy's. Not now.

"You're very quiet," Amy said when they were on the second train, from Victoria down to Box Hill in the Surrey Hills. "Want to share your thoughts?"

She was perched on the edge of the seat in front of him, her knees brushing his when she moved. She wore a dress with a printed flower pattern. Her arms were bare, and she had a straw hat, which she'd placed for the moment on top of the small basket on the seat beside her. The basket contained sandwiches and a bottle of homemade lemonade. Amy had embraced the idea of a country picnic with her usual gusto.

Jake looked around to ensure they were not overheard. "Just wondering if we'd notice any changes because of what we're doing."

"What, going to Box Hill?"

"You know what I mean, me being here in a time I shouldn't be. You..." Jake hesitated. "Well, you not being in Lewisham today."

"We should've warned people."

"You know we couldn't do that," Jake said. "It would guarantee we'd be found. That would just stop you getting away, it wouldn't save anyone else. Even if anyone believed us."

"Maybe, but I don't like it." Amy gazed out of the window, at the small backyards of terraced houses beside the railway line. "Anyway, me being around tomorrow isn't going to make a difference to anyone else. I won't notice in any case; I don't know what happens in the future like you do. Tell me if you notice the world going off track."

"I'll keep an eye on it." The train was almost empty, and he put his hand gently on Amy's knee. She tapped him gently on the back of his wrist.

"Naughty. You're not allowed to go off track like that."

"Pity."

"Least, not until we're in the woods." She winked. "So, what kind of changes do you think we might notice? If we make our mark on history?"

You'll be alive tomorrow.

"It's impossible to guess," Jake said. "In any case, I'm going to try really hard not to make a mark on history."

"No more bets on the horses?"

"I'll be discreet."

Amy looked out of the window for a few moments and then turned back to Jake. "Tell me something," she said. "I can keep a secret. When this war ends, is that it? Does that end the fighting? People thought there would be no more wars after the first one, but then along came Hitler. Is this it, are there no more wars after this?"

Korea. Vietnam.

"Well, not exactly *no* wars."

Iraq. Afghanistan. Venezuela.

"It'd be hard to have no war at all," he said. "But at least London doesn't get bombed again."

"Except by people who live there, you mean. With explosives in their handbags."

It was still early when they reached Box Hill station, and a thick morning fog clung to the ground. They were the only ones to leave the train at the tiny rural station, and they had the world to themselves as they walked along a misty lane toward the invisible bulk of Box Hill.

A wooden signpost directed them down to the banks of a small river, which they crossed on stepping-stones. Jake went first and leaned back to offer his hand to help Amy over some of the gaps. She didn't really need help, but he liked the fact that she accepted it, and her hand felt cool and small in his. When she jumped from the last stone to the river bank, Jake caught her briefly in both arms, and she leaned against him, the basket squashed between them, and their lips briefly touched in a kiss like a brush of soft velvet.

They stood close together for a long time, neither saying anything. Amy held Jake's gaze so firmly it felt like she was searching for something deep in his eyes. He knew what he saw in her eyes—everything that mattered to him.

"I'm glad you came back with me." Her words were almost inaudible over the murmur of the water.

"Me too."

"We better get moving. This hill won't climb itself."

The mist laid a blanket of moist stillness on the woods, pressing any sound into the leafy earth. A few paces beyond the river the ground climbed sharply upwards. Broad, shallow steps had been cut into the slope. The only sounds were their breathing and the faint drip of water from the trees.

As they climbed, the mist thinned out. This place felt more significant than a patch of misty woodland—the tap of water on dead leaves, golden ingots of sunlight slanting down between the pillared trees, the murmur of his and Amy's breath—it all combined to make him feel he was in a holy place. The world opened to him as a vast, open cathedral on the damp hillside. They climbed hand-in-hand toward an unseen altar at the top.

Perhaps he was influenced by the knowledge that miles away from them, back in London, the hand of Amy's death was falling from the sky, clutching for her and coming up empty. Catching sight of Jake watching her, Amy smiled, and he felt his heart falling into a deep, dark well. Behind Amy, a shaft of sunlight lit up a tree from behind, making it look like a bright X-ray of itself.

"Come on," Amy said. "No rest until we reach the top."

"You promised me a view. What're we going to see in this fog?"

"Have some faith. It isn't going to last long on a summer's day, is it?"

The path turned to the right, and they emerged from the trees into full sunlight. They were on a broad, open hilltop, meadowed in thick grass. Above was a pale blue sky, clear except for a few strands of cloud, forming parallel lines like ridges of sand on a beach at low tide. The hilltop fell away sharply, and everything below was lost beneath a carpet of fog. It looked like a white sea had rolled over southern England, or the glaciers had silently returned in the night. A few miles south, the low hump of a hill poked above the mist like the curved back of a whale, the only sign the rest of the world was still there.

"I didn't know there could be places like this," Jake said.

"It's just a hill in Surrey. Surely you still have things like this in your time?"

"Maybe I never noticed."

Maybe I never looked.

In 2040, no one slowed down enough to do this kind of thing, take a day out and go walking in the woods. Amy walked forward a few paces onto the brow of the hill. Her thin dress briefly caught the sunlight and Jake saw the shape of her body silhouetted through it. For a moment, he imagined Amy fading away to transparency. He wondered if this was the precise moment the V-I was falling on the busy shopping street they'd left behind. He shivered, despite the growing heat of the morning.

Amy turned and smiled. Behind her, the sky was an empty canvas on which her future remained unwritten.

They sat on the surprisingly warm, dry grass and drank lemonade. Already the mist was thinning, with the tops of tall trees showing through. Jake lifted his face to feel the sun on his skin. The air tasted of spring clouds and warm grass. Had he ever been happier than at this moment? Could anyone be happier than this?

If he'd been offered the chance to stop time, he would've chosen here and now, alone with Amy on this impossibly beautiful hillside. He was at peace; released from the cold chains of history, he and Amy could do anything. He'd cheated Hitler of one of his victims, and surely nothing else could touch them.

As if reading his thoughts, Amy said, "How can people fight, in a world that's so beautiful?"

Jake thought again of the conflicts to come after this one, and the messy world he'd fled in 2040, its beauty long faded.

"Cleverer people than me have been stumped by that one." He took Amy's hand in his and brought it to his lips. Her skin smelled of lemons. Maybe she'd spilled some of the lemonade. "Shall we have our picnic, then decide what to do with the rest of our lives?" he said. "Or is it too early for the picnic?"

Amy kicked off her shoes and lay back on the grass. Her legs were pale as marble.

"Never too early for a picnic."

XLVII

At last, Hannah got the message that Jake had been located, and Ed Robinson wanted her to go back to 1944 with Lew. He told her to keep it secret but to come to his office early, an hour before the Jump.

Hannah couldn't sleep, as so often these days, with Jake gone. She found herself at the Office half an hour early. Her name was on the list with Security, who waved her into the lift, and her pass took her to the normally off-limits eleventh floor. She made her way to Robinson's office. The door was partly open, but there was no noise from inside. When Hannah knocked, there was no response, but the door moved in a few inches and Robinson's chair was empty. His jacket hung on the back of the chair.

She stepped into the room. Maybe he was in the Gents. She could sit and wait.

Most OffTime offices were sparse in their furnishing. Ed Robinson's was, if anything, emptier than most. There were no pictures on the walls. Robinson had no personal effects on the desk, apart from a framed photograph of a ruined red London bus. It was a double-decker, but the roof was missing, and shreds of metal hung in ugly strips from the top deck. Daggers of metal and broken glass carpeted the road around the bus wheels. It was a familiar photo; the bus destroyed by a suicide bomber in 2021.

There's a limit to how long you can look at a picture of a bus. Hannah's attention drifted to Robinson's desk. She didn't even register that she was reading the words on the display until her attention was snagged by the word 'Reset.' She leaned forward and looked more closely. Half her attention remained on the open door behind her, fearful that Robinson would come in, so she did no more than skim what was on the screen.

'...impossible to isolate OT intervention responsible for subject slippage in 1944...cumulative impact of repeated missions...up to 35% chance of Category One change, before 'Project Reset'...'

'.... adjustments necessary...risk to TempIntegrity amber-red...Subject AJ remains main risk...Agent W responded as per psych assessment but under review...'

'...K team delay launch event, enabling corrective impact...backup option remains K team termination of subjects...estimate below 10% chance of Category Three violation on Reset completion...'

There was a soft sound behind Hannah, and she lurched quickly back in her seat, turning to see Ed enter the room. He had a paper cup in his hand.

"Hannah, you're impressively early. I would've got you some coffee."

"I'm fine."

Robinson settled into the chair across the desk from her. He glanced down at the screen as he put his cup down, and looked quickly up at Hannah. He thumbed the desk display, which went dark.

"If you read any of that, you'll have an idea what I'm going to say."

"What?" Hannah willed her features into an expression of polite, innocent interest. "Oh, the screen? No, I didn't look."

"Well, I'll tell you about it." It was clear Robinson didn't believe her.

Some of what Robinson told Hannah was no surprise. It was obvious Jake going missing in 1944 was serious. Doubly so because the reason he'd gone off the rails was to save the life of the Jenkins girl. It didn't take a genius to realize OffTime would want to try very hard to stop Jake interfering with her death. Things that happened in the past needed to stay happened. That was the core purpose of the Office, the thing she'd spent all her adult life working for.

Along with Jake, of course, Hannah thought bitterly. Although, as she was discovering, there were other ways in which Jake seemed prepared to cast aside the things she thought he cared about.

What was more surprising was what Robinson thought would happen if Amy Jenkins didn't die on schedule; that she might meet Axel Darnell's father, heading off the birth of the father of time travel. This prospect carried such a dizzying freight of contradictions; Hannah's mind flew at them softly but fluttered away like a moth, and all she could think was—*waste of time saving her, Jake. She won't stay with you.*

"Nothing's certain, Hannah." Robinson misinterpreted Hannah's brief shake of her head. "But we can't risk it. The thing I want you to understand is that there's nothing to be done for Amy Jenkins. You can't save her."

Like I care.

"But there's a chance to save Jake." Robinson looked at her from beneath thick wire-wool brows. Hannah had never noticed before how much he resembled a sad, bald owl. "If you do as I say."

What Ed had to say was simple enough, but he stressed she couldn't share any of it with Lew Brockley. Lew thought he was leading the mission, and Hannah wasn't to tell him of the backup plan. Lew's plan was to travel to Blackheath and make discreet contact with Jake. Lew's orders were to try to persuade Jake to come back to 2040, leaving Amy Jenkins to her fate.

Lew had authority to try any method he could devise to bring Jake back. He could make all kinds of promises—indemnity from disciplinary action, a promotion, early retirement with a generous golden handshake, you name it—to get Jake to come with him. Hannah didn't think any of it would work.

If all else failed, Lew was authorized to call in a special Jump pick-up. OffTime had set up a mobile Darnell facility in Blackheath, close to where Jake was living in 1944. The Darnell team could lock onto Lew's tracking chip, and the last resort was for Lew to confront Jake and grab hold of him as the pick-up happened. Timed right, Jake would be pulled back to 2040 with Lew. Hannah wasn't sure this plan would work either. Lew seemed to have persuaded Ed Robinson that he was on board with the plan, but she had serious doubts Lew would ever force Jake to do anything he didn't want to do.

The briefing over, Hannah traveled with Ed from his office to the Darnell Suite. When she entered the changing room, Lew was already stripped to his underpants, stuffing his clothing into a locker.

"Hello, Lew. Surprise," Hannah said. He opened his mouth to reply but stopped himself when he saw Robinson enter the room behind her.

"Late change of plan," Robinson said. "I've asked Agent Benedict to join the mission."

Several different responses came and went on Lew's face as he looked from Robinson to her and back again. Finally, he shrugged. "Your call. I could do it on my own, but obviously, it'll be good to have Hannah along." He spoke directly to Hannah, giving her a smile like ice on a dark road. "Better be quick. Jump's in ten."

Lew said no more as they made their preparations. Hannah was sure there were things he wanted to say, but Robinson would be listening from the control room.

Their Jump was targeted on the early morning of July 21, 1944, a week before the V-I attack. The weather during most of that week had been warm and dry, and both Hannah and Lew traveled light, with a couple of changes of clothing in their canvas bags. They lurched in rapid sequence from the Darnell Suite to a narrow alley in east London. They were alone, but they could hear the noise of motor-vehicle engines beyond the mouth of the alley. When their bags popped into being at their feet, they picked them up and retreated farther down the alley from the road and crouched down to pull on their clothing.

"Nice of Robinson to send you along." Lew was putting on his clunky 1940s shoes, and he didn't look up from the elaborate task of tying the antique laces.

"I couldn't warn you, Lew. He sprang it on me late. Said I could help."

"Yeah? Not sure how."

"Come on, Lew, ease up. I'm as involved in this as you are. More involved in some ways."

"That's what I worry about."

"You don't need to worry. I'll do my job. But I have a stake in this."

"I know you do." Lew straightened up and looked at her. "The kind of stake that complicates things."

"Like it wasn't already complicated."

"Hannah, I'm sorry about what's happened with you and Jake. But if this is going to work, you need to follow my lead. I've got the orders and the mission lead, and I'll tackle Jake. You need to stay back unless I call you in."

Lew took Hannah's silence for agreement, and they picked up their bags as Lew led the way to the mouth of the alley. Hannah stared grimly at Lew's back as they walked. There were things Lew Brockley didn't know, and she wasn't going to tell him. Sure, he had his orders, but she had hers too. Nor did he know that a backup team was already in place, tasked with shadowing her and Lew, and stepping in if needed. Robinson said this B team was led by a man called Dave Kavanagh. The point was that Lew could run the mission his way, but she knew he wasn't going to get anywhere with Jake. Lew could never persuade Jake of anything if Jake's mind was made up.

And I saw him with her. That's a mind that's made up.

When Lew failed, Hannah would be ready. Robinson had told her—*you can bring him back, Hannah. I can tell you how. When Lew fails, you can intervene. But you have to do it exactly the way I tell you.*

Hannah followed Lew Brockley out of the alley and along Thames Street toward London Bridge. Lew didn't look back at her, and he didn't seem inclined to make conversation. A warm breeze brushed Hannah's hair back from her forehead and moved scraps of paper along the pavement beside her feet.

"Hang on, something's wrong."

Lew stopped suddenly. He was looking up at the sky. Hannah remembered their first trip to 1940s London and wondered, for a moment, whether Lew heard an approaching aircraft. But she heard nothing apart from the thin clatter of a bus pulling away from them on the far side of the road.

"What is it?"

"That's not right," Lew said, more to himself than to Hannah. He turned slowly round, still looking upwards. Hannah followed his gaze but saw nothing remarkable—blue sky, a few lonely scraps of high cloud, behind them a bright sun level with the top of Tower Bridge.

Lew turned without warning and walked quickly across the street. On the far side, an old man in a long coat and flat cap sat on a stool beside a wheelbarrow piled with newspapers. A wooden hoarding next to him held a flysheet for the Daily Mirror with a headline in thick capital letters: US MARINES CAPTURE GUAM—TOTAL JAP DEFEAT. Lew leaned over the barrow, peering at the front page of the paper on the top of the pile.

"Oi, gotta buy it to read it, squire."

Lew backed away, waving an apology. He walked back across the road to Hannah, his face pale.

"The weather isn't right. Most of the week was dry and sunny, but July 21st was overcast until late afternoon, with a light shower or late morning rain."

"So, is it evening instead of morning?"

"No." Lew nodded at the sun, which was in the east. "This isn't July 21st." He looked around, biting his lip.

"If it's not the right day, when is it?"

"The newspaper says it's Friday, July 28th." Lew fixed Hannah with a miserable gaze. "What time do you reckon it is?"

Hannah knew what he meant. It was clearly morning, and still relatively early. But how close were they to 9:41 when, five miles to the southeast, Amy Jenkins' V-1 rocket was due to fall from the sky?

XLVIII

London, 1944

Jake saw what was wrong as soon as their train passed through Lewisham station on the way to Blackheath. Amy spotted the change in his face.

"What is it?"

"We can't talk here." He couldn't prevent himself staring out of the train window. The railway track ran on a bridge over Lewisham Hill, and from this elevated position there was a clear view to the top end of the High Street. There were two trams passing in front of the Victorian clock tower, market traders packing away unsold fruit and vegetables, a line of black cabs outside the Gaumont Cinema. All of it was exactly like countless other evenings. All utterly, absurdly normal. All of it—on this day, when it should've been a scene of carnage and devastation—impossibly wrong.

They left the train at Blackheath, and Jake carried the empty picnic basket as they walked up the hill from the station. Amy was calling in on her parents before she went away with Jake the next day.

"Jake, there was no sign of a bomb back there."

"That's just it." Jake's head felt thick and heavy. He couldn't have got the date wrong.

"Wasn't it meant to be this morning?"

"Yes. Something's happened."

"Or not happened," Amy said. They stopped a dozen paces short of her parents' house and stepped to the side of the path, into the doorway of the post office, which was closed. "Isn't that good? No bomb after all; so not only am I still here but all those other people, too."

"That's one way of looking at it." Jake bit his lower lip. He was struggling to think straight. How could events in the past have changed so sharply, so soon? That couldn't be a result of his presence, surely? Amy took the basket from him and kissed him on the lips. A frown clouded her brow like a warning of a distant storm.

"Are we going to be all right?"

"Yes. I need to think this through," Jake said. "Maybe you should stay with me tonight."

"Your Mrs. Downing would have a seizure. I'll be fine here with mum and dad."

"If you see anything strange, anything at all, phone me or just come over." As he said it, Jake made a promise to himself that he'd check on Amy's house during the night. One thing he hadn't sent back to 2040 was his stunner, and he was ready to use it.

"We'll be fine," Amy said. "I've had a lovely day. And tomorrow will be even better."

Jake said, "And every day after that."

They'd agreed to meet the next morning at Lewisham Station, at 9:30 for the train to Waterloo, where they were due to take a second train to Bourne-mouth. Jake offered to meet Amy from home, but she insisted on meeting in Lewisham. Her parents thought she was going on holiday with two women from her old job at the ARP station and she didn't want them to see Jake.

They said goodbye and Jake walked back in the direction of Blackheath village, toward his flat. When he came to the first road junction, he looked back. Amy had disappeared. Jake turned right, away from his home and walked down the hill toward Lewisham.

The sun was low, and the evening was warm, with a rich fragrance in the air—a mixture of rose blossom from the well-tended gardens of some of the large houses on the hill, wood smoke, and the smells of dinner cooking in nearby homes. A group of three young women passed Jake, walking up the hill. They wore the informal uniform of office workers—white cotton blouses and narrow skirts, and they laughed over some private joke, nudging each other and clutching each other's arms.

It was a perfect summer evening, under a deep blue sky that promised fur-ther days of sunshine and sleepy afternoons. If you didn't know there was a war going on, you'd never guess. And that was why Jake's stomach felt as if it contained a large block of metal. He walked toward the High Street feeling like he was encased in a Perspex bubble. Everything was fine, and that was what was so wrong.

In his own time, when he'd discovered Amy's fate, Jake had seen photographs of the High Street after the V-I explosion—grainy black-and-white images of a crater wide enough to swallow a row of houses. Tiny figures stood at the edge of the crater. Farther back, heaps of splintered timber and shattered bricks, stumps of ruined buildings, and a bus on its side. In one picture, a woman stood with her head bowed into the chest of a man who held her shoulders in a strangely formal pose, as if they were about to dance. The woman wore a long, dark coat that looked too heavy for the season but was apt for the funereal gravity of the destruction around her. The features of the man and woman were unclear in the photograph, but Jake couldn't help imagining that this was Amy's parents, holding each other upright against the weight of grief bearing down on them.

The photographs he'd seen were probably taken during the afternoon following the explosion—that was earlier today. Yet the High Street Jake walked down was eerily unchanged from the last time he saw it. The market stalls were closed and shuttered, and a group of council workers swept up scraps of paper and discarded pieces of fruit and vegetables. The sweepers prompted a blustering flap of pigeons to scatter into the air from the rope fence around a hole being dug for waterworks.

Instead of mounded piles of powdered stone and charred wood, Jake walked between rows of shops. Here and there the shops were abridged with gaps that must've been caused by bomb damage, but most of it looked old and strangely tidy. Woolworths, Marks and Spencer, Chiesemans, and the Post Office; all the stores that should be damaged or destroyed by the V-I were still here, impossibly intact.

Jake went into the Market Tavern, which should've been closed, all its windows blown out and basement flooded by a burst water main. The saloon bar was quiet, with a couple of solitary drinkers hunched over their pints at opposite ends of the bar. He ordered a beer from the middle-aged woman behind the counter top.

When she delivered his drink, he said, "How's your day been? Busy?"

"Pretty quiet for a Friday, my love. You?"

"I've been out of town. You've not noticed anything unusual?"

"Depends what you mean, dear." The woman got a distant gleam in her eyes. "Actually, one thing I never noticed till you asked, I haven't heard no more doodlebugs today."

"How many have you noticed before?" Jake spoke casually and took a sip of the beer.

"Gawd loads, love. Past couple of weeks it's every day. Do you think Jerry's given up? Maybe our boys have reached the launch sites. In Belgium, the wireless said."

"Let's hope so."

Jake idled back up the hill, struggling to fit the evidence of his eyes into what he knew he should've seen. Could he have gotten the day wrong? There was no chance of that, so deeply was July 28th burned into his memory.

There was no doubt about it—in the world, as it should be, this was the day Lewisham suffered London's worst flying-bomb explosion of the war...which could only mean the world was no longer as it should be. Of course, he'd intended to change events all along, but only by keeping Amy out of the way of the bomb. Fifty dead instead of fifty-one seemed a trivial change. And yet Lewisham High Street on the evening of July 28th was transformed, or rather not transformed—it was exactly as it'd been before. The destruction of the flying bomb had passed it by.

Jake felt a shapeless fear that he'd never experienced in all his time as an agent. He was off the map and didn't know why. He didn't see how his actions so far could possibly have had such an effect. How could coming back with Amy for these few weeks affect the actions of the Germans in northern Europe, or change the flight path of their missiles? Inducing Amy to leave the ARP station, taking lodgings in Blackheath; none of this could possibly make so much difference.

He felt a strong rope of unease coiling inside him, anxious that he was so soon in uncharted territory, worried his recklessness might've set in motion forces he couldn't predict and had no chance of controlling. Jake was adrift in a version of 1944 that was already diverging sharply from the one history knew. If what he'd done could already have this much impact, what did the future now hold?

Jake was about thirty yards short of his lodgings. He could see the window of his flat in the tall house overlooking the heath. A man about Jake's height stood under a tree across the street, directly opposite Jake's balcony. Unusually for the 1940s, the man wasn't wearing a hat. His hair was dark, drawn back slightly from his forehead in a thin widow's peak. As Jake approached, the man stepped forward from the shelter of the tree and turned to face him.

It was Lew Brockley.

Jake felt two conflicting emotions. First, he couldn't help himself, his face split in a grin with the pleasure of seeing Lew again, seeing his partner and old friend when he'd assumed he'd never again see any familiar faces from his own time.

This was followed by the grip of a cold tension in his spine as he digested the implications of Brockley's appearance. Jake stopped walking and took a step sideways. He looked quickly up and down the street, ready to run.

"I'm on my own, Jake." Lew took a few more steps toward him, his hands spread out at waist height, his palms upturned. "I just need to talk."

XLIX

London, 1944

Jake took Lew inside and dug out a bottle of whisky he said he'd been saving for emergencies. They sat on the tiny balcony and watched the sun go down over Deptford. Jake watched Lew sip his drink.

"That's not completely bad," Lew said. His throat felt like it was lined with straw. "Almost like a decent whisky. Apart from the color and the smell."

"And the taste," Jake said and smiled for the first time.

"I can't tell you how relieved I am to see you, Jake. We were aiming for July 21st. I couldn't believe it when I found out the date."

"We?"

"Me and the team at the Darnell Suite," Lew said. He was leaving Hannah out of it for now. "The geniuses who can put you down with such unbelievable accuracy. Like, a week later than planned."

"Or nearly a century too early in my case."

"My point exactly."

"I'm not so sure it's all accidental."

"Hard to be that incompetent without trying, you mean?"

"I'm not joking, Lew."

"Me neither." Lew drank more of the whisky, which traced fire down his throat. "But what about today? What happened?"

"I was wondering if you could tell me."

"I'm as baffled as you, Jake. I thought we— I was too late."

Jake watched him over the top of his glass but said nothing. Behind him, the sky glowed the same color as the whisky. A last red strip of sun hung above the red-brick houses across the street. As the sun inched lower, the red strip thinned, flowing sideways along the roof tiles.

"When I got to Lewisham," Lew went on. "I expected to see, well you know."

"Hitler missed after all."

"Seriously, what do you think happened?"

"Why don't you tell me? You've just come from the future."

"No one knew anything about this."

"Really? No one?" Jake said. "I doubt that. Someone knows. Someone must've done something to make such a big change."

"Maybe not," Lew said. "Maybe it's you, and Amy. You were back here for six months when you shouldn't have been. She was in 2040 and then back here these past weeks. We don't know what impact that could've had."

"Nothing I've done or Amy's done could stop the Germans launching a V-1," Jake said. "How would we do that? They fall on London, they're not launched from here."

"You can't tell what impact you're having on the past, Jake. The longer you're here, the worse it might get."

"It's done," Jake said. "Right now, I don't care. No bomb falling today means Amy's still alive."

Something Jake said nagged at Lew. Like Jake, he couldn't see how their presence in London could change something as big as the V-1 attack. The bombs weren't launched from here but from Belgium. Lew remembered Nancy talking about her encounter with her old friend, Kurt, just back from his mission in Belgium.

"There may be nothing in this, Jake, but I heard about an OffTime mission to Belgium around now. Secret, led by a guy called Kavanagh."

"Never heard of him."

"Remember the guys who got away on our 1941 trip? The bald guy with the beard? His mate called him Kav."

"You think it's the same man?" Jake said. "And, what, he went to Belgium to stop the V-1?"

"I don't know," Lew said.

"I don't understand why they'd stop the bomb," Jake said. "But it's no surprise to me there's another team meddling in this. Right from the start, there have been too many so-called accidents. Dumping me in 1943, the agent I saw the night of the air raid, now this; someone's pulling strings."

They both fell silent, sipping their drinks. The sun slipped from sight and the evening abruptly felt colder.

Lew said, "I came to take you back, you know."

"*Take* me?"

"I told Robinson I could persuade you to come with me."

"And do you think you can?" Lew shrugged, and Jake continued, "What if you can't persuade me? What're the rest of your orders? March me to a pick-up at gunpoint? Have you got a backup team waiting in those trees?"

"I can't guarantee the Office hasn't got some plan like that. But I won't use force with you. You know that."

"So how do you plan to persuade me?"

"The first part of my plan was to be here a week ago. Now, I don't know. I guess the lack of a V-I attack alters the picture. Amy's still alive. Robinson was very keen to convince me no one at the Office wanted to cause Amy's death. They just wanted to stop anyone interfering to prevent it."

"It's been prevented, so what now?" Lew's glass was empty. Light was fast draining from the sky, pushing shadows into the street below. "All bets are off now, I guess," Jake said, answering his own question. "No one knows what to do next."

"What do you want to do, Jake? Now Amy's safe, don't you think you should come back with me? Don't take any more risks."

"I'm going to stick to what I planned. Amy and I are going away from London for a few weeks. While we're away, I'll think about whether she's really safe, and whether I should come back. But I'll be honest with you, Lew, if there's a way for me to stay with Amy, I'll take it."

"I thought you'd say that."

"So why did you come?"

"I couldn't just give up on you. You wouldn't give up on me."

"You've done enough." Jake picked up the bottle and splashed more ration-book whisky into their glasses. "Go back, tell them I couldn't be reasoned with, I've disappeared without a trace."

"Not sure that'll work."

"Whether it works or not, you just need to go home and leave me to it," Jake said. "I wish there was more I could say."

"Maybe there is something I could do. It bothers me that the bomb didn't fall today."

"I don't suppose it bothers the fifty-one people still alive."

"Something that big, a fixed point in history, shouldn't just fail to happen."

"I'm sure you're right, but I'm not worrying about it." Jake drained his glass, wincing a little. "As far as I'm concerned, Amy dodged the bullet today. Now she has a future that isn't written yet, that we can make up together."

"But the bomb not coming," Lew said. "We don't know what the effect of that'll be."

"You can go back to the future and look it up. Me, I'm in the same place as anyone else. I don't know the future anymore. Most people live with that all their lives."

Lew studied Jake's face, unable to tell if he really was as relaxed about it as his words suggested. After a career spent preventing time crimes, Jake had embarked on the biggest time crime he'd heard of.

"Here's what I'm going to do," Lew said. "You're going away tomorrow?"

"I'm meeting Amy at Lewisham Station at 9:30."

"I'll leave you alone tonight and try one more time in the morning to persuade you to come home."

"There's no point, Lew."

"Duty. Anyway, assuming I fail—"

"You will."

"Assuming I fail, I'll go back home and say I lost track of you."

"If you think you can. Don't take any more risks for me."

"Then I'll try to find out what happened to the V-I. Why it didn't come. And whether that has any implications for you."

"Apart from the obvious one."

"Apart from that. If I find out anything I think you should know, I'll try to get a message to you. If anyone ever lets me Jump again. Otherwise, you're on your own."

Lew left soon after. They shook hands at the front of the house, and Lew surprised Jake by stepping forward and hugging him with a force they both knew held the finality of their parting buried in it.

"Careful, men didn't hug in the 1940s," Jake said. "I think it was still a crime."

"Take care." Lew's voice sounded, even to him, like dry leaves. "You both take care."

L

London, 1944

Before he went to bed, Jake turned out all the lights in his flat and sat for ten minutes on the balcony. He kept very still and watched the street below and the heath beyond, scanning every shadow for suspicious movements. He saw none.

He slept surprisingly deeply, despite the events of the day and his anxiety that Lew might not be the only OffTime agent who knew where he was. When he woke in the morning, the sun was already high and the day warming fast. As he carried his case down the hill to Lewisham, sweat tickled between his shoulder blades.

He pictured himself and Amy on the beach at Bournemouth. He wondered how she'd look in a bathing suit. Bikinis didn't exist yet, but that didn't stop him imagining her in one. And, after a hot day at the beach, there'd be the cool privacy of the hotel room. Walking down the hill under the copper-sulphate bowl of the late July sky, there was nothing ahead of them but endless days of promise, waiting to be filled with whatever they wanted.

He reached the station at around nine-fifteen. Shoppers were already walking toward the High Street from the roads around. He put his case on the pavement and sat on a low brick wall outside the Flower of Kent pub to wait for Amy. Closing his eyes, he raised his face to the sky, feeling the sunlight almost uncomfortably hot on his skin. The air smelled clean and earthy, with an undertone of beer from the open door of the pub where a woman mopped the stone steps.

When he looked up, a familiar figure walked toward him. He was so shocked to see Hannah, that for an instant his mind spun helplessly round without giving him her name. She wore a dark jacket, patently too heavy for the warm weather. Her right hand was in a pocket. A thin smile looked stapled to her lips; her eyes narrowed like someone concentrating on threading a needle.

She planted herself in front of him, about six feet away. Her hand still in her pocket.

"Surprised to see me, I bet."

"You could say that." Jake looked past Hannah, checking the street for other agents. Could she really be here alone? Was Lew involved? "How are you?"

"Could be better. But you know why."

"Look, I really don't—"

"Where is she, your antique girlfriend? The war-widow? Still alive?" Her stare was a gauntlet thrown at his feet. Her nostrils flared as she breathed loudly, her jaw tight and her head moving very slightly from side-to-side as if the weight of her emotions made it too heavy for her shoulders.

Jake flinched as Hannah, at last, pulled her hand out of the pocket. It was empty, although her jacket hung low on the right side, weighed down by something. She raised her arms toward him, and for a moment he thought she might hit him. To his surprise, she stepped close, leaned in and kissed him full on the lips. Her hands gripped his upper arms, and she pulled back to stare into his face with fierce eyes.

"Does she kiss like that? Your whore?"

"I'm sorry, but this isn't—"

"Isn't what? Isn't what you planned? I know what you planned. You think it's all going your way, don't you?"

"Hannah, I never wanted things to be this way. I never meant to hurt you. If I could've avoided it, I would."

"Hurt me? You say it like it's a small thing. Like you just caused me a little inconvenience. Hurt is too small a word for what you've done to me. Do you think I'll just get over it? Think you can disappear into history with her and I'll just wipe away a tear and move on?"

Hannah's voice rose in pitch and volume, and Jake was conscious people were looking at them.

"I'm sorry. I really am. But I can't help the way I feel."

"Oh, don't insult me! Who cares what you feel? This is more important than you. Do you think you can just have what you want, whatever the cost to everyone else? She should be dead now, your tart. It's what history wants, it's what everyone needs."

Hannah's hands dug into Jake's arms through his clothes. He took a step back, but she hung onto him. Something behind her head caught his eye. Amy stood some thirty feet away, her face frozen into blankness as if she was trying to remember something. His attention was drawn back to Hannah when she released his arms and took a step away from him.

"Keep out of it!" she shouted, looking past him. Jake stole a quick glance behind him. Lew Brockley stood maybe twenty feet away. "Stay where you are!" Hannah yelled. "I'm handling this."

For a frozen moment, the four of them stood in a ragged line along the pavement: Jake and Hannah face-to-face, Lew behind him, and Amy behind Hannah. Jake wanted to warn Amy, tell her to run, but for the moment Hannah was the only one who didn't yet realize Amy was there.

Not for long. Hannah must've seen something shift in his face because she turned and saw Amy. Her hand went back to her pocket, and when she brought it out again, the sight of the gun clenched a tight fist in Jake's chest. Hannah stepped sideways so she could point the gun at Jake without it being visible to most passers-by. It was, however, visible to Amy, whose eyes went wide.

"Over here," Hannah said, gesturing Amy closer with a shake of her head. Amy moved closer, stopping a few feet away.

"Leave him alone," Amy said.

"You're dead," Hannah said. "Didn't you see the gravestone?"

"Please," Amy said. "We're not hurting anyone."

"How do you know who you've hurt?"

"Hannah," Jake said. "You don't have to do this."

"Someone has to stop you. You can't be allowed to mess with the past to suit yourself."

"It's too late, Hannah. The bomb should've been yesterday. Let it go."

"Some of us have a backup plan," Hannah turned to Amy, keeping the gun pressed hard against Jake's ribs. "Listen to me, Amelia Jenkins. Here's what you do. I need you to walk away from here. You go down to the high street and wait for me on this side of the road, twenty yards past the clock tower. Is that clear?"

"Yes," Amy said. "But why?"

"No questions! If you don't do it, or if you're not there when I get there, I'll kill Jake. Clear?"

"You wouldn't do that," Amy said, her eyes on Jake. He nodded slightly, urging her to go. If he could get her away from Hannah, maybe there was hope.

"Believe me, you don't know what I can do," Hannah said. "Now go!"

Amy backed away a few paces, turned, and continued walking. Hannah watched her leave.

"Hannah, this isn't the way to handle it," Lew said.

"Stay back, Lew," Hannah said, giving him a swift warning glance and prodding Jake harder with the gun. "You're out of this now."

Amy was almost at the corner. A few more paces and she would be out of sight. Jake prayed she'd keep going, and not wait for Hannah to find her.

"You're not going to shoot me, Hannah," Jake said. His own gun was in his bag at his feet. There was no chance of reaching it unless Hannah was distracted.

"This isn't about you, Jake. It's about her."

Amy had disappeared.

"What will you do when you go after her?"

"I'm not going after her," Hannah said, with a sly smile. "I've just sent her where she needs to be."

"What do you mean?" But Jake knew. He heard a familiar engine sound, like a motorbike climbing uphill. It came from the east, beyond the corner Amy just rounded. Jake looked that way and saw something he should have registered properly before. A man with a beard in a long coat had watched Amy pass. He was now the only person on the street not looking at the sky. Instead, he spoke into an object in his hand.

"Is that your backup? Kavanagh, is it?"

His words distracted Hannah, who followed his gaze, absently moving the gun away for an instant. Jake swept his left hand upwards, chopping the underside of Hannah's arm with his wrist. She leaned away and lifted the gun high to keep it from him. Jake grappled in close, and she swung the gun down, and Jake took a glancing blow on the forehead.

Ignoring the pain, he thrust his head upwards and into Hannah's face. At the same time, he grabbed her wrist and twisted hard. She gasped in pain, and with his other hand he got hold of the gun and wrenched it out of her grasp. Hannah took an unsteady step backwards, holding one hand over her face.

"Jake, don't." It was Lew's voice behind him.

Jake ignored him and lunged forward again, shoving Hannah hard, so she fell back over the low wall beside the footpath and into a narrow, rubbish-strewn flowerbed. Jake threw the gun in a high arc up onto the railway bridge behind them. It thumped with a metallic sound on a rail out of sight above. He sprinted in the direction Amy had taken, vaguely aware Hannah was back on her feet behind him. The noise from the east had grown to a roar.

"Amy, wait!" But she was out of sight, and probably out of hearing.

A single impulse burned in Jake as if he'd been doused in petrol and set alight. Catch up with Amy and get her to safety. A flickering succession of thoughts flashed through his brain as he ran. They could still go away. Just get her away from here and out of London. Their bags were abandoned on the footpath back at the station, it didn't matter. Take a train from another station, it didn't matter. Buy them new clothes. He still had a wallet bulging with his Ascot winnings and could get more money. Everything could still work out. They could still have the future they'd promised each other on Box Hill. Just get Amy to run.

Hannah came after him, shouting something but he ignored her. He was at the top of the High Street, where the pavement was crowded with people shopping at market stalls. A tram stopped outside the co-op, coughing a stream of people out onto the footpath. Some of them stopped at the edge of the road and turned their faces to the sky, blocking the way for the people behind. Amy stood where Hannah had told her to go.

"Amy! Run!"

She showed no sign of hearing him. She was looking upwards, like the people around her. The street was full of waxworks, necks bent back, looking up.

A man close to Amy pointed high into the eastern sky. The roaring noise was so loud it could've been inside Jake's head. But it wasn't—a flying bomb moved fast across the glassy sky.

It was yesterday. It can't come today.

But he saw it all clearly now—Kavanagh in Belgium, Hannah marching Amy into the impact zone.

He pushed a woman aside and reached Amy, she looked round in surprise and appeared not to recognize him for a moment. He got an arm round her shoulder and pulled her into movement. There was only one chance—if the bomb was exactly the same as history's V-I, but a day later, perhaps the impact would be the same. Where in the street had the damage been least? He and Amy moved, running and stumbling south, away from the area where he'd seen the crater. Ahead of them was a rope fence. A sign hanging from it read, "Metropolitan Water Board."

He didn't hear Hannah's approach, but she was suddenly on him. She pulled his arm away from Amy and jabbed an elbow into Amy's face, pushing her back the way they'd come.

"Hannah, no! Run this way." But he couldn't even hear his own voice. The noise of the V-I was a living thing.

It's okay, if the engine keeps going, it won't come down.

It was as if his thought flicked a switch, the roaring noise stopped, leaving them in the grip of a choking silence. Everything froze for an instant. The three of them looked up at their death falling from the sky. The empty air between them soaked up all sound and energy.

It struck Jake how falling in love—really falling in love, in a way his own time had forgotten—was like the moment before the flying bomb came down. You knew you were truly in love when all the background noise fell away and in a frozen silence, you could only wait to learn your fate, because life was no longer yours to control.

His love for Amy was so big it forced everything out of his life, made him cast aside everything he'd known, everything he thought mattered—his friends, his job, his home, even the world in which he was born and belonged. He didn't care. All that mattered was being with Amy, to hold her in the hungry silence of the falling bomb. Nothing else mattered; not OffTime, not Lew, Hannah, or Nancy, not the chilling but undeniable fact that yesterday's bomb was falling today.

Jake punched Hannah in the side of her head, and she released her grip on Amy. He pulled Amy with him, throwing them both toward the rope fence. There was a man in front of them crouched down, running away from his abandoned vegetable stall.

Someone behind him, maybe Hannah, shouted something and there was a whistling sound from above. He had Amy in his arms, and they were falling as if the world had been snatched away from under them, and then all sound went away as the world turned silvery white and dissolved into a million sparks of light before it sucked them down into darkness.

LI

There was a silence so entire it was like Lew was under water. He lay face down on the road, his head covered by his arms. Small pieces of wood and stone pelted him. A plank of wood wind-milled down from the boiling gray sky and struck the ground next to him before striding end-over-end down the street. It made no sound.

I'm deaf.

The street was transformed: the market stalls gone and a row of shops with them, leaving a smoking heap of masonry with sharp fragments of wood sticking up like splintered bones—the air full of chalky dust. In front of him, where Jake, Hannah, and Amy had run into a crowd of shoppers, even the pavement and the road were gone. In their place was a crater forty feet wide.

Lew dragged himself to his feet. There was blood on the ground and ragged pieces of meat scattered in the dirt. He peered down into the crater, wondering where the crowds of shoppers had gone. He moved back from the blast zone, uncertain what to do. His hearing slowly returned with the distant bells of fire-trucks, and somewhere, someone wailing like an injured cat.

A hand on his shoulder turned him round, and he found himself face-to-face with the bald man called Kav, whom he had encountered all those months ago when they were in the more innocent London of 1941.

"You're Brockley, aren't you?"

"And you're Kavanagh?" The other man nodded. "What's going on?" Lew asked.

"Robinson can explain when we get back," Kavanagh said. "For now, we need to finish our job."

"Yeah? What's our job?"

"Help with survivors, like any decent human being would," Kavanagh said. "And stay long enough to find out if any of them are ours."

Lew wasn't happy about working with Kavanagh, but he accepted the need. They exchanged barely another word through the rest of that long day, as they joined a growing crowd of volunteers—digging casualties out of the smoking rubble, occasionally helping injured people into ambulances, too often retrieving body parts from beneath bricks and splintered wood. The wrecked street quickly became chaotic as emergency services flooded in and local residents joined them.

Lew soon lost the little hope he had of finding Jake, Hannah, or Amy alive. Indeed, it was nearly impossible to identify even the dead. The estimated casualty numbers fluctuated during the day, as did the typed lists of names posted on a surviving noticeboard beside the clock tower.

One list named the dead, while another listed the missing not yet identified as casualties. A third, much larger list showed the injured, in some cases with a note of the hospital they'd been taken to. As they labored in the wreckage, a policeman came and went at the noticeboard, bringing updated lists. Lew and Kavanagh took turns checking them.

"She's on the missing list," Kavanagh reported at around three in the afternoon, returning from his latest visit to the board. "Amy Jenkins."

"Anything on Jake or Hannah?"

"No," Kavanagh said. "I don't think they'll make the lists. Certainly not Benedict, she won't be on any records here. Not sure about Wesson."

"His name was Jake."

"Whatever."

At five, Lew found the name 'JENKINS, A.C.' on the list of those confirmed dead. They'd seen no trace of Hannah or Jake, but many bodies were unidentifiable. Not even the number of dead was clear at this stage, so severe was the destruction. The final tally would probably depend on assumptions about the missing, and testimony of friends and relatives. Hannah and Jake might not even show up in the numbers.

In the evening, Lew and Kavanagh split up and toured the hospitals. Kavanagh traveled up to Guy's, while Lew took Woolwich and Lewisham. The corridors were crammed with casualties on trolleys and sobbing relatives. In the confusion, Lew wandered largely unhindered, looking for familiar faces. He fantasized about entering a ward and finding Jake propped up in bed, sipping tea. But he found no sign of him or Hannah.

It was dark when he met Kavanagh again at London Bridge. They walked in silence to a deserted side road off Lower Thames Street and stripped down to their underwear. Lew looked around as they stood a yard apart in the dark, imprinting on his memory his last view of London in 1944, sniffing the dusty air he thought would forever remind him of this terrible day.

Kavanagh's bald head shone purple, and there was a smell of ozone. With a soft puff of air in his face, Lew was dropped back downtime.

LII

London, 2040

Nancy Ahmed was in the Darnell Suite when Lew Jumped back. She instantly took in the rigid expression on his face, the stiff silence between him and Kavanagh, the dust on their clothes.

"Where's Hannah?"

"Not now."

"Jake?"

Lew shook his head. The realization of Jake and Hannah's deaths landed in Nancy's eyes, closing her face as if he'd slammed a door in it.

After a shower and change of clothes, Lew gave Kavanagh the slip and went straight to the Office. He didn't know how it was possible to keep moving when he was so tired, but somehow, his anger and grief drove him on.

The guys on the desk told him Robinson wasn't available and invited him to wait in a windowless room behind the reception desk. He thought about going up to his floor. Maybe there was something to do while he waited for Robinson to show up. But he honestly couldn't think what that something might be, apart perhaps from breaking some furniture. In any case, he noticed the beefy security guy eyeing him sideways. Lew stepped into the waiting room and sat. Maybe he'd be grateful for the delay. If he got in to see Robinson straight away, he didn't know what he might do.

After twenty minutes, Mister Beef, the security man, said he could go up. Robinson was sitting behind his desk when Lew stepped into the room. He jumped up and ushered Lew into a seat.

"I've heard all about it. I can't tell you how sorry I am." Robinson looked tired as if it had been him dodging bombs in the past and seeing his friends blown up, instead of Lew. "Terrible. There are no words for it."

"I can think of some. You set this up, Ed. Why did Hannah have different orders from me, and why was that guy Kavanagh there?"

"We've talked about this, Lew," Robinson said. "We talked about Amy Jenkins. We couldn't afford her timeline to be changed. But what happened with Jake and Hannah was terrible. No one could've predicted that."

"I get the impression you can predict quite a lot," Lew said. "I'm getting the feeling that the Office can do a bit more than they put in our training manuals."

"I don't know what you mean," Robinson said. "Are you sure we need to talk about this now? Everyone's upset."

"Why was Kavanagh there?" Lew repeated. "And why was he in 1941 when we were there? That time you let us think he was trying to assassinate Churchill."

"Some things need to be kept classified," Robinson said. "You understand that."

"Bullshit! I don't understand why you've been playing us like this."

"Look, you're tired and upset, with good reason," Robinson said. "We can talk all this through when you've had a chance to calm down. I'm sorry about Jake and Hannah. But I can't say I'm sorry that Amy Jenkins died the way history said she should. It's what had to happen."

"Shame about Jake and Hannah, though."

"I've known them both years before they joined the Service," Robinson said. "If there were anything I could've done, I would've done it."

"Even if that meant saving Amy too?"

"That wasn't possible."

A tense silence slipped into the room. Lew didn't know what to say next; he wondered if Ed was right, that this was a conversation better had when he'd been back a while, rested, and collected his thoughts. The memory of Jake, Hannah, and Amy running toward the V-1 was still too fresh.

"Why did the bomb come a day late?"

"I'm sorry?" Robinson looked surprised.

"The flying bomb. How could it come a day late?"

"I'm not sure what you mean."

"The bomb was meant to fall on July the 28th."

"I don't think so," Robinson said. "July 29th, 1944. A German V-I hit Lewisham High Street, killing over fifty people. It's a matter of record. Look it up."

"It was July 28th," Lew insisted. "Hannah looked it up. Jake saw the grave. July 28th. But something happened and the bomb didn't come that day, the day Jake arranged to keep Amy away from that place. Somehow it came the next day."

"Like I said, I don't regret Amelia Jenkins being there," Robinson said. "I'm just horrified Jake and Hannah were with her at the time. How did that happen?"

"Never mind that," Lew said, unwilling to be diverted. "I don't know what the historical record shows now, but I do know the V-I was meant to land on the 28th of July 1944. We were due to Jump back a week earlier and get Jake out. But somehow, we ended up coming out on the 28th of July itself. I thought we were too late for the bomb, but it hadn't come."

"I've got people looking into your Jump," Robinson said. "I don't know why you arrived late. That shouldn't happen."

"Seems pretty standard lately, Ed. What with our 1941 mission ending in an air raid and Jake getting dumped in 1943 instead of coming home."

"Look, you're emotional right now, I understand that." Robinson leaned forward and steepled his fingers in front of him. "We'll need a full debrief before long, but maybe you should get some rest." He stood up, signaling the audience was over.

"Was it Project Reset?"

Robinson blinked several times and reached into the pocket of his tweed waistcoat. He put his cigar in his mouth and sucked on it a couple of times as he sat down again.

"I don't know what you mean."

"Is that why we arrived late?"

"I'm sorry; I don't know what you're talking about."

"Just something I heard Kavanagh was working on," Lew said. "Nice guy, by the way." Lew thought back to the evening with Nancy and Hannah on the balcony in Deptford, with Jake missing in the past. Nancy was late because she ran into that guy she knew, just back from his secret mission in 1944. The team leader was someone called Kavanagh. What Kavanagh and his team were doing in July 1944, disguised as Germans in Belgium, Lew hadn't a clue. Coincidentally, the same place and time the retreating Germans were playing their last desperate cards in the war against Britain—the V-I flying bombs.

"You've lost me." Robinson stood again. "I really think we need to get some rest and talk about this later."

They were interrupted by the buzzing of Robinson's desk phone. Ed let it go to voicemail, but for a brief moment he was distracted, bending forward to check the caller display. Lew decided this wasn't the moment to push any further. He needed to think.

"Okay, Ed," he said. "I guess you're right. I woke up this morning in 1944, and I feel I've been awake for the whole century since. But I want to know more. I've still got questions, and I need answers."

"Of course," Robinson said, back in his seat, already looking more relaxed. "We'll talk again soon."

LIII

London, 2040

Before he saw Ed Robinson again, Lew met Nancy Ahmed the next evening in the Adam and Eve, a pub not far from the Office. Nancy was there when he arrived, sitting in a corner booth, looking fresh-faced and younger than he'd ever remembered being himself. She stood up and hugged him when he reached the table.

"That feels good," he said when she let him go.

"You looked like you needed it."

Lew got them both a drink and told Nancy everything that had happened. When he finished she sat for a long moment, slowly shaking her head.

"They made it happen," Lew said. "I'm sure of it."

"Me too," Nancy said. "What do we do now?"

"Nothing's going to bring Jake and Hannah back."

"I know. But we've got to do something." Nancy drained her glass and leaned back against the side of the booth. "Jesus, what a mess. I thought time travel was a good thing, but everything about it just seems to fuck up the world more. Maybe we'd be better off without it."

Lew picked up his pint to give himself a moment to think, but Nancy, observant as ever, spotted something in his face.

"What is it, Lew?"

"You've given me an idea."

Lew arranged to see Robinson again three days after his return from 1944. Arrangements were already in hand for the memorial service for Jake and Hannah. They'd get the full treatment, and Ed was no doubt already working on the moving speech he'd give for the fallen heroes. Lew was confident there'd be no mention of Agent Wesson's unfortunate insubordination or the way Agent Benedict got them both killed seventy years before they were born.

Lew had had time to recover his composure, and they talked in Robinson's office, just the two of them, each with a mug of coffee on the desk between them. Robinson had his feet up on a spare seat. His tweed waistcoat had two buttons undone, allowing his paunch to swell out a little like he was hiding a basketball.

"I've been thinking, Ed. I've worked a few things out."

"Go on."

"I'm not the best for sticking to the rulebook, you know that. But you need to know I'm on the right side here." Robinson picked up his coffee mug and took a sip. Lew had rehearsed this with Nancy. "I was a bit overwrought when we spoke before. I'm cut up by what happened with Jake. I wish I could've prevented it. But it's done. This whole thing has made me realize just how fragile things can be, and how important it is to protect the foundations of the world we're living in."

"Good to hear that, Lew."

"I loved Jake like a brother. I'd give anything to have been able to save him. But in the end, I've got to admit he made mistakes. Whatever anyone else did, Jake brought some things on himself."

"Some people would say that's harsh," Robinson said. "But I agree. No one made him break the law."

"So, I've been thinking." Lew could hardly believe Robinson was swallowing this shit, but he ploughed on. "All the things that went wrong—Jake ending up in the wrong year, me and Hannah Jumping a week late in 1944, the flying bomb coming a day late—"

"It came when it came. Check the history books."

"Anyway, the point is, it can't all have been an accident, coincidence."

"What was it, then?"

"I don't need to tell you, do I, Ed? It was the Office. Someone from here was interfering. There was more than one team working on this."

"Why would you think that?" Robinson's eyes were like dark magnets.

"I don't expect you to confirm it, Ed. But it's obvious. Your man Kavanagh was the clincher. But there's something else, something more important."

"Yes?"

"We're always told that our job is to stop people messing with the past."

"That is our job."

"But there's more to it than that, isn't there?"

"Is there?"

"Come on, Ed. I've got more missions than I can count. You can level with me. I've made up my mind. For Jake and Hannah, I'm going to do the right thing from now on. Do my best to prevent this from happening again."

Robinson said nothing for a long time. Then he gave a sigh like a balloon deflating. He put his feet down and leaned over the desk, thumbing the display. After a moment, he nodded to himself and sat upright again.

"What I'm going to tell you is something you cannot repeat to anyone else."

"I won't."

"Ever."

"Ed, I know the score."

"There are things about the Darnell Jump that we don't advertise." Robinson's shoulders slumped, and he looked suddenly very tired. "It can do more than we've ever made public."

"I guessed that. Jake said when he was dumped in 1943 he moved across London in location as well as forward in time."

"And Amy Jenkins came forward in time."

Lew didn't reply. He wasn't going to confirm that, or his part in Jake's return to 1944.

"The Darnell process is more flexible than we let on," Robinson said. "But there's more. It took a while to discover, but traveling into the past has an unpredictable impact. It can disrupt the fabric of the past, change the pattern of events."

Wow, hold the front page.

"That's not exactly a secret," Lew said. "Otherwise, why have OffTime to stop people changing the past?"

"That's not what I'm talking about, Lew. Of course, there's the risk of deliberate interference. People try that, and a lot of our work is aimed at stopping them. But there's something else." Robinson ran a hand across his shiny scalp. "Something harder to detect but ultimately more dangerous. Every time we use the Darnell Jump, it has a side effect. Usually so small it's undetectable. For a long time, we weren't aware of what was happening. But it seems there's a cumulative impact. We can make a whole load of Jumps with no apparent effect and then somehow, taken together, they can add up to some tangible change."

"What kind of change?"

"It's hard to pin down. We have a ton of people monitoring this stuff and most of the time we don't spot it. There's a kind of, well, *leakage* you could call it."

"What is it that leaks?"

"Reality. The millions of tiny facts that make up the way the world is. There are the big things, the things we'd notice, like the way clothes are designed and made, the kind of coffee that's been sourced overseas, the layout of the Tube and the style of road signs. But think of the smaller things. Everything around us is the product of millions of decisions and actions too minor to be noticed."

Robinson leaned back in his chair and waved a hand airily at the room around them. "The men who painted this building made thousands of individual brushstrokes, each one subtly different. The same for whoever made the furniture and decided the layout of the rooms. And it isn't just the products of people's actions. It's events no one can control. You buy a coffee on the way here today. Let's say it takes two minutes and after you've got your coffee you enter the station and get on a Tube train straight away. That kind of thing happens hundreds of thousands of times every morning. But what if another customer walks into the coffee shop just in front of you? It then takes two and a half minutes to get your coffee, and you miss the Tube train."

"Doesn't sound like a particularly big deal."

"To you, it's no problem, there's another train quickly after. But who will you now meet that you wouldn't have met? Or who will you miss who you might've seen? Most of this probably makes no difference," Robinson said. "Or it seems that way. For us, living in the present, it doesn't matter which way we go because we'll never know what the alternative path would've been like."

"But in the past, we do."

"Yes. Or at least we know a lot. Obviously, if something big changes, then history changes with it and that's that."

"We talked about that before."

"There are times when an accumulation of small changes can shift the probability of something going the way it should, and we get worried. If we detect it."

"Isn't this what a lot of our training is about? We have it drilled into us to minimize our impact on the past environments we visit."

"True. But there's a limit to it. You might be the anonymous stranger who walks into the coffee shop and makes someone a minute later than they would've been. However hard you try, you can't avoid that kind of impact."

"What should we do?" Lew said. "The only safe thing is to stop time travel altogether."

Robinson looked at him for a long time. His eyes were tired and watery like he might be about to cry. The thought horrified Lew.

"That genie is out of the bottle, though, isn't it?" Robinson said at last. "Whatever we do, someone will try to kill Churchill, steal Da Vinci's paints, stop Marx publishing any books. And we have to stop them. How can we not?"

"So, we can't stop using the Darnell Jump, but every time we do, it undermines the present, chips away at the real world in ways we can't always detect?"

"What we think of as the real world, yes."

"So, what happens? You have a team of guys trying to trace where the damage is and then fix it?"

Something deep in Robinson's eyes, the impression of a shadow that just slipped out of sight, jarred with the surface impression of candor carried by his words. There was something he wasn't saying.

"We try. We monitor what we can. There was a special project a few years ago to identify the key events and people, the foundations of the modern world."

"A long list, I bet."

"Very. We try to keep a fix on them, looking for any sign, the slightest shift in the surrounding detail."

"Where did Jake and Amy fit into this?"

"What do you mean?"

"How did they show up on your monitoring?"

"I told you about that." Robinson frowned. "The possible impact of Jake's action, or at least what he intended, was pretty obvious. If Amelia Jenkins survived because of his interference, I told you what could've happened."

What if she survived without his interference?

Something didn't add up, at least not the way Robinson laid it out. There were too many loose ends, too many coincidences. Lew now knew the extent of the covert monitoring and intervention. He also knew Kavanagh had been in 1941 playing some double game. Jake met Amy Jenkins, and then what should've been a routine Jump back home went tits-up because somehow the Office scheduled it in the middle of London's biggest air raid of the war. And, surprise, Amy Jenkins was right there too, and someone—probably an OffTime agent—drew Jake's attention her way. Having saved her, Jake gets dumped in 1943 and—another surprise—bumps into Amy again, this time believing it's for keeps because he's been lost in the past.

Too many coincidences.

Now that he knew how closely OffTime monitored the past, it was odder than ever that it took so long to pull Jake out, giving him plenty of time to get attached to Amy. Lew didn't suppose Amy's accidental arrival in 2040 could've been foreseen or manipulated. That must've happened just as it appeared. But practically everything else was suspect, even the ease with which they sneaked Amy back to 1944. Now that his suspicions were aroused, he saw a hidden hand behind everything that happened.

"I need to know where you stand, Lew." Robinson studied his face. "The work goes on, it's constant. There's always a new risk. We can't put the Darnell genie back in the bottle, but we have to manage it. We can't help Jake and Hannah, but we can try to stop it happening again."

You can't control it. We're riding a tiger. What happens when you want to get off?

Lew sensed everything he knew, the world he took for granted, was built on sand. Every Darnell Jump shifted a few grains. For a long time, you didn't notice, and then a chunk of the sand moved, and a corner of the building you thought was solid collapsed. Sometimes, the world changed, and you never knew. And even if you detected it, how did you prevent it? By shoveling more sand under the walls? How could anyone know for sure what action would put things right? How many more times would an Amy Jenkins need to be thrown under a bomb, and would it do any good?

"You can be part of it, Lew," Robinson said. "It's our most important work, and we always need good people. Now that you know what's going on, I want you to help."

"What can I say?"

What could he say? It was obvious—in the tent, pissing out or outside, getting pissed on? He thought again of Jake running after Amy, trying to reach her as the V-I came sharking out of the sky toward them. What would Jake want him to do?

"You can trust me, Ed," he lied. "Count me in."

LIV

Lew filled Nancy in during a walk through the park near the Office. It was a Sunday, so they didn't expect to be seen, but even so, they kept to the paths among the trees on the far side of the lake from HQ.

"It wasn't accidental," Lew said. "They manipulated Jake from the start, I'm sure of it. There are too many coincidences."

"Manipulated, how?" Nancy asked. She trudged alongside him, hands thrust into her coat pockets, head down watching her feet on the grass. They both kept their voices low, although there were few people nearby. "We were there for some of it. I don't see how they could manipulate everything that happened."

"Not everything," Lew said. "But our 1941 mission was never to save Churchill. Amy Jenkins was always the target."

"How do you figure that?"

"I've thought about this a lot, Nancy. History says Amy died in July 1944. But let's say their probability analysis flags up a growing risk that she might not. If she lives, she may go on to meet the father of Axel Darnell. They can't afford that to happen. If it did, no time travel, and no chance of putting it right."

"But it was Jake who caused the risk of Amy surviving," Nancy said.

"Just bear with me," Lew said. "I'm saying, what if the risk already existed. They'd want to correct it."

"Simplest just to send someone like Kavanagh to put her under the bomb."

"They did that too. That was the fallback," Lew said. They were at the western end of the lake. The ugly façade of Buckingham Palace loomed beyond a high hedge. They turned and began to walk back toward Whitehall.

"Kavanagh's team was in 1941 with us. They'd already saved Churchill, and their other job was to be a decoy for our team. Our real job was to influence the behavior of Amy Jenkins, by inserting Jake into her life."

"That's a stretch, Lew," Nancy said. "I was there, remember? No one was telling us what to do. I never met Amy then."

"Remember how detailed our instructions were? Where to be and when? Jake told me he and Hannah met Amy first on the way to Blackheath. Kavanagh led us to her wedding and then disappeared. Then the Office had us Jump back in an air raid where Amy's husband was killed, and Jake was lured into rescuing her. Lastly, he gets Jumped to 1943, with a survival plan that guarantees he'll meet her again when he finds a job. Coincidence?"

"Okay, I agree it looks screwy," Nancy said. "But none of it guarantees Jake does what he did."

"True," Lew agreed. "But say you want an agent in place who can influence Amy, make sure she dies? They'd have a good handle on how Jake was likely to act from his psych analysis. I bet that showed he was likely to fall for Amy, as well as having commitment issues."

"Is that what it was?" Nancy said. "Hannah would've loved to hear it."

"I agree the events were too complicated for OffTime to predict everything in advance," Lew said. "But they could put the right elements in place and then manipulate Jake to do what they wanted. Maybe they were confident, in the end, he'd do his duty, but he surprised them by the strength of his love for Amy."

"Different commitment issues there," Nancy said.

"Kavanagh and your mate, Kurt, in Belgium are the clinchers," Lew said. "They fixed the launch of the V-I for twenty-four hours later, and Ed set up Hannah to make sure Amy was in the right place. Job done."

"If you're right, they used us like puppets?" Nancy said. "That's sickening, but what can anyone do? It's happened."

"It's worse than that," Lew said. "There's no end to this. They'll go on manipulating events forever. What they did to Jake and Hannah is bad enough. But it's only a small part of the mess we're in.

"Everything OffTime does," Lew went on, gesturing around them absently as they paced along in parallel with the Mall. "Every trip into the past has an impact. One leaf brushes another, one grain of sand tumbles against others, and over the centuries the world in which time travel is possible lives under the threat of an avalanche, sweeping away our reality."

"Maybe," Nancy said, "but mostly we'd never know."

"Sure, but the cure is worse," Lew said. "To shore up reality, OffTime plays God. Robinson and his bosses watch over everything and choose who lives and who dies, who gets born and who never exists. Anyone, anywhere, at any time, who threatens the erosion of the world as the Office wants it, can be wiped out. Killed or prevented from ever being born."

"Do you really think there's much of it, Lew? The kind of thing they did with Jake, Hannah, and Amy?"

"I don't know, but it can't go on. No one should have that sort of power."

They were now at the end of the park. Ahead of them, across a wide road, was the fortified wall of Downing Street, flanked by the Georgian government buildings of Whitehall. The paranoid direction of his thoughts made Lew uneasy. Was someone listening to them right now, pointing a directional microphone at them and recording their words? And if not, even if they were unobserved now, who was to say someone at some time in the future might not come back in time and spy on them?

"Even the worst tyrants in history only controlled their present," Lew said. "Death always broke their grip in the end. But OffTime has power over the present and the past, which gives them control of the future. That kind of power shouldn't be in anyone's hands, least of all the cold, dead grip of bureaucrats like Ed Robinson."

"But what can anyone do about it?" Nancy said.

"Jake had an idea," Lew said. "But I'll need your help."

In the coming weeks, Lew kept his head down and did everything Robinson asked. He played the part perfectly, keen to toe the corporate line and do his bit to keep the future safe from a crumbling past. But however much Ed Robinson appeared to trust Lew, he was on probation. He had to constantly show he was thoroughly with the program, that he could be trusted. The last thing he needed was for anyone to become suspicious about his interest in events in Germany in 1952. That was where Nancy came in. Fortunately, Agent Ahmed, Miss Goody-Two-Shoes, attracted less suspicion. She could do the research they needed.

One day, three months after he left Jake and Hannah in 1944, Lew withdrew his modest savings from the bank and walked into the east London Darnell suite late in the evening. As arranged, Nancy was already there. Lew gave all the money to the two guys in the control room. Four days in 1952 was what he bribed them for. He didn't know how long they'd keep their mouths shut. Long enough, he hoped.

By the end of the first day, he and Nancy were in Germany, on a train up the Rhine Valley from Cologne to Koblenz. As the train sped south, the bluffs rose higher on each side, topped here and there with ruined blockhouses from the recent war and castles from earlier centuries. The river the train followed twisted tighter and narrower, giving Lew the feeling that with every mile they burrowed deeper into the past.

In Koblenz, they checked into separate rooms at the Triererhof Hotel on Clemenstrasse. It was only a couple of minutes away from the riverside café where Nancy's research told them they needed to be the next morning. It took Lew a long time to fall asleep that night.

He was nervous and excited about what they planned to do, and he couldn't disentangle the logical paradoxes embedded in their plan—to come between Frank Darnell and Heidi Kastelein and ensure their son was never born—to change Heidi's life and the world, to do the impossible—and by meeting her ensure they could never meet. If they succeeded, would any of it ever have happened?

EPILOGUE

Koblenz, Germany 1952

The next morning, to Lew's despair, all was lost. He and Nancy stood at the river wall, with Kavanagh's concealed gun pointing at them. In the next few minutes, they'd witness the historic meeting that they came so far to prevent. Darnell would meet his young German sweetheart. On top of all the other things that had gone wrong, this would be the crowning failure. Maybe Kavanagh would let them watch the happy couple stroll away arm-in-arm, before marching them back to whatever fate OffTime had for them back in the future they thought they'd abandoned.

"I'm sorry, Nancy."

"It's okay," she said. "I got to visit Germany. Never been before."

"Make the most of it. They won't be letting you come again," Kavanagh said.

There were worse places to stand while you waited for your plans to crumble. They were in the sun and sheltered from the wind, with a view across the Rhine. The river bent slightly east as it met the Mosel beneath the Deutsche Eck, a monument to German unity, which in 1952 seemed a little ironic.

In years to come, there'd be a cable car across the river here, but for now, they had a clear view on their left of a pedestrian precinct between them and the café and other buildings set back from the river. On their right, the broad river was uniformly gray except where the wind whipped up shoals of white-caps.

Lew saw the table outside the café, where he'd sat before Heidi Kastelein's arrival and Kavanagh's intervention. He had left his German-English dictionary there. The pages flapped weakly back and forth like the wing of a drowning gull. He pointed it out to Kavanagh.

"Maybe I should go and get it," Lew said.

"Forget it."

"What if young Heidi sees I've left it and comes looking for me, to give it back? She might miss Frank."

"You don't give up, Brockley," Kavanagh said. "I'll give you that. But I'll take the chance."

They were silent again for what felt like several minutes. Lew watched gulls dip over the chilly Rhine water. A scrap of newspaper wriggled past them on the pavement, in the grip of the capricious wind. A couple of cars passed on the road behind them. Nancy looked at Lew with a question in her eyes, but he couldn't tell what it was. The bell in the clock tower rang, clanging the hour, slow and heavy. Despite himself, Lew counted the peals under his breath. Beside him, Kavanagh looked at his watch. The bells fell silent after eleven.

The door of the café opened, and a couple came out, pulling on coats. Neither of them was Heidi Kastelein or an American airman. They glanced at Lew's dictionary on the outside table but then walked away toward the Old Town. Lew looked at Nancy again. She gave him a full, eyebrows-raised stare.

"In your research, Nancy," Lew said at last. "Did you find out what time the Darnells met?"

"Just before eleven. The mother talked about the church bells."

Kavanagh looked again at his watch. There was a waxy sheen of sweat on his upper lip. Lew cleared his throat theatrically. "I don't want to worry you, Kav old fruit, but—"

"Shut it, Brockley! He'll come." Kavanagh looked up and down the riverside boulevard. There were very few people around; the woman with the pram whom Lew had seen earlier was throwing some bread to gulls, a tall man in a gray overcoat stood in front of the church, looking up at the façade. He was too far away to see clearly. There was no sign of the American airman whom history was supposed to be sending to cross the path of Fraulein Kastelein, who even now might be finishing her coffee inside the café.

They stood like this, in silence, for another few minutes, until the café door opened and Heidi Kastelein emerged. She was alone, no future husband having slipped in the back way while they were distracted. Kavanagh breathed out with a noise like a car tire deflating. Heidi walked along the boulevard, on a track that would take her close to where they stood.

"Maybe I should talk to her," Lew said from the side of his mouth. "Persuade her to stay a bit longer."

"Don't move," Kavanagh said.

Axel Darnell's once, but maybe not future, mother passed them and walked on. Everything about Heidi was tidy. Tidy Heidi—her eyebrows were clipped into thin lines, her red hair pulled back tightly from her forehead and fixed behind her head with a small metal clip. Her lower lip was as full as a summer berry, and she chewed it thoughtlessly as she walked by, deep in thought.

Kavanagh had a look on his face like someone just shot his puppy, as Heidi Kastelein disappeared around the corner into Rheinstrasse. Lew had no idea why, but he thought now she'd never be Frank Darnell's German teacher and wife, probably never meet him. She'd never be the mother of their talented and history-making son. Poor Frank, he thought. He didn't even have the compensation of meeting Amy Jenkins instead.

He knew it must be imagination, but again he had that feeling of everything around him wheeling ponderously about. He felt a spasm of dizziness and leaned against the river wall. From the look on his face, Kavanagh also felt dizzy.

"So, Kavanagh," Lew said. "What now? Got a backup plan?"

Before the other man could answer, Lew noticed Nancy staring along the river bank, a frown creasing her brow. Lew followed her gaze. The sun was behind a cloud again and fifty yards away the tall man in the gray coat, whom he had previously seen in front of the church, was walking toward them. Now that he'd moved closer, Lew recognized him, and the shock made him reach out a hand once more to hold the wall.

"It can't be," Nancy said, shaking her head.

But it was. Jacob Wesson was approaching. His hair was shorter than before and flecked with gray, and he had a thin beard. He looked older than Lew, but there could be no doubt about it. Jake was alive, and he was here.

"Well," Lew said, as Jake stopped a few feet in front of them, a grin splitting his face. "Life is full of surprises."

"Wesson?" Kavanagh said. "What? How?" He was leaning against the river wall as if someone had hit him on the head with a mallet.

"Jake," Lew said, and stepped forward to hug his partner, but he was too slow for Nancy, who was already squeezing Jake and saying something through her sobs.

"Where have you been?" Nancy said. "You died."

"I can explain," Jake said. "Why don't we sit at the café table over there? Now that the Darnells won't be in the way."

"Fuck you, Wesson," Kavanagh said. "I've got a job to do."

"Suit yourself, Kav," Jake said. "Here's what we'll do. We'll sit outside where you can see us. You can join us whenever you like. Stay here and wait if you want, but Frank Darnell's not coming. He's on a train to Cologne."

"How do you know?"

"I bought his ticket," Jake said. "He was a little fragile after our drinking session last night. But, hey, it's your choice. Stay here if you like, but I think you might need to think about a new job."

Jake, Nancy, and Lew moved to the table Lew had before, reserved by his dictionary. Nancy and Lew had so many questions—What? How? When?—that they couldn't get them out, and Jake held up his hands. "Let's order coffee, and then I'll talk."

The waiter brought the drinks, and Jake told his tale. He answered Lew's question first— how could he be here when Lew saw him run into the blast zone eight years ago?

"The one bit of luck I had was what I remembered of the original V-I blast," Jake said. "Where the damage was worst, and places that didn't suffer as much. One of the market traders had a miraculous escape when he fell into an exposed drain, where there were water works going on. In that chaotic final second, I saw a man disappear down the hole, and I dived after him. The bomb came, and it was bedlam afterward."

"I saw it," Lew said.

"The chaos meant I could get away without being discovered. I was happy to let OffTime think I was dead. I'm sorry you had to think it too."

"What about Hannah?" Nancy asks.

"I'm afraid she was killed in the blast," Jake said.

"Are you sure?"

"Yes. She was—" He rubbed at his temples with his fingertips, suddenly looking tired. "Her body was almost unrecognizable, like many others. But I knew it was her. I identified the body."

"And Amy," Lew said. "I'm sorry about her, Jake. After all you went through."

Jake took a sip of his coffee and looked from Lew to Nancy and back again. Behind him, Lew saw Kavanagh, still by the river wall, holding his head in his hands. The woman with the pram had stopped feeding the gulls and was close to Kavanagh, perhaps asking him if he was all right.

"Amy survived," Jake said at last.

"What?" Nancy spilled some of her coffee before she could put the cup down.

"But I saw her name," Lew said. "And her grave."

"Like I said, I identified Hannah's body," Jake said. "I just didn't say it was Hannah. I said it was Amy."

"Where is she?" Nancy asked, but for Lew, everything had come into focus. He watched Kavanagh slowly raise his head and talk to the woman in front of him. She wore a headscarf, but a flash of red hair beneath it told Lew who she was.

"I remembered our conversation, Lew," Jake said. "About when Darnell's parents met. I thought Amy and I would never be completely safe while someone could travel back and change things. I've waited eight years to come and make sure Axel Darnell was never born."

"We had the same idea, as you can see," Nancy said.

"Which is a nice surprise," Jake said.

Lew watched the woman with the pram pat Kavanagh gently on the shoulder. The two of them turned and walked toward the café, where Lew, Jake, and Nancy sat. Kavanagh looked calmer now, perhaps beginning to accept what had happened. Maybe it was just that talking to Amy had put him in a happier frame of mind, as she had a way of doing.

"What now, Jake?" Lew said, ignoring the cry of surprise from Nancy beside him, as she finally saw who was walking toward them and pushed back her chair. "What do we do now?"

"After all that's happened," Jake said, "This can still be a beautiful world."

Lew thought of the younger Jake and Amy, walking away from him and into the sunset that evening he went with them back to 1944, the way they held hands and didn't look back, walking into a future that until now he had thought they were denied.

"Anything is possible," Jake said. Over their heads, two gulls croaked a farewell, wheeled in a wide circle, and swooped away over the river. Nancy hugged Amy and then bent down to look in the pram. Amy saw Lew watching, and her smile was like the sun breaking through after a storm.

"Yes," Lew said to his friend and partner, back from the dead. "The future is unwritten."

Again.

ACKNOWLEDGEMENTS

Small parts of this book appeared (in very different form) in two short stories published a few years ago. The ghost story, 'Fifty One', featured the same flying bomb explosion as in the present book and also carried the seed of the love triangle. It appeared in Dark Tales 16 (2015). The science fiction story, 'How Stanley Spencer Painted the Cookham Resurrection,' appeared in *Phantaxis* magazine, issue number 1, in November 2016, and featured a little of the time travel activity also used here (and one of the characters).

Naturally, in a work of fiction, stuff is made up. But to the extent that events taking place in the 1940s are true to life, I have drawn on some history books. I found the following really helpful: *Waiting for The All Clear, True Stories from the Blitz*, by Ben Wicks (Bloomsbury 1990); *The Flying Bomb War*, by Peter Haining (Robson Books, 2002); and *Children of the Blitz* by Mike Abraham (Pamick Books, 1994). As for the accuracy of events in 2040, we will have to wait and see.

It's easy to write a book on your own. But to write a good one, you need help. To the extent that this is a good book, I'm grateful to a whole bunch of people. They include early readers Laura Cunningham, Jeremy Hodgen and Neil Grant, and Vin Miles who hunted down typos.

✦✦✦

ABOUT THE AUTHOR

Chris Barnham worked for two decades for the British government, advising Ministers on education and employment policies. In 2013, he decided it was time to make stuff up for himself. He now combines writing with running a small business, and active involvement in community politics in south London, where he has lived since the 1980s. His short fiction has appeared in a range of magazines, including *Compelling Science Fiction*, *Black Static*, the UK's premier horror magazine, and the late-lamented *Pan Books of Horror*. His first novel, *Among the Living*, was published in 2012 (revised 2nd edition, 2017).

Chris lives in London, England, with three tall children and a scary wife. Whenever work allows, he spends as much time as possible out of town with mud on his boots. His latest walking challenge is the 630-mile South West Coast Path, around the Devon and Cornwall coasts. You can follow his (slow) progress on his blog.